I0726492

THE XERXES FACTOR

An Intergalaxia Novel

Anna Zogg

The Intergalaxia Series
By
Anna Zogg

The Paradise Protocol
The Xerses Factor
The Terran Summit

The Xerxes Factor
An Intergalaxia Novel
© 2016 by Anna Zogg

Published Mountain Brook Ink, White Salmon, WA 98672, creating fiction you can believe in.

Scripture quotations taken from the New American Standard Bible®, Copyright © 1960, 1962, 1963, 1968, 1971, 1972, 1973, 1975, 1977, 1995 by The Lockman Foundation. Used by permission." (www.Lockman.org)

Edited by Sharon Hinck
Copy edited by Ginny Smith
Cover design by Nick Delliskave

Library of Congress Control Number: 2016902564

Print ISBN- 978-1-943959-18-1

To my daughter, Geneva Bennett,
the smartest, strongest and most beautiful woman I know

Acknowledgement

As always, I am overwhelmed by the support and encouragement of so many. My deepest appreciation to Virginia Smith and Sharon Hinck: you are both fantastic editors and writers. A special thanks to Marilynn Rockelman, Licensed Clinical Mental Health Counselor for her advice about professional counseling, including the information about hypnotherapy and PTSD.

Chapter 1

Sean was ordered to kill the woman. Not marry her.

The thought pounded Kelli Layne as she watched the happy couple at their celebratory reception. Across the grand ballroom, they embraced. Her fingers tightened around a flute of pink synth-ale until the glass threatened to crack. With the party in full swing, everyone appeared in high spirits. But neither the exotic space station nor the triple moons of Xerxes IX could banish her melancholy.

Long ago, she'd lost her heart to Sean Reese. How could she have made that clearer?

As Kelli leaned against a column, she identified several high-ranking guests who attended the white-tie event. Even delegates from the formidable Intergalaxia organization made an appearance. When Sean and Aric had saved a primitive planet from being plundered, they had vaulted into celebrity status. Not only that, but rumors abounded he was up for a big promotion.

Even though technically he failed his last assignment. The woman at his side wasn't supposed to live.

Kelli pressed fingertips to her temple, battling the headache that had plagued her all day. Caused by the artificial gravity or the overly crowded outpost? Seemed like twenty parties were happening on the space station all at once. A security nightmare.

Glad I'm not on duty.

She rolled the cool syntha-ale glass across her forehead, trying to alleviate the discomfort. Hours before, a bellhop had delivered an aspirin derivative to her hotel room—two tablets. Though she'd taken one, it had done nothing for the pain. She rummaged in her purse for the second. A passing waiter exchanged her drink for champagne, which she used to down the pill.

She should leave. Especially as the revelry—and her headache—escalated.

When she snapped her clutch closed, Jayden Song caught her eye. Kelli hiked up her smile as Sean's best friend and fellow USF agent approached.

"Well, well. Aren't you distracting." His gaze remained locked with hers, belying his words.

Speak for yourself. He cut a dashing figure in his black tuxedo, which contrasted with the white waistcoat, shirt and bowtie. The ensemble complimented his taupe complexion and dark hair.

"Haven't you been trained not to be distracted?" She spoke coyly.

"No man could resist you in red silk."

Except you?

"Really, Jayd, I've heard better pickup lines from a dozen men already."

"Only a dozen?" He grinned. "Well, I can't blame 'em. You're drop-dead gorgeous."

Gorgeous? Ha! In the six years they'd known each other, Jayd had always treated her like "one of the boys." Because they served on rival USF teams? Or because he was a senior agent? However, their paths usually intersected at the gym.

"You're wrong about one detail." She adjusted the long scarf of her sheath dress.

He glanced pointedly around. "Unless you hid the bodies, no one's dead. Is that what you meant?"

She smirked as she smoothed her hand over the soft material. "This is Xerxian textile, not silk. Bought it this afternoon."

"Nice choice." His dark eyes met hers. Funny she'd never noticed before that he was about the same height. Most times, her five feet ten gave her an advantage over shorter colleagues. In her heels she stood a mere inch taller than Jayd.

Suddenly, he leaned in. "So what's bugging you, Kel?"

How'd the punk guess? When she'd once voiced frustration about his ease in reading people, he told her all Asians had that mystical ability.

She blinked innocently. "Who said anything's bugging me?"

One eyebrow rose. "The truth's written all over you."

In spite of herself, her smile faltered. Give her an assignment and she could pull it off without a flaw.

She lifted her chin. "I have no idea what you're talking about."

For a few moments he appeared to weigh her comment. Finally, he shrugged and turned. "I'm curious. What's your assessment of the new Mrs. Reese?"

Kelli shifted from one foot to the other as she glanced at the woman. "Surprised to learn she has a kid. Can't believe Sean stuck around when he found out."

Across the vast room, Aric held her daughter's hands and twirled to the music. The girl giggled before collapsing against her mother. Arms linked, they headed to Sean.

"She's one special lady." Jayd pressed one finger to his chin. "I've never seen a guy so much in love. Although, when I first met her, they both stank of rotten eggs."

"Who said men were logical?"

He grinned without looking at her. "Because of Aric, Sean's a new man."

Guess he would know. They had been friends long before USF.

"What'd you mean he's a *new man?*"

Jayd faced her, a glint of mischief in his almond-shaped eyes. "You're gonna hate it."

"Oh?"

"To use one of your phrases, he 'got religion.'"

"She suckered him into that?" Kelli let out a breath of incredulity. "I knew his marrying her was a mistake."

As soon as she spoke, she saw the trap.

"So *that's* it." Jayd's eyes narrowed. "You have a thing for Sean. You're disappointed he didn't pick you."

Kelli gritted her teeth. A series of retorts flashed through her mind—agree with sheepishness, disagree with indignation, punch him.

To her credit, she didn't flinch when he leaned closer and spoke in her ear. "Don't worry, Kel. Your secret's safe with me."

He strode away, the crowd swallowing his lean form.

Blinking rapidly, she willed the burn in her eyes to ease. Jayd had an annoying knack of cutting to the heart of a matter. This wasn't the first time.

Hang him.

A passing waiter took her unfinished drink, but she declined a fresh glass. Her three swallows of alcohol were a mistake, proven by an overwhelming desire to cry. When the persistent waiter hovered, Kelli waved him off.

If she didn't get out of there soon, she'd start blubbering. Then her colleagues would dub her Big Baby rather than Ice Queen. Everyone would know about her feelings for Sean. She had to leave. Now.

She turned and in four steps ran headlong into her supervisor.

"Ms. Layne." The man spoke with the warmth of

granite. "Just the person I wanted."

"Sir?"

"How much alcohol have you had this evening?"

Odd question. "A couple swallows, sir."

"Perfect." He spoke in an overly loud voice, rocking on his feet. "Someone told me you're next in line on the roster."

I'm not, but… Wisdom sealed her lips. Her boss had a nasty way of punishing any perceived insubordination.

"You need to take over Runkle and Munly's assignment."

Kelli resisted the urge to cite regulations—she carried no badge or weapon, hadn't been prepped. And she was taking over for two agents?

She carefully crafted her question. "What assignment, sir?"

"Protection of Reese's stepdaughter."

A protest nearly burst from her. Clenching a fist, she smoothed her expression into serenity. "There's nothing I'd like better than to take care of that kid."

He nodded, shoulders relaxing. Obviously he missed her sarcasm.

"Wait here. Reese is on his way with the girl." The man reeled away.

Her jaw jutted. If only she'd gone to her hotel room fifteen minutes ago. If only she'd dodged Jayd and his intrusive questions.

"Kelli?"

Sean's voice jerked her from introspection. She willed her heartbeat to stop its erratic cadence as she turned to the man she still desperately loved. Her throat went dry at how his amazing physique filled his formal attire.

Play the part. Pretend. She'd done it before.

"Sorry to spoil your fun." His baritone sent shivers down her spine.

"No problem." The lie fell glibly from her lips. "I was hoping for a little action."

"Afraid there won't be much with a seven year old." He smiled at the solemn girl beside him, hand in his. A miniature of her mother, the child was kind of cute in violet taffeta. "Ella, this is Ms. Layne." Sean looked up. "Can she call you Kelli?"

"Sure."

"Kelli's going to watch over you until midnight. That work for you both?"

Midnight? *Gah!* That was hours away. Nodding, Kelli managed a frozen smile.

Sean clasped his stepdaughter's hand between both his. "You don't have to stay here the whole time. Head up to the suite whenever you want."

Kelli's veneer threatened to crack. The honeymoon suite?

He knelt before the girl. "I'm going to go back to your mom now. Okay?"

"Okay," Ella whispered.

Sean bent to kiss her cheek. "If you need anything, let Kelli know."

He started to rise when the girl threw her arms around his neck. When her hold tightened, his expression flashed pure wonder.

Kelli had never seen that kind of look on her father's face.

"Have fun, sweetie." His voice grew husky. He rose and touched Kelli's elbow. "Thanks a lot. I appreciate this more than I can say."

She stared after him, skin tingling where his fingers had brushed.

I'd do anything for you, Sean. Anything.

But the words were much too late. And best left unspoken.

She started when a small, frail hand slipped into hers.

"So, um, you hungry?" Kelli struggled to find her voice.

With brown eyes fixed on her, Ella shook her head.

She cleared her throat. "Then how about something to drink?"

One shoulder lifted as the girl turned her face away.

"Okay." Kelli spoke with more assurance than she felt. By the stars, she hadn't a clue what to do with a kid. She herself was an only child with one cousin eighteen years her senior. "I wouldn't recommend the synth-ale. Stuff tastes terrible."

Ella grinned as she continued to study her shoes. Good sign?

"How about some punch? That sound all right?"

"Yes, please."

A server magically appeared and took their drink order—slushies for two.

Hand in hand, they waited. Kelli intercepted the smirks of her colleagues, which she doused with a glacial glare. If anyone ribbed her, she'd pummel them the next time they met for physical training. As a bonus, she'd give them a nice bruise or two. And they knew it.

The waiter brought drinks, a garnish thoughtfully added to Ella's. Since the girl liked the punch so much, they got a second. Slightly salty, the icy blue slipped down in the growing heat. Kelli marveled that the little girl didn't grow weary of hanging onto her hand. Perhaps the kid was lonelier than she?

A distant memory hit Kelli, one where she'd been to a party as a child. No one had watched over her. A picture of a large, dark dining hall buffeted her. *I was eleven.* The memory sharpened and came into painful focus. Not a party. It had been her mother's funeral.

She pushed the thought away, fighting weepiness. What kind of imported champagne were they serving? She grabbed two orange Xerxian berries from a nearby platter and wolfed them down. Their waiter appeared again, but she declined. No more drinks. Not even slushies.

The room dimmed. A spotlight snapped on Sean and his wife as they took the dance floor.

"Can I see?" Ella craned to look.

After leading her to a chair, Kelli helped her balance on it.

Ella's parents made a beautiful couple. Sean's sandy hair contrasted with Aric's brunette. Towering over her, he escorted her gracefully across the dance floor. Kelli marveled at his ease of movement.

I should be in his arms. Oh, Sean.

But he had eyes only for the woman who smiled up at him.

Kelli sucked a deep breath, unable to tear her gaze away. Even when Ella leaned against her shoulder, she couldn't stop watching them. Couldn't stop torturing herself with, *Why not me?*

When Sean kissed his wife, the crowd murmured approval. The smattering of applause broke her trance.

The girl tugged on Kelli's scarf. "I have to use the bathroom, please."

Glad to escape, she snagged their waiter and asked for directions to the nearest facility. Instead of merely telling her, he led them through an exit. "The one down here isn't as crowded."

Before she could ask which way, the door shut. The ill-lit hallway apparently doubled as a storage area with chairs and tables lining the walls. Where was the restroom? She considered going back into the ballroom, but Ella started walking on tiptoes. Time to hurry.

"Let's go...*this* direction." It took forever to pick their way through the dizzying maze. When they turned the corner, she found a promising sign.

They rushed inside. While Ella went into a stall, Kelli set her clutch on the counter to rummage for lipstick. She stared at her pasty skin in the mirror. Her blue eyes looked so bloodshot, they appeared fueled by neon lights. "Ugh, I look ghastly."

"I think you're pretty." Ella's voice came from behind a slatted door.

"Thanks. I think you are too." When her scarf slipped yet again, she wound it once more about her neck and flung the ends over her shoulders.

The girl washed and dried her hands, countenance...adoring? Kelli smoothed on lipstick, then tucked a stray tress into her bun.

The girl continued to stare. "I wish I had blond hair."

"Changing brown to blond is easy." She paused, sensing the girl needed assurance. Why the empathy for a lonely girl? Like Kelli cared what the kid felt. "What's harder to change are your features. Someday everyone will envy your pretty lips and cute chin."

Ella shyly smiled.

"I like you. You're nice." The child's expression added a dimension of seriousness that left no doubt of sincerity.

Kelli released a breath, not even aware she'd been holding it. Heedless of her long gown, she knelt before the girl.

"I like you too, Ella. You're a very special person." She pressed her lips together before adding, "And you have two wonderful parents who love you very much." She blinked rapidly. What was wrong with her? She felt about ready to lose it.

"When I grow up, I want to be like you."

Kelli resisted the urge to say, *No, you do not.* Instead, she smoothed a strand of hair off the girl's forehead. "That's a sweet thing to say. Thank you."

Ella's skin was soft. Eyes so trusting. She radiated innocence.

Had Kelli ever been like that?

Behind her, a whisper of sound alerted her that someone entered the restroom. Ella's eyes widened. Still kneeling, Kelli glanced over her shoulder.

Black shoes. Dress pants. A man?

Feet lunged forward. Kelli struggled to rise. Her heel caught on her gown. Off balance, she teetered. *Too late.*

A fist swung. She flinched, avoiding most of the impact. Pain exploded in her head. Her scarf tightened. Weight pressed downward. Tile dug into her knees.

Where was Ella?

Kelli slid fingers between the material and her throat. "Ella." She choked out the word. "Run!"

Flailing, Kelli sought to strike her assailant. A door banged. Footsteps pattered out of earshot.

Vision blurred. Air became precious.

Her fingernails connected. The man grunted, hold loosening. Again she struck, gouging skin. He retaliated by stomping on the back of her ankle. She screamed, the sound gurgling.

The noose constricted. Gagging, she tried to push up. One leg flopped. Useless. Her gown imprisoned the other. Flashes of light exploded in her vision.

Her world plunged into dark pain.

Chapter 2

"Kelli! Do you hear me? Dear God, please…"

The faraway voice battered her. Cold riddled her body. Hard tile ground into the back of her head. Warm hands chafed hers.

She inhaled, air rasping into her lungs. Back arching, she gagged.

Strong arms raised her as a paroxysm seized her. Planets tilted as Kelli fought for equilibrium. She groaned. Arms encircled her as she pressed against a stiff starched shirt.

Was she alive? She had to be. It hurt too much.

"Thank You, Lord." The familiar voice came again. "Thank You…."

Who…? She pried open reluctant eyes to see Jayd's mouth flattened into a grim slash.

For now, she merely breathed.

"You're okay. You're going to be okay." Jayd's voice soothed as he cradled her. Fingers brushed hair from her face.

"Ella…" Another coughing fit demolished the sentence.

"Gone." His tone grew terse. "Taken."

"My–my responsibi–" Kelli couldn't articulate the words. Her throat burned. A burgeoning dizziness engulfed her. Her ankle screamed in agony.

"You were outnumbered. I saw one man. Had to be more."

She shook her head.

"There was nothing you could do, Kel. I'm glad I got to you in time."

She fought to speak.

"Wait." He pressed an imbedded security chip behind his ear to activate a hidden mic. "South hallway. She's alive but needs a medic. Yes, sir, I'll stay with her."

Floor tilting, Kelli slumped against him. How could she have knelt with her back to the door? How could she have been so stupid? She'd been oblivious to danger.

"Ella," she whispered, then blurted, "Sean!"

How could she admit she'd let him down? When he found out, what would he say? She would never be able to look him in the eye again.

Wheezing intermingled with hard coughing. She clutched Jayd's tuxedo.

"Take it easy, Kel." His calm voice fell low on her ear. "Your ankle's broken. God knows what else they did to you."

It didn't matter. She wanted to shriek her utter failure and self-loathing. Instead she buried her forehead against Jayd's chest, fighting an overwhelming urge to bawl. His hold tightened, fingers stroking her head and bare shoulder.

"I've got to go after her." The words grated through her raw throat. "They couldn't have—"

"You're not going anywhere. You can't."

Medics arrived. One attempted to pry her grip from Jayd. "We've got her, sir. Step back please."

"No!" Kelli fought them. "Jayd, we need to find her..."

Sharp glances passed between him and the two medics. Why were her words slurring?

"Every available agent is looking for Ella." He grasped her arm. "I'm not leaving you."

They allowed him to hang onto her hand while they examined her. What were they saying? Heart rate escalating? Blood pressure rising? Time passed in agonizing slowness while the medics hastened to stabilize her. The whole time she kept her gaze focused on Jayd.

"A gurney's coming," one EMT said.

"No. Jayd, help me." When she pushed up on one wrist, the room swam crazily. She slumped back against him. Her pulse thrummed through every nerve in her body. What was pounding on her eardrums?

Again, the mute communication passed between

the three men.

One medic shoved his face into view. "We need to take you to the clinic now. Your ankle is—"

"No." She struggled for breath. "I'll be fine."

"Kelli." Jayd's pinched face captured her attention. "You're *not* fine. I'll stay with you, but you need medical attention."

She shook her head. "I have to find Ella. I have to."

At least, that's what she thought she said.

He squeezed her hand. "You need to take care of yourself. Then we'll find Ella."

"Promise?" A half-sob choked her. She rallied. "You have to promise me."

Stupid weakness!

"I promise."

From what seemed a great distance, she heard others enter the room, static communication, shouts, loud talking. She closed her eyes at the barrage, hanging on to one sanity—Jayd's hand holding hers. Nausea, pain, vertigo. All threatened to overwhelm her. She refused to open her eyes as several people called her name. One medic responded curtly to the harsh questions fired at her.

The near-hysterical babble of a crowd. The ear-piercing wail of a medic cart. The cool air of the sub-rail. A bumpy ride through the outpost. Lights. More noise. Adrenaline-laced voices.

The hand that wouldn't let go.

"Kelli? Kelli, look at me." Jayd's voice pierced the shroud of agony. "I can't go with you any further. But I'll be here when you get out of surgery."

She couldn't speak, but she made him promise

with her eyes. Tears pooled at the bridge of her nose.

"I'll be right here." His warm fingers trailed across her cheek.

A sharp hiss at her neck and darkness engulfed her.

"You came in with...with the girl?" The medic yawned while he spoke.

Girl? Jayd stifled his irritation and merely nodded. His gaze raked the surgeon, automatically assessing the man.

Mid to late forties. Overweight by fifteen to twenty pounds. Likes synth-ale a little too much. Divorced? His unkemptness comes from more than the late hour. Slight discoloration on ring finger. Missing band. Recent.

The man yawned again. "She's going to be fine."

Jayd released a breath he didn't know he'd been holding. "Good to know."

Out of habit, he scanned the doctor's ID microchip with his comm-unit. For the last several hours, he had been doing nothing but check USF's progress on the case as per the director's orders. And wait.

Agents and other authorities had been alerted and were in place. The search was on for Ella. Jayd's one and only assignment was to remain at the medical center, monitor Kelli, and report back once he knew her status.

"She's suffered a MTBI—layman's terms: mild concussion. Fractured ankle. Pretty severe. Hematoma. Bruising at her throat, obviously. Mild abrasions." The man ticked off the injuries like he was reciting a grocery list. He stifled a third yawn. "Her voice should come back without therapy. She was lucky."

Lucky? Jayd clenched his jaw.

The man frowned. "I probably should've verified first. You're her…?"

"Friend." The man didn't need to know more.

The doctor's eyebrows raised, a slight smirk on his face.

He met the medic's gaze steadily, detaching himself from his growing fury. *Overinflated ego. Used to throwing his weight around.* In a cool voice, Jayd added, "I'm responsible for her."

"Oh, really? That include her level of partying?"

Habit and training tamped down a retort. Instead, icy calm flowed through him at the man's insulting tone. "Excuse me?"

"Don't play stupid. This is a big weekend here. You brought her in, you know what she's been doing."

"Look, Doctor…" Jayd leaned forward and pretended to read the man's nametag, "Deitman. I need to know everything about Special Agent Layne's condition. Right now. You can make my life easy or I can make yours uncomfortable."

Jayd seemed to recall the clinic repeatedly paging Deitman. For Kelli's surgery? Because the doctor didn't take his responsibilities very seriously or because he was distracted by something else?

The man shrugged, a sneer marring his face. "It'll all be in my report. Should be done tomorrow. Or later today." He looked at the chronometer on the wall. "Say noonish."

Information on the surgeon started popping up on

Jayd's CU's screen. Including some intriguing red flags. "I'll take the verbal one now. And I need to know where she is."

"You're not seeing her tonight. My orders."

This was a game Jayd was not going to play. The usual bluff would have no effect on this idiot, so he pulled out his ID and held it in front of the man's nose. A deliberate four inches. "I *will* be checking her." He paused to let the physician read his security level. "About that report?"

Deitman glowered. "Layne's blood alcohol level was abnormally high. She also had some unusual substances in her system. She's stable now, but the drugs complicated surgery. She'll need to be detoxed for at least forty-eight hours."

"Drugs? What kind of drugs?"

Still cynical, the man rolled his eyes. "Illegal ones."

Jayd clenched his fist. "What did you say?"

"Like I told you, it'll be in my report."

"The lab made a mistake."

"You know where she got the hyper-flavones? Maybe you provided them." Deitman radiated hostility and self-righteousness. "I'll need to contact the Xerxian authorities. Recreational drugs are strictly forbidden here. Even though this space station is disputed territory, it's the gateway to their world. We abide by their laws."

Jayd drew himself up and spoke in frigid tones. "You will do nothing of the kind. This is an internal matter for the Universal Security Forces. And as for your veiled insinuation about my providing illegal drugs to her, I'll try to overlook that in my statement to the director when I personally report to her."

Deitman's mouth flattened into a white line.

Still rebellious. And stupid.

Details about the doctor glowed on the screen of his CU. "Well, well, look at this." Jayd allowed his shoulders to relax and a smile to grace his lips. "Says you're behind on two child-support payments. And a four-year old parking ticket is still outstanding in Chicago City." He let his gaze flick to the doctor. "Trying to dodge those by hiding on this outpost?"

"I'd never… How dare you insinuate that I'm…?" The man blustered to a stop. "What gives you the right to check into my personal rec—?"

"Oh, this is fascinating," Jayd interrupted. "Apparently Xerxians take financial support of offspring very seriously. Missing even one payment is punishable by twenty days of manual labor."

"I'm a Terran citizen. You can't turn me over to the Xer—"

"This station is disputed territory, remember?" Jayd deliberately kept his tone soft. "It's the gateway to their world. Didn't you say we abide by their laws?"

The medic fumed noisily for a couple more seconds.

"Good thing I happen to have the Xerxian embassy's contact info right here." Jayd tapped c-mail's quick-send.

His finger paused when the doctor sputtered. "Don't send that. I'll cooperate."

Amazing what a few well-placed threats could do. Deitman visibly trembled from pent-up fury. But he had the wisdom to keep his mouth shut. Finally.

"Now, as I was saying…" Jayd paused, letting the man sweat a moment. "I want you to personally check the lab report. I'll need a complete list of all the drugs and their side effects. I want to know exactly how they could have gotten into Kelli Layne's bloodstream. Furthermore, I'll be posting two guards at her door. Make sure your staff has proper identification or you'll be treating their injuries too."

The man folded his arms. "I don't have time to be an errand boy. I have other duties which—"

"Consider yourself relieved until further notice." He tapped out a communiqué to the director. *Urgent: Increase security level of med clinic to one. Protection imperative for Layne.*

The doctor blanched. "You didn't…I mean, please don't send anything to the Xerxians. I swear I'll catch up on payments as soon as—"

"One more thing," Jayd interrupted yet again, not even bothering to relieve the man's anxiety. "I don't want to hear gossip about Special Agent Layne's medical condition. Anywhere. Understood?"

He swallowed convulsively. "Yes. Yes, of course. Anything."

"Good." Jayd smiled expansively. "We're going to her room now. And then you're going to call a staff meeting so that everybody understands the new rules. Got it?"

"Yes, sir." The doctor's chin quivered. "I got it."

As they walked down the hall, the director's reply scrolled across the screen of Jayd's CU. He blew out a breath. Regardless of Kelli's condition, he was to get her report as soon as possible.

Guarding her had been the easy part. Getting her to spill her guts would be a whole 'nother matter.

Kelli was bound to hate him for it.

"Hey, Kel." Jayd's voice and face floated into focus.

She stared at him. Why was he in her apartment? She closed her eyes again. This had to be a dream.

His gentle touch on her hand pulled her from the abyss. "You're in a hospital on the Xerxes space station. Ring a bell?"

When the head of the bed began to lift slowly, she winced at the grinding noise. This hurt too much to be a dream.

Kelli assessed the room between sleepy blinks. Metal bars on the bed. Open curtains. Artificial light from the window. Muted beeping. Comm-panel.

Jayd's worried face.

Sitting up felt good, although it made her head swim. Again she focused on him. "How long since *you* slept?" Her voice sounded raspy.

A grin split his face. "Good to have you back. And your voice sounds better than expected."

She evaluated his condition. "I'd say three days. That how long I've been out?"

"Give or take. They kept you sedated—detox protocol. And you had some nasty injuries."

Detox? She pressed her head against the pillow, trying to remember. Anything. When she tried to lift her hand, the med cuff imprisoned one arm.

What had happened?

Jayd answered as though she'd asked the question aloud. "You were assigned to guard Ella Reese at the reception. You were attacked. Ella taken. We don't know by whom or how many. I saw only one man. So far no contact, no ransom demands. Technically, this is Intergalaxia's jurisdiction. For now, USF's director has been authorized to remain abreast of any information pertaining to this case."

Her eyes squeezed shut. "I remember now." She swore softly, then fixed her gaze on Jayd. "I was out three days? Who authorized that?"

"You needed time—"

"No, I need to find Ella." She struggled to sit upright. "Who's the idiot that let the kidnappers get a head start?"

Jayd pressed her shoulder with a warm palm. "The director."

The only one who could override her protest. Kelli wilted against the sheets. Though this director was new—the last one had resigned under a cloud of suspicion—she was a "by the book" administrator.

"There's more." His lingering fingers tightened. "You not only had a blood alcohol level of over point one-zero, but it was climbing—indicating you'd assimilated something that caused your B.A.C. to escalate. Good thing we caught it in time."

"I didn't take anything. I only had a little champagne." A memory slipped from her grasp, then returned. "I told my sup that when he asked." She looked at him. "I had a couple sips. The drink was in my hand when you talked to me, remember? I never finished it."

"Lab tests say otherwise, Kel. I checked and re-checked them myself."

Her breath came more rapidly. Vaguely, she heard the beep of a monitor speed up as well.

Jayd's gaze pinned her. "Drugs were found by your purse in the bathroom."

"What?"

He said nothing more, his brow drawn, mouth tight.

"I don't do drugs, Jayd." She coughed to dislodge the annoying hoarseness in her voice. "You know that."

"Guests say otherwise. They saw you pop a few at the party."

Clutching at the recollections, she fought to form coherent thoughts. "Wait. Yes. I took something for a headache. The bellhop brought meds to my room just before I went to the ballroom."

Could the pills have been something other than an aspirin derivative?

"Somebody set me up." When Jayd didn't answer, she grabbed his wrist. "You believe me, don't you? I swear, those weren't mine. And I didn't drink any alcohol after I was assigned. I don't know how..." She broke off, again feeling like a memory danced on the edges of her mind.

"What do you recall?"

"I–I remember..." She stared at the tan dimpled ceiling tile, piecing together the events. "A waiter. Seemed like we always had the same waiter." She met Jayd's gaze steadily. "He got punch for Ella and me. I thought it tasted a little funny, but I'm not a slushy expert."

He didn't grin as she expected. Instead, his jaw tightened. "Want to tell me about that night?"

She withdrew her hand to rub her forehead. "We hung around the party for a while. Ella had to use the restroom. We ended up in a back hallway."

"How'd that happen?"

She couldn't recall exactly. "Guess I got turned around."

"Why didn't you go back to the ballroom?"

Why hadn't she? Kelli lowered her eyes. Yes, she had a legitimate excuse—Ella's need. But that wasn't the whole truth.

"Because of Sean, right?"

Kelli plucked at the sheet, refusing to look up.

"You couldn't stand to see him and Aric together." He leaned closer. "Admit it, Kel."

"Okay, it was a stupid mistake." She glared at him. "But did you have to mention Sean again? You said my secret was safe. I remember your exact words."

He took his time answering. "True. But I *didn't* say I wouldn't bring it up again."

Beep, beep, beep. The monitor sounded louder in the intolerable silence.

Jayd sighed. "Then what happened?" His softened voice invited confession.

"It's kind of fuzzy." She chewed her lip. "We found a bathroom. And I was kneeling on the floor."

"Why?"

"I was..." She pressed her fingers to her forehead. "I was talking to Ella. Someone came in."

"Man or woman?"

She reflected. "Man. He had on dress shoes."

"A guest?" Surprise flitted across Jayd's face.

"Possibly. Or one of the servers. I never got a good look." She took a shaky breath. *Beep-beep. Beep-beep.* "He must have been waiting outside. Watching. Listening." She stared at the impressionist painting on the wall. "No doubt a professional. Knew what he was doing. I was incapacitated fairly quickly."

"Not an easy thing to do."

"I acted like a noob. A stupid noob!" Kelli again passed a hand over her face. "I had my back to the door. I was kneeling. I felt tipsy and never thought it strange."

"Sounds like you didn't take your assignment seriously."

He was right, of course. She'd been so focused on her disappointment, on self-pity, that she'd let down her guard. Useless to say her sup also hadn't thought the job significant. He'd given her an assignment meant for two agents. No use pointing fingers now.

Hating the weakness, she fought the burn in her eyes. "What am I going to do, Jayd? How am I going to explain my actions?"

How could she ever face Sean?

Eyes full of pity, Jayd said nothing.

She pressed her lips together, then plunged on. "Can you access my hotel room? Get my comm-unit?"

"For?"

"So I can make notes on what I plan to say when I give my official statement. I'm sure USF won't wait long."

"They haven't."

What did that mean?

Jayd cleared his throat. "You just gave it."

"What?"

Beep-beep, beep-beep, beep-beep.

His face was shadowed, the artificial light streaming behind him. He retrieved his CU from his pocket and snapped it off. Then he removed a tiny pin from his lapel. A camera?

If she'd been stripped naked before a crowd, she wouldn't have felt more violated. "You...?" She clenched her teeth. "How could you?"

His dark eyes flashed regret, but ever the professional, his shoulders stiffened. "I have already confiscated your badge and weapon from your room. And I've been instructed to inform you that until further notice, you are suspended."

Chapter 3

Kelli clutched the door jam in her apartment, battling the occasional lightheadedness that had plagued her for two weeks. Not only that, but she felt like she had gained twenty pounds overnight. Because she hadn't yet readjusted to Earth's gravity?

Craning her chin upward, she checked her neck in the mirror. Good. The ugly bruise had finally faded, giving her the confidence that it would draw no unwanted stares. Gingerly she tested her ankle, grateful that the outpost had one of the most advanced bone menders. It wouldn't do to fall flat on her face when she walked up to Sean. She wanted to put her best foot forward, so to speak.

How would he react when he saw her?

He might slam the door in her face when she showed up—unannounced—at his home. But this was the only way she could see him. Her calls to USF to arrange a meeting had failed. As a newly promoted division chief, Sean was booked for the next month.

While she'd been recovering on the Xerxian space station, she'd expected him to pop in. Nothing. Only later did she learn the Reeses had departed with an armed escort the day after the kidnapping. Had they no choice but to leave?

The moment Kelli's therapist released her, she had returned to Earth. Her impromptu stop at USF headquarters to see Sean had failed. Security wouldn't let her past the foyer. That left only one thing to do—go directly to his house.

And if USF or Intergalaxia didn't like it, tough.

"Besides, what are they going to do?" Kelli asked her reflection as she smoothed the collar of her teal-colored pantsuit. "Suspend me again?"

USF hadn't reinstated her. Hadn't debriefed her. Hadn't bothered to request a face-to-face meeting.

Her mouth tightened as she thought of her ignored calls and unanswered c-mails. Even from her teammates. Were they afraid to talk to her? Or was something more sinister going on?

The only way she'd been able to keep abreast of the kidnapping news was through the regular media channels. According to them, Inter-G was heading up the investigation, but they had made no arrests.

She slipped on earrings. "Fifteen flippin' days on the case and nothing yet?"

Clenching her teeth, she refused to dwell on Ella being in the hands of ruthless criminals. The longer she was missing, the greater the chances she was dead.

No. Ella *had* to be alive.

Once she was rescued, USF would reinstate Kelli. End of story. But for now, she had to take care of this one vital task.

Meet with Sean.

She limped to her aero-car, strapped herself in and locked the apartment door with voice command. Though the weather advisory warned against air travel because of high winds, she bypassed the automatic lockdown. Her Class A license allowed her to fly, even in rough weather. The extra cost to travel by air instead of by ground would be worth all the fees she would pay if it meant getting to Sean's sooner. With it being Saturday, he was likely home.

After setting the coordinates into the GPS, she took off. Once she cleared the building's parkspace, she switched back to manual. The difficult flight kept her mind off the speech she'd rehearsed to death over the last couple weeks. Kelli blew out several cleansing breaths.

This would be no big deal. She would admit her failure and move on. Perhaps this would be the first step in smoothing things over with USF.

All too soon, she reached his exclusive neighborhood and found the house number. After parking on the street, she gave herself a last-minute pep talk. "You can do this. You've *got* to."

She stepped out of the car. As she walked up the driveway, she gaped at the size of the house. It had to be a Level Five home, complete with a second story. Did it also have a basement? Extravagant. Her Level Two apartment was dinky by comparison.

A private yard and fence surrounded the house. And it had trees. Lots of them. Hanging from the eaves, a humming bird feeder danced in the wind. An expensive glider rested on its charge pad, humming in rest mode. A doll lay on the cushions, forgotten.

Did Ella like to sit there? Kelli imagined the seven-year-old, legs swinging as she watched birds flit around the feeder. Or her skipping across the grass. Did Sean play hide-and-seek while his stepdaughter hid in the shrubbery? Or behind the trees?

Catching her breath, she grew aware of how forlorn this place must feel without that little girl.

At the sound of the front door opening, she swiveled. Aric strode out.

No. *Not her!*

Where was Sean? Kelli glanced at the house, searching the windows. Empty. *He* was supposed to be there. To be alone with Aric...

This was going to be awful.

"Kelli!" Several yards away, Aric stopped. In the darkening afternoon, her skin appeared anemic, starker because brown hair framed it. Her green eyes were red-rimmed, face haggard. She wore jeans and a royal blue cotton blouse, nothing like the elegant woman of the reception. More down to earth.

Vulnerable.

Kelli's mouth moved, but no sound came out. *Does*

she know I am in love with Sean?

Expression suddenly melting, Aric strode across the expanse and flung arms about her. "Thank you so much. Thank you for all you did. Words cannot express..." She broke off, a deep sob choking her. "You nearly died for my daughter. I cannot begin to tell you..."

A storm of emotion slammed against Kelli. She couldn't breathe. Couldn't think. A crumbling flood-wall pressed against her, the monstrous waves threatening to overtake her. The tempest continued to build as Sean's wife sobbed, her slim body shuddering against her. Everything Kelli needed to say jammed in her throat.

I'm sorry about Ella.

I wish I'd been stronger.

I'm so sorry I failed you.

Tears strangled her, colliding with a swell of self-recrimination. How could she have been so stupid? How could she have allowed Ella to be taken?

She refused to give into weeping. Anger overcame the desire to melt in sorrow. Kelli gritted her teeth so hard her jaw ached.

Finally, Aric pulled back. "I'm so sorry. I ruined your beautiful outfit."

Kelli fought to answer. "No big deal."

"I guess you've heard?"

Uncertain what she meant, Kelli nodded nevertheless. Besides, she couldn't trust her own voice.

"The kidnappers..." The grieving mother retrieved a wadded tissue from her pocket and blew her nose. "It's awful. The waiting." She pulled out another tissue, then shredded both as she talked. "I can't sleep. I don't know what to do. What not to do. I keep imagining I hear my phone. Even when I sleep. I wake up a million times a night, thinking I hear Ella. I'm afraid to leave the house in case—" A sob cut off her words.

Kelli awkwardly patted her shoulder.

With a heroic effort, Aric gathered herself. "But I'm glad you came. I've been so worried about you."

"I'm...I'm fine."

"You were injured." Her mouth quivered. "Trying to protect Ella."

Kelli's eyes burned. "I was so inadequate."

"No, you were incredibly brave."

"That's kind of you to say." The words came out barely above a whisper.

"I wanted to visit you. On the space station. But they..." Aric's mouth tightened. "Inter-G wouldn't let us even talk to you. I was so angry. I'm *still* angry."

"I understand." Kelli dislodged the frog from her throat. "It's okay."

The wind whipped around them and roared against the house. In her peripheral vision, she saw the bird feeder swing crazily as it spun.

"What am I thinking?" Aric cast a glance into the sky. "Let's go inside before the storm breaks and we get drenched."

"No, really I—"

"Come on." Ignoring her protest, the woman tugged on her arm. "I made a pot of coffee a half hour ago. Please don't make me pour it down the drain."

Where were all her handy excuses? Kelli had been so prepared to give Sean her speech that she'd not considered he might be absent.

Mind blank, she let Aric shepherd her toward the front door. What could they possibly have in common to talk about?

Of all the stupid things Kelli had done in her life, allowing Sean's wife to get chummy would top them all.

"How're you liking the soundproof room downstairs?" Jayd propped up his feet on the leather ottoman.

Sean slumped in the seat opposite him. "Great."

"Workers did an awesome job laying the slate in the entryway too."

"Um-hmm." Sean nodded, smile vacant.

For fifteen minutes, Jayd had attempted to get his friend talking. About anything besides the one topic that hounded them day and night—Ella.

Ensconced in his friend's private home office, Jayd fingered his mug of coffee. Not that he was really interested in it, but Aric had been insistent. If making the brew helped occupy her, he gladly would provide a respite from agonizing over her daughter's disappearance. She was starting to appear gaunt, like she hadn't eaten or slept since the kidnapping.

The way I must have looked after my wife's death.

Sean's sigh drew his attention back to him. "I don't understand why..." He leaned forward to rest his head between his hands.

Why the kidnappers hadn't made contact? That

question seemed to be on everyone's lips. The longer no one communicated with the Reeses, the greater the probability that Ella would never come home.

A dozen useless phrases barraged Jayd's mind. What could he say that hadn't already been voiced by well-meaning friends and colleagues? Take heart? Don't fear?

"How's Aric doing?"

Sean shook his head. "She stuffs it. Won't open up. Won't cry. I hear her roaming the house at night. Since her mother left, she barely talks. Even to me."

Again, Jayd remained silent. The USF psychiatrist had told his friends to stay busy, to get on with life. He didn't need to repeat it. "I pray for you. All the time."

"I know." Sean's mouth spasmed as he stared at the floor. "Thank you."

Jayd studied the *Rachael D.* paintings in the office, which depicted images from her *New Worlds* collection. The searing whites and brilliant yellows of birthing stars bespoke hope in the relentless space black. The burgundies and taupes were a perfect match to the dark woods of the furniture and studious atmosphere of Sean's office. Appropriate. No doubt Aric chose them.

How would Jayd's house be decorated? Had his wife lived, he imagined she would have chosen a more traditional Chinese décor. Like Sean and Aric, they would have lived just outside New Washington. Jayd's parents would have insisted. They despised big city apartments with foldable rooms and enviro-life systems that controlled all aspects of high-rise living. Back then, both he and Liu always sought to keep the in laws happy.

But that was another life. Hard to believe nearly ten years had passed since her death.

Jayd shifted his attention back to his friend. Time to get on with what he'd come to do. But he had to proceed carefully. He wasn't even supposed to ask about the investigation.

"So, what's this about a body?" Jayd lifted his mug, but realized how his question could be misconstrued. He quickly added, "From the space station?"

Expression leery, Sean raised bloodshot eyes. "Where'd you hear about that?"

Keeping his face neutral, Jayd shrugged. "Word gets around. You know USF." He refused to compromise his Inter-G informant. Ryan and he had swapped inside information ever since they'd begun working at their respective organizations.

Plausible deniability. Jayd would merely get a reprimand, but Sean risked his career. The less his friend knew about his sources, the better.

When he remained silent, Jayd pressed. "One of the waiters, right?"

"We're not supposed to be having this conversation." Sean's fingertips dug into the leather armrests. "Inter-G made it clear that USF needs to butt out."

"Yeah, I know." He bit off a scathing addendum.

The space station was intergalactic territory, therefore Inter-G was in charge. Or so the logic went. They wanted no help—or interference—from any other organization.

However, Jayd refused to sit on his thumbs. On his own, he'd done some quiet investigation. Like visit the former director of SARC, a man incarcerated because of Sean and Aric's testimony. Though Jayd had found no direct evidence linking him with the kidnappers, he had no doubt the guy was involved. Somehow. Unfortunately, Jayd had to drop the inquiry. Inter-G would find out.

He waited until his friend took a sip of his coffee. "Think the waiter was Kelli's attacker? He fits the details she gave us about him."

Setting his coffee down with a clunk, Sean noisily cleared his throat. The meaning was clear—*back off.*

"They match the DNA?" Ignoring the warnings, Jayd leaned back in his seat. "If she clawed him, the skin under her fingernails would positively ID him."

His friend's jaw morphed into stone. The gesture proved to be exceedingly informative.

"Ah." Jayd straightened. "The sample got contaminated? That the hospital's fault or Inter-G's?"

Sean growled. "What is it with you? Can't leave well enough alone?"

"No. And you know that."

His friend shook his head, but it appeared as though he was softening.

Jayd leaned forward. "So which was it?"

"Hospital." His friend spoke out of the corner of his mouth as he pretended to study the wall art.

"Figures." Jayd squelched a desire to denigrate them even further. First they delayed Kelli's surgery because they couldn't locate the surgeon, then they botched the sample. "I never did tell you about the idiot doctor I encountered there. Acted like he was God's gift to humanity."

His friend snorted, shoulders relaxing. "I know the kind."

"Treated Kelli like she was some drunken prom queen on a binge." And Jayd, her date with a sinister agenda.

Like Kelli would ever date me. Especially since she admitted to being in love with Sean. Not that Jayd planned to ask her out. The idea was stupid on so many levels. Relationships at work were always a bad idea. Though they were on different teams, he was a senior agent.

And he was a follower of Christ. She definitely was not.

How many times had he heard her deride anything religious? She mocked Christians the most. In the years they'd known each other, he had avoided that topic, even hiding the fact that he was one.

Sean cradled his mug. "How is she, by the way?"

He took his time answering. "Okay, last time I saw her." Since the Xerxian Outpost, she wasn't too happy with him. "She's on Earth now. Got in the day before yesterday."

"Really?" His friend got a speculative look. "I should go see her."

Jayd shook his head. "Wait, I thought talking to her was strictly prohibited." He recalled the grilling he himself had received from USF and Inter-G.

"I don't plan to discuss the kidnapping."

"Okay, but are you sure visiting her is a good idea?" Jayd didn't need to spell out the reasons. Several people had commented on her stricken look at Sean's reception. Though Jayd had edited his report, the gossip still multiplied.

"She needs closure."

"There's talk of further repercussions."

"Which I'm adamantly against." Sean's jaw flexed. "She's a fine agent. We'd be foolish to lose her." Before Jayd could respond, his friend added, "I'll never forget her professionalism when we were both undercover at SARC. Her ability to maintain a convincing persona. Well, you know. You were her handler."

Yes, Jayd did know. That year they'd worked together had fired his admiration for Kelli. It had given him a chance to really get to know her.

And her to get to know Sean.

Jayd studied his friend. Was that when Kelli had fallen in love with him? When Sean had posed as a security guard and romantically pursued the supposed shy admin assistant? Maybe she had taken his act a little too seriously.

Pushing away that thought, Jayd debated whether or not to share the rumors he'd heard at work. If nothing else, they would serve to warn Sean about the general consensus at USF. "You know what they're saying about Kelli, don't you? That she purposefully let down her guard, hoping something would happen to Ella."

"There's nothing I'd like better than to take care of that kid." Though he was certain Kelli had meant nothing by the comment, her supervisor now attached an ominous significance to her words. So did other witnesses.

How had Jayd missed the fact that everyone got drunk so quickly? Or that one specific waiter had hovered around Kelli and Ella?

He'd been so focused on Kelli that he'd thought of

nothing else. Yes, he had saved her life. But if he'd paid attention to the big picture, he could have saved her *and* prevented the kidnapping.

Sean's mouth set. "People say the stupidest things."

Shifting in his seat, Jayd cast about for a way to bring the subject back to the investigation. Nothing subtle came to mind, so he decided to be direct. "Any info about that mystery woman on the outpost? The one with unexplainable injuries?"

His friend frowned.

Jayd spread his hands. "This isn't about the kidnapping."

"Right." Sean drew out the word.

"Just tying up loose ends."

His friend's eyebrows rose, but he finally answered. "If you're talking about the woman with the broken collarbone—dead end. Obviously a tourist. We estimate over a thousand extra people were there that weekend. Lot of stupidity going on too."

"With so many getting hurt, it's a wonder anyone vacations there." Jayd loaded his tone with sarcasm.

Sean tapped the table as though to emphasize a point. "I'm reminding you again—it's out of our hands. You didn't hear it from me, but the director got a call yesterday. From Intergalaxia. To put it mildly, Rosborough *advised* us to back off."

"Humph." Jayd's fault. He had leaned on a few people pretty hard. "Since you're my boss now, you might end up having to fire me."

"You go, I go."

Jayd had no immediate response. His friend was

bullheaded enough to do it, too.

Somewhere in the house, a door slammed.

Sean's eyes met his.

"Visitor?" Jayd asked.

He shrugged. "Probably a member of our support group."

Jayd listened, but heard nothing more from downstairs.

The afternoon had darkened considerably. Envirocontrols snapped on, slowly bringing the lights to preset levels. Aric's choices, Jayd guessed, noting the glow of the Tiffany-style desk lamp and the spotlights on the paintings.

The disappearing daylight reminded him he had work to do. USF's director had personally tasked him with monitoring Kelli.

Just one more thing to cover with Sean...

Jayd leaned forward and folded his hands. "I have a confession to make."

"Oh?" His friend grinned, obviously recognizing a code phrase they used years ago while in the military. It usually meant one of them had done something foolish and needed the other to cover for him.

"Before the director hauls you into her office—I need to tell you I've been checking up on Aric's exhusband."

The grin blinked off his friend's face.

"You shouldn't discount him, Sean. He is a main suspect."

"He didn't know about Ella's existence until several months ago."

"That's what we're all assuming. But what if he did

know?"

His friend shook his head. "He could've kidnapped Ella at any time after our return from Empusa III. Aric was incommunicado for almost four years. No one at SARC knew about her daughter—not even Barkley. Besides, why would Harker wait? And why risk taking her at a high security location off world? We deliberately waited months before having a reception."

"I don't have answers. I'm just telling you what my gut says."

"I appreciate it, but Harker's been checked and rechecked. His alibi is tight."

"Did he contest your adoption of Ella?"

"No. According to his attorney, he said he 'didn't want to be bothered with progeny.' His words. He's a scientist, not an operative. That weekend, specifically that night, he was on Earth having a dinner party with a dozen friends. He's never been to the Xerxian Outpost. The guy's clean."

"Eh, you're probably right."

Jayd still didn't like it. The man was Ella's biological father, even if he pretended no interest. "Okay, another thing."

Sean's eyebrows rose. "For not telling you anything, I'm talking an awful lot."

"Yeah, sorry. I was curious about Kelli's supervisor. Any reason why he reassigned the two original agents who were guarding Ella?"

"Runkle had an emergency call from home. Her mother was in an accident so she had to leave."

"Someone check that out?"

"Yeah. Mom was mugged by some punk kids. Minor injuries."

"Hmm." Jayd absorbed the news. "What about Munly?"

"Food poisoning. Or flu. Not sure which."

"So I guess that means Kelli's sup is off the hook." When Sean's eyebrows rose, Jayd added, "As far as being in on the kidnapping."

"Yeah, he's been cleared. But he got a formal reprimand. Even though he and most of the guests were schnockered that night."

Jayd flexed his jaw. This whole kidnapping business had too many inexplicable events. And frankly, he didn't trust Intergalaxia. Next to the well-oiled machine of USF, their security division was a joke.

Jayd stretched back against the leather chair. "One thing for certain—I'm never going back to the outpost. A second visit might kill me."

His friend gave a half-hearted chuckle.

"Thanks for the coffee." Jayd rose. "I'd better be going."

"Not staying for dinner?"

"Not tonight. I have some, um, homework." Code word for date. However, Jayd used it to purposefully mislead his friend.

"Homework?" Sean cocked an eyebrow. "Blonde, brunette or redhead?"

"None of your business."

"Glad to hear you're back in the game." He slapped Jayd's shoulder, making him wince.

"Ok, Sean, I'll tell. Blonde."

The smile vanished from his friend's face. "You keeping Kelli under surveillance?"

How'd he guess?

He felt compelled to explain. "Director's orders."

Sean's surprise melted into speculation. "Obviously she picked you because she knows you'll do a great job."

Like when Jayd had tricked Kelli into giving her statement? Maybe that's why the director had tasked him.

"Why don't you wait here?" Sean motioned for Jayd to retake a seat. "Let me see if we still have a visitor."

Or was he worried they might be weeping? Jayd knew women didn't like to be interrupted if they were boohooing together. His three sisters had trained him well.

"No problem." He slid back into his chair.

"I'll let you know if the coast is clear downstairs."

"By sending up a flare if it isn't?"

"Something like that." Sean grinned.

He disappeared from the room. Except for the howling wind outside, the house settled into an eerie quiet. For a few minutes, Jayd waited patiently while the minutes ticked by. Curiosity overcame prudence and urged him to lean out the door and listen. Voices floated up to him.

Was that...? Couldn't be.

Chapter 4

"I'm so glad you came by." Aric stood at the kitchen island while she washed her hands. "I hope you know you're always welcome in our home."

Kelli slipped onto a barstool. The inside of the house was even more impressive than the outside. They had their own personal recycling center? And water reclamation unit? Either Aric was well connected or Sean's pay increase had been substantial. Maybe both.

When Kelli's gaze landed on an upright electronic tablet, her heart skipped a beat. The drawing on the display was obviously Ella's. The bright, orange words "I love you my family" jumped off the screen. She caught her breath at the three figures holding hands. The large smiles on each face. The pink heart above them. The bright, cheerful sun in an upper corner.

The screen faded to another drawing. Another happy picture with more smiles.

Her heart burned.

I wish...

Kelli couldn't name what she longed for. Something that went beyond solving Ella's disappearance. A deep emotion tugged at her inmost being. A yearning to have belonged to a family like that?

Aric followed her gaze. "Ella is a prolific artist. We have her drawings in almost every room of the house."

The use of present tense—*is*, not was—wasn't lost on Kelli. They hadn't given up hope!

"I know she'd want to draw a picture for you. Or six. Especially since you took care of her that night." Aric took a shaky breath. "I've wanted so much to thank you personally."

"But I didn't—"

"Yes, you did. You nearly died protecting my daughter." Her eyes welled with tears.

Kelli hung her head, hating to be thought of as a hero when she'd so miserably failed. Failed everyone. *Including myself.*

Her hostess leaned forward and rested a hand on her arm. "Please don't blame yourself for what happened. We chose the Xerxian Outpost to insulate ourselves. We thought we'd taken all the necessary precautions."

To protect them from whom? Barkley was in prison, but his head of security had never been apprehended. Was he responsible? Or someone else?

"Sorry to keep melting into tears." With the back of her hand, Aric swiped wetness from her cheek. She gestured toward Kelli's coffee. "I forgot to ask. Do you take cream? Sugar?"

"Both."

From a cupboard Aric retrieved sugar, stored in an antique bowl.

Outside the wind roared against the windows, but inside was still except the delicate ping of china. Again, Kelli's gaze was drawn to the electronic tablet. A photo of Ella was now displayed. Kelli's throat spasmed as she looked at the girl's wispy brown hair, large trusting eyes. Cute chin and mouth.

"I wanna be like you when I grow up." Kelli would never forget that sweet voice.

A distant sound caught her attention—like footsteps on carpeted stairs. She stared at Aric. They weren't alone? Shooting to her feet, she turned to face the one person she no longer was prepared to see.

"Kelli!" Sean stood in the doorway, shock plastering his face.

"Look who came to visit, Sean." Aric's soothing contralto took the sting out of his obvious disapproval.

Kelli opened her mouth, but nothing came out. What had she planned to say? Her entire speech had evaporated.

In a few strides, he closed the gap. He pulled Kelli into his arms and crushed her against his chest. Her hands hung limply at her sides while she endured the embrace, painfully aware of Aric watching.

"I'm so grateful to God you're all right." He stepped away and held her at arms' length. "I'm so grateful..." He gulped as though struggling to contain his emotions.

Words utterly failing, Kelli could only gaze at him. He looked so tired. So careworn. His brown eyes swam with unshed tears.

Oh, Sean. I never realized...

Her emotions tugged. Hard. Kelli felt like she was seeing him for the first time. A man with a huge heart who didn't deserve the sorrow he carried.

They—the kidnappers—had done this to him. And to Aric. Not only had they maliciously endangered Ella, they had destroyed a happy family.

Unforgivable.

"We should've taken out stock in a paper company." Aric came around the island and extended the box of tissue.

Sean grabbed a couple handfuls and noisily blew his nose. Only then did Kelli realize tears had slipped down her cheeks. She snatched a tissue and dabbed her face. When was the last time she'd cried?

I was eleven. I sobbed all night after Mommy died. And I vowed never to cry again.

"I'm sorry to have barged in." Kelli crushed the tissue in her hand. "I tried to set up an appointment with your secretary, but..."

Sean held up his hand. "No need to apologize. I'm glad you came."

"Thank you." She could barely get the words out. Ducking her head, she stared at the slate floor at her feet. Pink toenails shone against the subdued taupe.

"Would you stay for dinner?" Aric asked. "Both of you?"

Both? Looking up, Kelli noticed Jayd standing in the doorway. Realization exploded in her.

He heard everything.

He saw me in Sean's arms.

She had committed a breach of protocol, which Sean might be kind enough to overlook. Not Jayd. He had to report her to USF.

Is he recording this on his comm-unit?

"Whoa, Kelli. Sit down." Sean grabbed her arm and helped her to a chair. "You went white."

"I–I'm sorry." She pressed fingertips to her temple. "I get lightheaded sometimes."

He patted her other hand. "Aric, see if our concierge doctor is available."

"No, please no. That's not necessary." Kelli pulled her fingers away. The last thing she wanted was more medical people bombarding her with questions. "I'll be fine."

She would *not* look at Jayd.

Sean drew a chair closer. To be ready should she pass out? His knee was mere inches from hers, arm resting on the table between them.

Go away. Please!

As Aric set a coffee mug on the table, Kelli shot her a glance.

"Oh, right. Cream and sugar." Obviously she misinterpreted Kelli's look. Aric hurried to the cooling unit and was soon back with a small carton along with the sugar bowl and spoon.

Sean scooted the mug closer to Kelli.

Didn't they understand how this tortured her? It was bad enough that Sean was being so solicitous. But to have Jayd watching…

When she poured cream into her coffee, her arm spasmed. Liquid splashed over the rim and onto the table. "I'm so sorry!"

"That definitely decides it." Sean leapt up from the table and got a dishcloth. "You aren't leaving until you have some of my wife's awesome cooking. You, too, buddy." He pointed at Jayd. "No excuses."

"I really should be—"

"That's an order. From your boss."

Jayd's mouth tightened in a semblance of a smile. He shrugged. "Okay." He slid into the chair next to Kelli while she stirred her coffee.

Though she refused to look at him, she could feel his dark gaze boring into her.

"Let me help you with dinner," she told Aric. If she didn't escape Jayd's proximity, she'd end up dumping her entire drink.

"Not yet. At least finish your coffee."

Kelli was tempted to gulp it down. Instead, she swiveled in her seat until Jayd was no longer in her peripheral vision.

"Sorry to say, I have nothing prepared. We're having something rehy'd." Aric pulled a jar of food discs from the cupboard. "Not as awesome as homemade, but rehydration is faster and easier."

Kelli couldn't help a sigh of relief. The sooner dinner was done, the sooner she could get out of there.

"Oh," Aric said. "Sean told me they found a body

yesterday. A waiter from the reception. I wonder if he was the one who attacked you."

Kelli heard Jayd's sharp intake of breath.

Apparently unaware of her error, Aric continued. "Think you might be able to identify him? Maybe get a lead others haven't thought of?"

"That won't be necessary." Sean's voice held a hint of warning.

"Kelli has a right to know." His wife met his gaze squarely. "And we could use all the help we can get."

In amazement, Kelli watched Sean back down. At any other time, she would have found the exchange comical. Not many could make the big man retreat.

"I'm at your disposal." Kelli risked a glance at Jayd. "Unofficially until—or *if* I am official again. I'll do whatever I can."

Sean shook his head. "Your offer is—"

"*We* would appreciate it." Aric glared at her husband. She included Jayd in her tightlipped challenge. "And don't give me a stupid jurisdiction speech. So far nobody's come up with any good leads or plan of action. Everyone's so busy protecting their turf that nothing is getting done." Though her eyes glistened with tears, she held her ground. The room reverberated with the awful truth.

The two most powerful men Kelli personally knew had nothing to say. If she hadn't seen it herself, she wouldn't have believed it.

Part of her wanted to stand next to Aric and wave a solidarity fist, but prudence demanded she be wise. Inter-G wouldn't hesitate to flex their muscles and force USF to assign her to the Dzardian penal colony.

"Ready for my help?" Kelli rose. "With dinner," she added quickly.

The woman nodded, her mouth a slash of pain.

Aric was right. And everyone knew it. The different police and government organizations were jealously guarding their domain while a little girl's life hung in the balance.

"How about I set the table?" Kelli asked.

"That'd be great." Aric pointed her in the direction of dishes and flatware.

Wordlessly, she set out the items. No one said much beyond Jayd's comment about the stormy weather and Sean's subdued reply. In no time, Aric assembled a rehydrated casserole. She provided a few side dishes from the cooling unit.

Since the men hadn't moved from their places, Kelli found herself sitting between them at the square table. Like they were on a double date? The obvious pairing made her squirm.

She glanced at Jayd. His dark eyes met hers. Was he thinking the same thing?

"Sean, would you say the blessing?" Aric took the remaining seat.

"Of course." He held out his hands, palms up, one for his wife and one for Kelli.

Gulping, she hesitated to touch him. She could see Jayd's speculative gaze. After resting her fingers against Sean's, Kelli closed her eyes. She couldn't squelch a small gasp when Jayd grasped her other hand. Try as she might, she couldn't will her arm to not twitch.

What Sean prayed was completely lost to her. All

Kelli knew was it was long. Way long. How much thankfulness did he need to express for his God to be pleased? From her childhood, she recalled her mother saying, "God is great, God is good, let us thank Him for our food. Amen."

Obviously Sean didn't know the abbreviated version.

Keeping her eyes tightly shut, she schooled her features to remain neutral as the prayer went on and on. Jayd was staring at her. She could feel it. Her arm started to shake from holding it so stiffly. She wished she had leaned it on the table. Too late now.

Finally, Sean said, "And Lord, please protect Ella. We ask that you bring her safely back to us. We rest in Your love and mercy. Amen."

Before Kelli could pull her fingers away, Jayd squeezed them. What did that mean? She busied herself putting a napkin in her lap. It hid her scorn at the same time.

All this religious nonsense. Like there even was a God who cared about them. Nice sentiment, but praying would not change anything. If Intergalaxia was too inept to conduct a decent investigation and USF too whipped to challenge them, then maybe finding Ella was up to Kelli. Why not make her suspension work *for* her?

"So, Kelli," Aric's sweet voice rose above the clatter of dishes and utensils. "Is your ankle fully healed?"

"Almost. The occasional headaches are more annoying."

"Give it a few more weeks." Jayd held a spoonful of chicken casserole toward her, forcing her to meet his gaze. When she held her plate toward him, he continued. "You'll be back in top shape in no time."

"I hope so."

"She already *is* in top shape," Aric said. "I've no doubt she could hold her own against even Sean."

Kelli's cheeks blazed at the thought of wrestling him. *Gah, please don't let anyone suggest that for an after-dinner activity!*

As Jayd served Kelli some carrot salad, he tapped the spoon on the plate several times. "She's put me in my place a time or two."

What? Kelli stared at him. The closest she'd ever gotten in beating Jayd while they'd sparred was a stalemate.

"Then it's obvious why they..." Aric broke off what she was going to say.

Sean set down his fork. "What were you going to say, love?"

Slowly, she lowered the dish she was holding. "It's obvious why they drugged Kelli that night. They knew about her training. And how good she is. She would have killed them to protect Ella. And they feared that."

Sitting back in her chair, Kelli caught the look that passed between the two men. Like that hadn't occurred to them? She felt a rush of affection for Aric. Finally, an ally. Someone who believed her. Believed *in* her.

She waited until she could speak in a steady voice. "Thank you, Aric."

They continued the meal in silence. Determination continued to build in Kelli. Could she do her own investigation? Perhaps find vital clues that would help locate Ella? Kelli vowed to turn the universe inside out for Sean. No, not just him. She would do anything for him *and* Aric. Even if it meant losing her job at USF. Taking action of any kind would be better than sitting around waiting for someone to make up their mind about her. The limbo would kill her.

Not caring if her question sounded abrupt, she asked, "Would it be all right if I spent some time at headquarters? Maybe this upcoming week?"

Jayd shot a look at Sean.

"Since I'm on vacation, so to speak," she added diplomatically. "I'd like to access the library. Brush up on some subjects. Keep sharp."

Sean might have signaled Jayd because he was the one who answered. "I don't see why not. I'll get you clearance."

"Thanks. I appreciate it."

"I am tied up all day Monday, but I should have everything in place by Tuesday. That work?"

"Perfect."

After picking at her food, she found an excuse to leave the house shortly afterwards. Aric followed her out. The storm had drenched the landscape, but now the sky was clear. Exterior floodlights painted the foliage, driveway and nearby structures with glittering illumination.

She paused by her aero-car. "Thanks so much for dinner. And our conversation."

"And I meant it when I said you are welcome any time."

"Before I go..." Kelli paused, searching for the right words. "You may have heard rumors. Mind if I say something in my defense?"

"Not at all."

"Believe me when I say I did not—and never would—intentionally compromise your daughter's safety. Regardless of my personal feelings, I take my job seriously. Ella..." Kelli paused, recalling how that little girl had affected her.

Aric rubbed Kelli's arm as though to comfort her. "I think I understand. You don't have to explain."

"But I want to." She clenched both fists. "Can I tell you a little bit of what happened that night?"

With obvious reluctance, Aric nodded.

"Not everything, just toward the end." Kelli stared toward the city's glow on the horizon, trying to piece together what she remembered. "We were in the restroom. And I think I said something silly about how horrid I looked. Ella chided me and told me I was pretty. She was amazing. I feel like—like..." She stumbled over the words. "Like we bonded. Somehow."

"Ella has such a sweet spirit."

"I was kneeling on the floor, talking to her, when..." She broke off, unwilling to describe the attack. "I remember screaming for Ella to get out of there. And she did. I swear I heard her running away. I'm glad she didn't see any more of what happened. The rest is a blur."

Aric managed a tremulous smile.

"That's all." Kelli released a huge breath. "I thought you should know."

Head barely reaching Kelli's chin, Aric hugged her. "Thank you for sharing. I will treasure your friendship the rest of my life."

Friendship? The word caught her off guard. Yet, it

brought comfort. After she climbed into her vehicle, she rolled down the window. "Can I call you tomorrow?"

"I would love that."

Inexplicably, her eyes teared. "I'm so glad I came." Kelli nodded as though to emphasize the truth.

"Me too." Aric reached through the window to squeeze her hand. Then her expression grew stern. "And you let me know if those two big goons give you any trouble. I'll take care of them."

Kelli laughed. The first time in weeks. "I believe you."

Chapter 5

"Do you believe her?" Jayd asked after Aric shared what she'd learned about the night of the kidnapping. Was it his imagination, or did she look less haggard? Even hopeful?

Her chin rose. "Without a doubt."

"What about you, Sean?"

His friend stared pensively at the spoon he twirled between his fingers. "I don't know anymore."

Everything Aric had relayed fit with what Jayd's gut told him. Kelli didn't have any malicious intent against Ella. No matter how she felt about Sean's marriage, she would never put her emotions ahead of her duty as a USF agent.

How could he forget her testimony in the hospital? True, she was still under the influence of pain meds and whatever they'd given to detox her—but the raw honesty with which she spoke couldn't be manufactured.

Jayd sighed. "For what it's worth, I believe her."

Sean dropped the spoon on the table. "A moot point, really."

"What does that mean?" Aric's gaze flashed between her husband and Jayd.

His friend answered. "It means what we personally believe is irrelevant. USF has washed their hands of her."

Though Jayd suspected this was true, hearing it come out of his friend's mouth still shocked him.

Aric took a couple shallow breaths. Her gaze remained fixed on her husband. "So they won't do anything to help her?"

"Correct."

"They? Or *you?*"

"Aric, that's not fair."

Her mouth quivered. "Isn't *one* victim in this kidnapping enough?"

Sean straightened with a jerk. "Of course. Nobody's comparing—"

"But Kelli is the other victim here. And you know that. We couldn't see her in the hospital. Couldn't contact her while she recovered. How do you think that made her feel?" Aric's voice rose. "Sean, she almost died trying to save Ella. *Our* daughter."

He covered her small hand with his. "I have not forgotten that. Nobody has forgotten that."

"But you're letting Kelli suffer while you worry about politics."

"It's not that simple, love."

"It's true, Aric," Jayd interrupted. "Kelli might end up in prison."

Disbelief rippled across her features as she faced him. "For what?"

"Breach of security. A mountain of evidence against her. Nothing but her word, which right now, is worth next to nothing."

"Only Jayd's rock-steady defense has kept her free," Sean added. "As long as he keeps her under surveillance—"

"You're spying on her too?" Aric blasted him with green-eyed indignation.

Without conscious thought, Jayd tensed as though prepared to defend himself. He didn't owe her an explanation, but still found himself mumbling almost apologetically. "For her protection."

"Unbelievable." Her chair grated on the floor as she swiveled to face her husband. "Don't you remember when you first arrived at Empusa III? How the so-called 'mountain of evidence' was stacked against me? You didn't let anyone stop you from discovering the truth. Why aren't you working as hard for Kelli as you did for me?"

Jayd watched his friend struggle with an answer. The reasons were simple. They were on Earth, not an isolated alien planet. A tangle of red tape masked the truth here. They were constrained by laws and regulations at every turn.

Not for one moment could they forget that Intergalaxia watched their every move. Anyone remotely associated with the kidnapping had a proverbial noose around their neck.

Were they watching now? Even listening? Jayd glanced out the dark windows, certain they would even stoop to spying on Ella's family. Especially since Sean was USF. The possibility worked on Jayd until he squirmed in his seat. Maybe they should go downstairs to the silent room where no one could eavesdrop.

His friend finally answered his wife, eyes narrowed. "I can't help Kelli. There's nothing I can do."

"Can't or won't?" Aric yanked her hand from under his and stormed from the room.

Jayd rose. "Aric, wait."

"Let her go." His friend grabbed his arm. "She'll cool off after a bit."

Would she? Uncertain, Jayd remained standing as he watched her fly up the stairs. A heavy door slammed, the boom echoing through the house.

While Jayd had been married, letting Liu "cool off" had never worked. Instinct pressured him to advise Sean to go after Aric, console her. Maybe even lie to her. But what did Jayd know about their marriage?

He lowered himself to the chair. After a long moment of silence, he spoke. "Aric's right, you know. Kelli *is* another victim in all this."

Sean's jaw flexed.

"We could be doing more." Jayd's fist tightened under the table. How far to push this? It was one thing to bate his friend with work related items, another to call his friend to account for how they treated one of their own.

Sean blew out a breath. "USF—"

"Forget USF. I'm talking about us."

A flicker of doubt tugged at Sean's lips. It seemed to take him several minutes to answer. "What do you have in mind?"

"Let's cut her a little slack. After all, Kelli is our main witness. If anyone's going to crack this case, it's her." To lighten the mood, Jayd added, "If that's all right with you, boss."

Sean frowned as he stared into space. "You can't let up on surveillance."

"I don't intend to."

"But I'd recommend you make all your reports as boring as possible. Let everyone think she's settling into retirement." His brown eyes pinned Jayd. "You realize the delicate line you'll have to walk."

"What do you mean?"

"You have to make USF—and Inter-G—believe that you're out to nail Kelli. Otherwise they'll bounce you from surveillance and get someone not so amenable."

"True." Jayd hadn't thought of that.

"Communicate with me only face-to-face. Nothing electronic. And of course, watch your back."

He nodded. "Can you arrange for me to be released from all other assignments?"

"Consider it a done deal. I'll clear it with the director."

"One more thing, Sean." Jayd considered how to word his question. "Do you want to know all the details of what I'll be doing? The things I won't put in my reports?"

Again his friend took his time answering. "Better tell me as little as possible."

He agreed. If anyone was going to hang from Inter-G's gallows, it needed to be Jayd. He was expendable.

And this is the way it should be.

When they were in Special Forces together, Jayd should have died in a routine parachute jump. Sean had saved his life. USF later doctored the event to make it appear as though it was Sean's fault that Jayd and another soldier had died. They'd used the incident as an "in" for Sean to gain access to SARC and ultimately to take down their corrupt leader.

That all seemed so long ago now.

Noticing the time, Jayd rose. "I'd better go. I've got work to do."

After Sean walked him to the door, he stopped him on the stoop. "I'm going to have my secretary set up an appointment with Kelli."

Jayd assessed his friend. "A goodwill campaign?"

He nodded. "Let's stop those wagging tongues."

"Want me to accompany her?"

"Hmm." Sean's chin jutted in thought. "An escort of honor isn't a bad idea."

"You got it, boss."

His friend grinned. "You know, that title is beginning grow on me."

"And I'm thinking you like it a wee bit too much."

"First time since my promotion. Let's make it work for us."

Jayd resorted to something he hadn't done in a while. Something that used to irk his friend. He saluted.

"Get outa here." Sean playfully punched his arm.

Grimacing, Jayd rubbed the sore spot. It was good to see his friend relax again.

Even if it hurt.

Kelli listened to the soothing music in Marion Larson's inner office. The counselor wasn't in the employ of the USF or anyone else, giving her the confidence to share things that had plagued her since *that night*. She didn't trust the so-called doctor-patient confidentiality at USF. Not since Jayd had tricked her into giving an official statement.

This woman seemed different. It might have something to do with the Bible verses and decorative crosses scattered throughout her office.

Not that they didn't also make Kelli uncomfortable.

For starters, the woman appeared as comfortable as someone's grandmother. A clip bound lustrous silver hair. Apparently she didn't believe in hair dye or a lot of cosmetics. Though stylishly dressed, she avoided high-dollar designer wear. This woman didn't look harried or as money-desperate as USF's psychiatrist.

A small stack of books sat on a side table. "Please take one," invited an elegant, handwritten sign. The blue booklet with gold lettering read, "Psalms."

Sunk in an amazingly soft sofa, Kelli willed her body to relax. A few days prior, she had interviewed Marion via tele-comm. During that initial meeting, Kelli shared what had happened to her almost three weeks before. She'd felt so comfortable with the consultation she had agreed to meet the counselor in person. Unfortunately, the first slot open was the same day she had an appointment with Sean at USF. Not optimal timing, but a counseling session sooner was preferable to later.

She had to get better. Prove to everyone at USF that she was ready for duty. Ready and willing to join the hunt for Ella Reese.

Stylo and tablet in hand, Marion took notes. The more they talked, the more confident Kelli grew that this woman could help. Even if she was old fashioned and a religious nut.

"Before we get started, let's review some info." The counselor consulted her tablet. "You met with a psychiatrist?"

"Couple times. Assigned shrink. Idiot."

A brief smile brushed her lips. "How so?"

"All he did was prescribe drugs. They're still sitting on my bathroom counter."

"Have you tried any?"

"No. I don't do drugs. Not even OTC stuff." Especially since that episode at the reception. No one had informed her what she had ingested.

"All right." The counselor made a note.

"And he talked and talked. Useless. Nothing's changed. Nothing's helped. I want to get over this so everything can get back to normal."

She had a little girl to find. The clock was ticking. Time was running out.

Marion smiled. "That sounds like a great goal."

"But he wouldn't shut up. Wanted to dissect every-thing." Kelli finally put a lid on her hostility. "I'm sorry. This whole thing frustrates me."

"I hope you find it's okay to be frustrated here."

Surprisingly, she did. However, she shrugged, still noncommittal.

"Did you get anything positive from your sessions with the psychiatrist?"

She thought a moment. "I guess. I remembered a peculiar ring my attacker wore. But we didn't need to talk about it for twenty-five minutes. I swear he's getting paid by the minute." When the counselor made no comment, she went on. "He said if I concentrated on its golden glow, it would stimulate a warm, fuzzy feeling. Or something stupid like that."

With a grin puckering one corner of her mouth, Marion continued to write. Nothing could be heard in the room but the slight scratching sound of her stylo and the muted music.

Kelli tilted her head, relieving the stiffness. "Aric says you do things differently."

"A little." The counselor adjusted her reading glasses. "Most would consider me 'old school.' I utilize neuro-connection when appropriate, although nowadays most use drugs, especially when dealing with trauma. I'm not opposed to meds, but I'm finding quite a bit of success without them."

"Neuro-connection?"

"It used to be called 'hypnotherapy' in the counseling setting."

"Oh." Kelli couldn't help making a face. Hypnosis?

"Let me assure you about one particular point. You can lay aside any fears that you'll end up quacking like a duck."

Kelli chuckled. That's exactly what she'd been thinking.

"I cannot make you do anything against your moral or ethical will. You are always in control of the situation. And yourself. More importantly, I will never impose my beliefs on you."

"That's good...to know."

They talked through a few more things, but Kelli found herself fidgeting. "Can we get on with it? If this isn't going to work, I need to know. I can't waste several weeks finding out."

Marion didn't appear offended by her abrupt demand. After muting the office's music, she powered down the tablet. "Why don't you settle yourself more comfortably and close your eyes. Lean your head back if you prefer." Speaking in a soothing voice, the counselor asked her to relax. After encouraging her to lay aside things that might cause her stress, she suggested Kelli imagine herself in a safe place.

Safe? Where could she find that? Her thoughts rushed through recent history. Nothing. College? No. Her teen years emptied into a black hole. What about before her mother died?

Kelli shied away from memories of hospitals. All that remained was countless dark rooms in lonely boarding schools.

When Marion asked her to name her safe place, she couldn't articulate one. Kelli opened her mouth to fabricate something, but strangely, no words emerged. The silence grew heavy.

"Perhaps this place is a mountain lake," the counselor suggested.

A sigh of relief escaped Kelli. That would work. She'd seen them in travel-grams.

Marion suggested sights, smells, and sounds that she could experience. The imaginary scene drew her into a deeper place of relaxation.

The pleasant experience helped her let go of anxiety about that night. Stresses that she didn't realize still lurked. When the counselor brought her back to full awareness, Kelli felt rested. The first time in weeks.

Only anxiety about Ella's safety continued to claw at her mind. As long as that little girl remained missing, Kelli would never fully relax.

Sitting up, she glanced at the chrono. Twenty minutes had elapsed? That long? In the distance, she could hear the faint roar of big-city traffic. For some reason, life felt different. For one thing, she had a new appreciation for how counseling could help. Her mind seemed clearer and more focused. No doubt the healing would be beneficial to tracking down Ella.

While the counselor quietly made notes, the imaginary mountain scene came back to Kelli. "You asked me to think of flowers I might see. And to imagine their fragrance." She leaned forward. "But I smelled something really odd."

"Oh?"

Kelli stared toward the shaded windows and shook her head. "I can't describe it. Something, I think, from that night."

The woman's eyebrows arched. "During your attack?"

"I believe so. Yes, it was there, in the restroom." She sought to recapture the scent again, stumbling over the words to describe it. "Not soap or cleaner. It was something that didn't belong."

Marion remained quiet.

"Oh, and this was weird too." Kelli rubbed her forehead. "While I was relaxed. I saw this mottled brown. Or gray." Trying to *see* it again, she concentrated. "Sheets of brown. Kind of like the color of high desert mountains. I have no idea where that came from."

The counselor merely nodded.

Failing to understand the imagery, Kelli slumped.

"Are you getting a headache?"

Kelli froze. How did she know that?

Marion pointed with her stylo. "You touched your temple. Twice."

"Yeah, I guess I am." Creepy that the counselor could read her.

"Anything else we should address today?"

"Sometimes I'm nervous about going to sleep." Although *afraid* was the more accurate term, Kelli avoided admitting it.

"Medication can often help. But if you prefer, I can c-mail you some relaxation techniques to help you unwind more fully. Try them at home before our next session."

"Sure, why not? I used to do meditation. Learned it in college."

"This isn't meditation. At least, not in the way you're thinking."

"Oh?"

"Identical word, contrasting meanings." Marion set aside her tablet. "The kind of meditation you probably learned involves emptying your mind. The kind Christians do, or are supposed to do, is meditate *on* something. For example, the goodness of God. His attributes. Or contemplating His Word."

"Mind *filling* instead of mind *emptying?*"

"Exactly." The older woman fixed her with a gaze. "I've no doubt you may receive some immediate relief from emptying your mind, from stress or ill feelings. However, in the long run, filling your mind with positive thoughts may yield a greater benefit."

"I suppose. But I'm not a Christian." The perfect excuse.

"You don't have to be to use the technique." Marion smiled, confident, serene.

Kelli crossed her legs. Had she ever felt like that? "Got any suggestions?"

"For?"

"For something to meditate on?"

"There are plenty of books to choose from. Check my website for suggestions. And always, you are welcome to call me if needed." Marion stood. "We need to wrap this up. Let me look at my calendar to see when I'm open for your next appointment."

While she checked, Kelli slipped one of the free Psalm booklets into her purse. Might as well get her money's worth. Even if it was Christian mumbo-jumbo.

This was for Ella. Kelli could put up with anything if it meant finding that little girl.

"Next Monday at ten or Tuesday at three are open. Which works for you?"

"Monday. I want to hurry up and get well."

Marion made a note in her appointment book.

"This isn't a race. Please think of it as a healing process. It's not something you can *will* to happen."

Kelli made sure to keep her face impassive. *I can.* Her ankle recovering so quickly was recent proof. According to her physical therapist, she had broken records because she pushed so hard.

"Okay, I've got you penciled in Monday." The counselor smiled. "Good to have met you."

"Likewise." They shook hands.

Kelli opened the door but stopped on the threshold.

Jayden Song sat in the waiting room.

Chapter 6

As the two women emerged from the inner office, Jayd rose from the hardback chair. Kelli's widened eyes and parted lips betrayed that she had not expected to see him there. *Unwelcome* was written all over her. He resisted the urge to apologize for his timing, but it couldn't be helped. Her counseling appointment and the meeting with Sean nearly overlapped. Jayd wanted to escort her in an official vehicle and he couldn't chance their being late.

However, by meeting her at the counselor's, he confirmed that he'd been following her. That he knew her every move.

"Good morning." He smoothed his yellow silk tie, aware that his dark suit wasn't his usual attire. The occasion demanded more formal attire, to alert everyone this meeting meant business.

Kelli appeared professional in a charcoal gray suit. The scarlet accents were a nice touch. As usual, she looked flawless.

Glancing at the counselor, Jayd needed mere seconds to take in her appearance. *Fifty five-ish. Lifestyle conservative, despite expensive rings. Happily married. Long-term health issues. Diabetes?*

"Friend?" The counselor, who'd watched the exchange from the doorway, spoke to Kelli.

"Colleague." Kelli spoke like she spat out something distasteful. Her expression wasn't as kind.

"Jayden Song." Extending his hand, he half listened as the older woman introduced herself. He couldn't miss the way Kelli edged away from him.

Marion Larson's firm grip and frank stare left no doubt she sized up Jayd as well. "Nice to meet you."

They all turned when the door burst open and a harried looking woman entered. After glancing at the three of them, her gaze settled on Marion. "I'm so sorry I'm late."

"No problem. Come right in." The counselor nodded a farewell to Kelli and Jayd as she ushered her client into the inner room.

As soon as he and Kelli were alone, she said, "What are you doing here?"

"Escorting you to your appointment at USF."

"You know about that?" She rolled her eyes. "Of

course you would."

"Division Chief Reese asked that I accompany you this morning." Jayd withheld the truth that the escort was his idea. And using one of USF's limos.

Her brow lowered. "To make sure I didn't skip out? Or embarrass someone?"

Why the more-than-usual hostility toward him? He deliberately softened his voice. "No, Kel. To protect you."

That got to her. Though her shoulders relaxed a mere fraction, she wasn't letting down her guard.

He continued. "Sean didn't want you running the gauntlet alone." Another half-truth.

Her mouth softened, gaze cast down. Was she feeling gratitude toward the man she still so obviously loved? It hadn't taken any skill to notice her tender glances toward Sean during their dinner five days ago.

Jealousy bit. Brutally he quashed it. "We'll leave your car here."

Her blue eyes snapped up. "Is that—? Oh, never mind."

At her sudden acquiescence, he grinned. She was learning.

Pausing on the aeropad, she motioned toward his ride. "Chauffeured limo?"

"For you, only the best." He helped her in and let the driver close the door. After giving instructions, Jayd walked around to climb in next to her.

She sat as close to the door as possible, maintaining a good three feet between them.

When would she stop treating him like an enemy? Pride kept his mouth shut. He would not explain himself.

Jayd stroked his chin. "Interesting, your choice of counselors."

"Why's that?" Her tone chilled.

"Just surprised you picked a religious one." He steered away from the word *Christian.*

"She came highly recommended. By Aric."

"Aric?" They were getting to be friends? "Aric Reese?"

"Don't act so surprised."

"I usually do. When I am."

"No." Kelli turned and gazed out the window. "You don't."

What was that supposed to mean?

Ever since she hired on at USF, they'd been on rival teams. Always at odds. Always competing. The only case they'd worked on together was the SARC. And that was the first time he'd taken serious note of Kelli—her professionalism, dedication, incredible talents.

Liar. She'd intrigued him the moment she'd shown up in USF's gym for physical training. He clearly remembered that was the first day he had stopped torturing himself about Liu's death. And beating himself up with the *if onlys.*

If only he had been the one to stop at the corner market that night. If only he had agreed to meet Liu there. If only the three gunmen hadn't panicked and fatally shot the young woman who walked in at the wrong moment.

Less than six months later, he'd let Sean convince him to start a career at USF. Crime prevention had become personal.

As bright morning light spilled into the moving limo, Jayd studied Kelli's profile, noting some changes. Gone was the pinched look she'd had in the hospital, the pallor of pain, the puffiness of the meds in her system. Though she appeared physically healthy, he detected a tense uncertainty that he'd never before noticed.

Was that why she'd taken Aric's suggestion and seen a Christian counselor? Surprisingly, the thought unsettled him. The old Kelli was gone and he had no idea how to treat this new person before him.

She suddenly straightened. "Where are we going?"

"We have a few minutes before your appointment. I thought you might like coffee."

She raised her chin a notch. "I'm not thirsty."

"Suit yourself. But I need caffeine."

He'd already put in nearly a hundred hours keeping an eye on her. Working *for* her. He was about wiped. All better left unsaid. Especially since he'd bent more than a few rules when it came to her.

They rode in silence until the car pulled up to his favorite coffee shop. Jayd leapt out, then stuck his head back in. "Sure you don't want a medium, double shot, caramel and white chocolate iced latte with whipped coconut cream?"

She looked taken aback. *Good.* He'd practiced saying her favorite drink until he'd gotten it down pat.

"No." Her mouth twitched. "But thanks."

When he returned with his coffee, he deliberately took out his comm-unit. Sipping his drink, he checked c-mail. As per his instructions, the driver remained in the parking space, waiting for Jayd's signal.

The longer they sat, the more Kelli fidgeted and sighed.

Without looking at her, he scrolled through a note from his father. "Change your mind about coffee?"

"No." She quieted herself, sitting rigidly still.

Jayd pressed his lips together and frowned, as though concentrating on a work related memo. It hid his smile.

She crossed her legs, started to swing her foot, but halted it abruptly when he glanced over. Her gray shoes with the scarlet heels acted like a flag to draw his attention. More than once. Kelli had long, slender legs that would turn any man's head. They were bare. Tanned. The only thing that marred the perfection of her skin was a thin scar along one ankle.

But to him it was a badge of honor.

"Shouldn't we go? I don't want to be late."

"I'm just following orders." He kept his voice low and eyes averted.

She crossed her arms. "Do you always?"

Interesting that she would bring up the very thing he'd begun to ask himself. He met her gaze. "Do you?"

"Of course." However, her eyes betrayed her by flickering. "Mostly. Most of the time." She growled. Low in her throat. "Okay. Some of the time."

"I like it when you're truthful with me, Kel."

Her chest heaved. "I've always been truthful with you." She said it with a heat that appeared to surprise even herself.

He waited, letting the car fill with silence. In a soft voice, he finally answered. "And I believe you. I never doubted anything you told me."

She turned her full gaze on him. Finally. The glitter in her eyes made him clench his jaw.

Let me in. Let me help you. I want to be your friend.

He waited, the plea on the tip of his tongue.

"I wish I could say the same of you," was her devastating comeback, delivered in a strangled voice. She turned to gaze out the window again. Her hand stole up toward the corner of her eye.

Jayd stared at her slender neck a long time. What had caused her to completely lose faith in him? A number of possibilities ran through his head, but the one that stood out was at the hospital. He could explain that if she gave him some indication that she wanted to mend their relationship.

Pride kept his mouth shut. What was that old saying? Trust broken could never be regained?

He'd lost her. Lost her before he even had a chance to try to win her.

Jabbing the intercom on the armrest, he spoke to the driver. "We're ready to go."

Not until they were a few minutes from USF did he again speak. "A word of advice about this meeting."

She turned in her seat, expression guarded.

"Don't stop to chat with anyone. We've arranged this meeting to crush any lingering rumors in the office. For Sean's sake and your benefit."

Face impassive, she nodded.

"You've done it before—pulling off a performance. Walk with confidence. Look proud. You've done nothing wrong, nothing to be ashamed of. Meet people's gazes and stare them down if necessary. Don't try to hide your limp. You're not a whipped dog begging favors. You're a valued agent who nearly lost her life in the line of duty."

By the time he'd finished his speech, Kelli's blue eyes were as huge as the moons of Xerxes IX.

The car pulled up to the front steps. The driver leaped out and opened her door.

Walking up the exterior brick stairs was one of the most difficult things Kelli had done in her life. With each step, Jayd's words pounded in her head.

"You're a valued agent. You're valued."

By the time she reached the top, she had to stop. Her ankle throbbed. High heels had seemed a great idea earlier. However, they weren't meant for semi-sprinting up steps.

"Y'okay?" Jayd's eyes flashed concern.

"Yes. Give me a sec." She took a deep breath and mentally shoved a steel bar down her spine.

Jayd went above and beyond being a gentleman. No one had ever treated her the way he did. As they climbed the last few steps he held out his arm, which she gratefully took. Once inside, he ushered her through security checkpoints with a steadying hand on the small of her back.

"This way, Special Agent Layne," he said frequently, loud enough for those around to hear. "You don't want to be late for your meeting with the division chief."

With each semi-smirk and sideways glance, Kelli's determination to pull off the performance grew. Raising her chin, she schooled her features and squared her shoulders.

They traversed the marbled foyer, past guards who nodded their direction when Jayd's electronic clearance pinged "secure." Up a set of escalators. More stares or nods from those they passed. Through another checkpoint to get a visitor's ID—an odd sensation for her—and on to the elevators. Thankfully, not many people were using them. She and Jayd had one elevator all to themselves.

He punched a button. The elevator locked until the system verified his level of clearance. "Keep it up. You're doing great."

She flashed him a grateful smile. For the first time since entering the building she really noticed his appearance. One thing about Jayd—he looked good in whatever he wore. But especially today in his tailored Heléna West suit that complimented his Asian complexion. He looked professional without being too dressed up. His unique aftershave, something woodsy, filled her with confidence.

The doors opened to Sean's floor. Kelli instinctively backed up, fingers making contact with the cold, metal railing inside the elevator.

Word had spread fast. Or someone had leaked the news about the meeting. The floor had way too many people who didn't belong there. Gulping, she gripped the elevator's handrail.

Jayd kept the doors from closing, giving her a moment before saying with more volume that necessary, "This way, Kelli."

To buy time, she tucked a strand of hair behind her

ear and took a deep breath.

He nodded, ever so slightly, his eyes gleaming with *what?* A plea to be courageous? With his back to the open doors, he mouthed, "You can do this."

Stepping out, she hissed when her ankle spasmed. She grappled for support. Her hand met Jayd's steady hold.

"Sorry. My ankle."

"No need to apologize."

She straightened, heading toward Sean's office, through a gauntlet of people. Several greeted her.

"Nice to see you, Kelli."

"Way to go."

"Glad you're back."

"Yo, Kel."

She greeted the well-wishers, but stiffened her back at the mute, less friendly acknowledgements. As per Jayd's advice, she met suspicious glares without flinching, walking with confidence.

I have done nothing to be ashamed of. I am valued.

She had another moment of panic when they approached Sean's assistant. The woman, a well-known busybody, buzzed the intercom to let the chief know they'd arrived.

How should Kelli greet him? Would he hug her? What should she say? She should have called and asked him. *Too late.*

"Courage," Jayd murmured, his mouth barely moving. No one could have heard him except Kelli. Had she only imagined it? His expression remained carefully blank.

"It'll be a few minutes." The assistant waved at the

nearby chairs. "Would you care to be seated?"

"We'll stand." Jayd's cool voice matched his expression. How had he managed to position Kelli so that her back was to the crowd?

She hoped they wouldn't have long to wait. Behind her, she could hear the curious creep closer *en masse*. Her kneecap twitched. She stilled it.

This was just like a mission.

No, it wasn't. She might tell herself the lie, but her psyche knew it. Her nerves felt stretched to the max.

Minutes ticked by. Stares bore into her back. She willed herself not to smooth down her skirt or to sigh noisily. Beside her, Jayd stared vacantly at the wall, like they were strangers waiting in line at the bank. The assistant's eyes flicked to them several times as she tried hard to look busy. The silence wore on Kelli's nerves until she thought she would scream.

Deep breath…slow. Easy.

She jumped when the office door abruptly opened.

"Special Agent Layne." Sean had eyes only for her, his tone radiating warmth as it rang in the space.

"Chief." Her voice nearly failed.

He strode toward her, hand extended. "I am very pleased to see you. How's your health?"

"Improving, sir."

"Glad to hear it." Sean retained possession of her hand. "I'm sorry I won't be able to meet with you today as planned. A situation has come up."

Relief flooded her. "No problem, sir." Then it struck her. Perhaps Sean had planned it this way. So their so-called meeting wouldn't be inside his office, but out here? Public and visible?

Jayd's relaxed body language confirmed her suspicions. This had all been a setup. And they'd done this for her?

Gratitude swept over her.

Sean squeezed her hand a fraction before releasing it. "On behalf of the director and all of us at USF, I wish to commend your bravery and sacrifice. For the sake of…of my daughter." His voice cracked a little.

No acting there.

Kelli fought for an even tone. "I'm privileged to be part of this great organization. I only wish…" Words stuck. Her mouth moved, but nothing came out.

"I only wish we had more agents like you," Sean finished for her.

"Thank…" Emotion created a logjam in her throat. Kelli coughed and tried again. "Thank you, sir."

Jayd stepped forward. "I know you have a busy schedule, chief. So we won't take up any more of your day."

"Thanks for stopping by." Sean fixed his gaze on her. "And thank you again for making time to meet with me. Sorry about the change in my schedule."

Kelli merely nodded. After taking her arm, Jayd steered her toward the elevator. How had he known that her knees felt ready to buckle? When her ankle again twinged, she leaned on his arm.

Someone—from somewhere—began to clap. Suddenly everyone appeared to be applauding. Only Jayd's grasp held her upright, kept her moving forward. The ovation, pounding in her ears, matched the thumping of her heart. Before the shiny doors shut, she attempted to smile at those who were still cheering.

The ride back down, the walk through the foyer and down the steps, took an eternity. Finally, they were back in the limo, seated next to each other while Jayd continued to hold her hand. She couldn't stop shaking, as though a fever ravaged her.

What was wrong with her? Never before had she felt so…weak. *Human.*

Only when they pulled up to her apartment did she realize they had traveled across the city.

"My car," she protested. "It's still—"

"I'll have it delivered." He helped her out, gripping her waist. "Give me your key."

Even if she'd wanted, she couldn't resist.

In no time, she was seated on her couch, a glass of red wine pressed into her hand.

"Take a sip." He sat beside her.

She obeyed, the glass clinking against her teeth. When she attempted to set it on the coffee table, she nearly broke the stem.

"Easy there." His warm hand wrapped around hers, fingers gently prying her tight grip off the delicate glass.

The wine hit her empty stomach like a tsunami. Kelli wilted against the cushions. Sucking a deep breath, she fought the urge to rest against his chest. Warmth brushed her cheek—a memory. From *that* night? Again his woodsy aftershave assaulted her. A sensation of comfort—security—wrapped around her mind. Soul? Was there any such thing as a soul? She hunkered more deeply into the sofa.

His quiet voice cut through the silence. "You were magnificent."

She managed a wan smile. "Thank you. For...for setting it up. Making it happen."

"Glad to." Was that tenderness in his eyes?

Jayd was the first to break eye contact. His gaze darted toward the window, then back at her. "Promise me you'll rest this afternoon?"

She nodded.

"And when I bring your car back, you won't drive anywhere? At least, not until this evening?"

She noticed he didn't say *someone* would deliver her car. Would Jayd personally bring the vehicle back to her apartment?

Again, she nodded. "Not after I finish this wine. I apparently can't handle alcohol."

She'd meant it as a joke, but his expression clouded. His mouth worked as though he was about to say something, but changed his mind. Maybe he really did believe her story about the spiked slushy?

"I'd better go." Jayd rose. "No, don't get up. I'll let myself out."

This time, she didn't obey. Unsteadily she stood. He wheeled about, worry flashing across his face.

"Jayd. Thank you again." She held out her hand.

He stared at it a second, then slowly took her fingers between his. They were strong. Competent. Tender.

Today was the nicest he'd ever been to her.

A muscle flexed in his cheek. "You're welcome." He swiveled and disappeared out the door.

Kelli collapsed on the sofa, all reserves of energy utterly depleted.

Chapter 7

"Kelli's good. No doubt." Jayd plunked into a chair in his friend's office at headquarters.

Sean grinned. "But not as good as you?"

"That goes without saying."

For some reason Sean had asked him into his office. Because he changed his mind and wanted to know more details about Kelli's pursuits? They'd been chatting for a few moments before his friend indicated Jayd take a seat.

"She's got computer savvy, but she can't hide everything from me." Jayd monitored her activities closely, curious about the sites she visited. As soon as he'd gotten her clearance to USF databanks, she'd been busy using them. The weirdest sites she'd visited were about near-death experiences.

"You cleaning up behind her?" Sean sauntered from around his massive desk and settled next to him on a nearby chair.

"Yeah. Added false trails, like she suddenly took an interest in junior agents' required reading. Just to be safe."

"Good idea."

Jayd debated telling him that her latest topic was Aric's ex-husband, Mitchell Harker. Not only did Kelli consume all the gossip about Harker, she even enrolled in a virtual course he taught on "Derek's Deck," which usually only scientists, mathematicians and other nerds followed. What did she find fascinating about Harker? From what Jayd could ascertain, the man was an egotistical prig.

"I think she's figured out a way to monitor what Inter-G is doing with the case." Jayd indicated the scattered info-chips on his friend's desk. A large "I" imprint left no doubt whom they were from. "Those reports about Ella?"

"Yes. They're *gracing* me with the courtesy of keeping me in the loop. Their words." Sean's fist tightened. "If I spill the contents, they will cut me off. And vital body parts most likely."

Jayd managed a small grin, but he knew Intergalaxia didn't mess around. This was a huge concession to USF *and* to Sean. But did the news comfort Sean or add to his frustration as he merely watched others conduct the investigation?

Inter-G might pretend to play nice, but this was still blackmail.

"So where is Kelli concentrating her studies?" Sean asked with a forced nonchalance that caught his ear.

He scrutinized his friend and decided to withhold the info about Harker. "The Xerxian space station — their history, economy and current business practices. Maybe to find something Intergalaxia missed?"

Sean nodded.

"And she's using USF's gym." Jayd volunteered. "A lot."

Kelli worked out with an intensity that screamed obsession. What was she trying to prove? More than once, Jayd made it a point to "accidentally" work out the same time. She doggedly ignored his presence, consumed in her strength routines.

Sean leaned back. "I hear she won't spar with any USF personnel. But with local professionals? At a nearby facility?"

"Correct." Jayd shifted in his chair, growing uneasy with the prolonged chitchat. This was not like Sean. Especially during the busiest part of their workweek. "You sure she's not assigned to any mission? She's acting like she's prepping for one."

"I'm sure." Sean's brow clouded. "Do you know she and Aric have gotten to be friends? They talk a lot."

Jayd carefully crafted his reply. "Must be therapeutic. For them both."

"Yeah, but I'd hate to see Aric..." A muscle twitched in his cheek.

Hurt again? Have her friendship betrayed? Jayd couldn't even guess what his friend was going to say. Especially after the little blowup he'd witnessed between Sean and his wife.

"I uh, have to admit something." Jayd waited until he had his friend's full attention. "I broke into her apartment a couple times. Just to see what she's up to. But of course, you didn't hear this from me." He smiled as he remembered their overuse of the phrase in a recent conversation.

Sean managed a half-grin. "Of course not."

"Would be nice if she discovered something significant. Maybe that would be the ticket to get her restored to full status." Jayd was about to say more when his friend abruptly rose and stalked behind his desk.

For nearly a full minute, he watched Sean shuffle some items around on the surface.

"All right." Jayd rose. "What are you *not* telling me?"

Sean's mouth tightened and relaxed several times before he ran one hand through his hair. "Kelli isn't going to be reinstated. No matter what she finds. Intergalaxia plans to call for a formal tribunal."

"And our director agreed?"

"This is completely out of USF's control. I thought you should know." The only other time Sean had worn an expression like that was at Liu's funeral.

"When?" The word rasped out of Jayd's throat.

"In a few weeks." Sean's gaze finally met his. "Expect to get a summons as well. I recommended you as a character witness."

"Thanks." At least, that's what he thought he said.

He pressed two fingertips to his chin, aghast at the implications. Regardless of how glowing a report he gave, Intergalaxia would crucify her.

Heart pounding, Kelli gasped for air. Cold, clamminess clawed at her. No matter how hard she fought, she couldn't escape. The vaporous grip solidified until countless fingers imprisoned her. They squeezed until she couldn't draw a breath.

Pillows flying, she bolted upright in bed with a shriek. It took many moments before she could comprehend where she was.

She was in her apartment. With the bedroom door open, the violet glow of her toaster's indicator light pricked her eyes. Next to her, the dim chrono said 4:22 a.m. Damp with perspiration, she flopped back. This was the third night in a row she'd had a nightmare.

What were those relaxation techniques again? As promised, her counselor had c-mailed information. Kelli tried to imagine her "safe place" and to slow her breathing. *No good.* Sleep had galloped off, not to be corralled again.

She flung back her covers and staggered to the kitchen. "Vi," she commanded the enviro-life systems, "light level three." The room gradually brightened. She selected an herbal for her tea maker. As she waited for the brew, her gaze landed on the Psalms book she'd picked up from her counselor's office. Kelli hadn't touched the pamphlet since she'd dropped it on her dining table.

Defiantly, she jabbed the blue cover. Despite what it claimed to offer, she didn't need religion. Regardless, she flipped through the pages.

"Vi, light level five." The additional radiance spotlighted a couple lines.

My enemies surround me.

Out of the depths, I cried to Thee, O Lord.

Rescue me, O God, out of the grasp of the ruthless man.

How precious are your thoughts to me, O God!

"Precious? Yeah, right." Kelli leaned against the table, ignoring the beep that alerted her the tea was ready. "God thinks of me? Who are they kidding?"

A phrase caught her eye. *Surely the darkness will overwhelm me, and the light around me will become night.*

Chills crawled across the back of her neck. Knees weak, she sank into a chair. Cottony dryness filled her mouth.

Darkness? She couldn't slow her rapid breath. *Overwhelming darkness* perfectly described her nightmare.

That's what had awakened her three nights in a row.

She recalled details now. Of someone—some *things* holding her captive with claw-like hands. Only *they* were too strong to be people. No matter what she did, she couldn't wrestle out of their grasp.

Squeezing her eyes shut, she fought to blot out the memory.

She was running and running, but a thick blackness closed around her. With living fingers, the icy vapor tore at her, grasping, suffocating. She tried to scream, tried to escape the darkness, but it overtook her no matter how hard she ran. No matter which way she turned.

A cold shaft speared her spine. Understanding flooded her. In her dream she had died…but was not dead. Her existence continued beyond the grave. Somehow. And there, *they* were waiting.

Where was the light at the end of the tunnel she'd read about for those who'd had a near-death experience? And the blissful peace? Where were her loved ones who were supposed to be on the "other side" to greet her?

Where was Mom?

In all the websites she had visited, none of them mentioned this terrifying darkness.

She pressed fists to her forehead. "Oh God, I'm going crazy."

Suddenly realizing what she'd said, Kelli caught her breath. *I don't believe in God.* He was a figment of people's imagination. A myth they turned to when they ran out of options. A last resort.

Yet, she'd just addressed Him.

After staggering out of her chair, she paced. "I am competent, strong, independent. Religion is for weak people."

Kelli stopped. She must really be losing it, talking to herself like this. Bracing her hands on the table, she took several cleansing breaths. *There.* That helped.

Her gaze lit on the psalm again. She read the rest of the sentence.

Even the darkness is not dark to You, and the night is as bright as day. She skimmed the rest until she got to the end. *Lead me in the everlasting way.*

Was that what her nightmare meant? That she was running away from God? That she was running *into* the darkness, rather than letting Him lead her to an everlasting way?

Her knees gave out and she crumpled to the floor. She curled into a ball.

"I am strong. I don't need a crutch. I don't need..." But Kelli didn't dare utter His name again aloud. What if God was real?

Stories that she'd heard in boarding school flashed through her mind. The omnipotent being who sat on a throne in heaven and cast lightning bolts at anyone who displeased Him. The one who wiped out entire populations because He didn't get His way. The One who could see her, right now?

For the first time in her adult life, she admitted the possibility that God existed. And she grew afraid.

During her third visit to the counselor, Kelli intended to tell her about the nightmare, but she couldn't. After all, the woman was a Christian. She wouldn't understand. And Kelli didn't need a religious lecture.

Marion is obviously one of those born-againers. She won't understand the church Mom took me to whenever I came home to visit. They hardly talked about God. He was more of a doting grandfather or a magic genie. Not some evil Father who let His own Son be crucified.

"Have you been sleeping well?" Marion peered over her reading glasses.

No use lying. "Not really."

"Would you like to talk about it?"

Kelli fingered her earring, looked about the room, and finally landed on a plausible explanation. "That odor I've mentioned before? I can't get it out of my head."

Thank goodness she wasn't talking to Jayd. He'd know she was lying. And he'd weasel the truth out of her.

She never could hide anything from him.

"Do you remember anything more about it? Where you smelled it before?"

Good. Her counselor took the bait. Kelli made certain not to change her expression. "I think it was during my high school...no, college days." Speaking aloud made her grow more certain. "It was so out of place."

"Should we concentrate on that today?"

"That'd be great."

Marion led her into a relaxed state fairly quickly. Without asking questions, she merely had Kelli "visit" her classes, like she was taking a tour. "Think about your favorite freshman class. Your favorite teacher."

They worked through each semester until they got to her junior year where they spent more time. Kelli had vacillated about her studies, provoking many arguments with her father. Out of rebellion, she dropped her major.

As she continued down memory lane, she mentally breezed through her senior year, then her counselor brought her back to the present.

"I didn't remember anything about an odor." Disappointed that the neuro-connection had failed, Kelli sat up.

"How would you rate your college experiences overall?"

"I enjoyed them, I guess." She spoke without thinking. "Especially my junior year. I loved that semester"

"Oh?"

"It really ticked off my father. That's when I finally stood up to that controlling...jerk."

Marion's silence invited further explanation.

"I dropped my business major. Took a bunch of electives. Useless classes, according to him. Music appreciation. Massage. I was good at that. *Too* good." She smiled at the recollection. "Acting. Didn't do too badly. Some anthropology course. Cosmetology. Oh, and painting, which I was terrible at."

"Remember any particular odors from that course?"

"Mm-hm. Actually, I didn't spend much time in the classroom. But I did meet a guy I liked. He did my paintings in exchange for massages." Again, she smiled. "Good thing. Kept me from flunking the class."

"Did you use oils for massages? Incense?"

Kelli grew pensive. "Yeah, I used oil. But my boyfriend was allergic to a lot of them. I bought some organic brands with no scent." A memory tugged at her. "We didn't use incense because he couldn't stand the smell of..." Her throat tightened. "*Incense. I think...*"

The room grew hushed as though holding its breath. Turned to stone, Marion didn't move. Kelli could swear that even her heart chugged to a stop as one thought crystalized.

In slow motion, she exhaled and inhaled. "Something my anthropology professor brought into class one day. I recall…" The memory began to cascade inside her mind. Words tumbled from her. "He brought in this jar—illegally obtained. A speckled jar, made out of some kind of pottery. We all gathered round. He removed the sealed lid. The odor was like nothing I'd experienced before. Like someone slapped my face. The taste permeated my mouth."

Chills ran through her body. Kelli stared at her counselor. *"I remember now,* Marion. I remember! On the space station, my attacker smelled of Xerxian ritual incense." Her breathing halted as she stared into the memory. "There's only one place your clothes can get saturated with that odor—you have to physically be on Xerxes IX."

"I'm sorry for the short notice." Kelli glanced over the top of her aero-car to the surrounding area before focusing on Aric.

"I got your text. Everything okay?" Face lined with worry, her new friend ran to greet her. Aric's long brown hair, pulled into a loose ponytail, bobbed.

Kelli studied the open front door. "Are we alone? Is anyone else home?"

"Yes, I mean no. No one else is here."

"I can't—we can't talk in the open." Unease clutching at her, Kelli scanned the area once more. Had anyone followed her? She and Aric had to get out of sight.

"Come with me." Her friend grabbed her arm. Once inside the slate-floored foyer, she shut the door.

Kelli gulped at air. "I need a favor. A huge one."

"Wait." The brunette held up her hand and motioned for her to follow her into the basement.

Didn't she say no one else was home?

When they reached the lower level, Aric snapped on a hallway switch. A shimmering blue force field lit up. "Leave your purse and shoes here." She pointed to a chair.

Together they passed through the glinting, transparent wall and into a room.

After Aric shut and sealed the door, she spoke. "Bug-proof room."

"Nice." Made sense for a division chief to have one in his home. "Eavesdrop proof?"

"Oh, yes." Her friend nodded for emphasis. "So what's going on?"

She grew sober. "Before I tell you anything, you have to swear not to say a word to Sean. Not until I check out some things. If I'm wrong, no big deal."

"And if you're right?" she spoke slowly.

"I can't even begin to comprehend the possibilities. Not yet." Her mind swam with a million *what-ifs*. "If Sean finds out, and he does nothing to stop me, it could mean the end of his career. I won't risk that. You *have* to promise."

Face pale, her friend bit her lip. "Okay. I promise."

"Thanks." Kelli felt like the anti-grav safety feature at the gym had suddenly activated and the barbells she held snapped to weightlessness.

"What's the favor?"

"I need something of Ella's. Like a lock of hair. Or a baby photo. Something you treasure. But, I warn you,

you may not get it back."

Aric's face tightened. "I'd sacrifice anything to help find Ella."

Kelli sighed in relief. So far, so good.

"Would a baby locket work?"

"Perfect." Kelli cleared her throat. "And one more thing."

"What is it?"

"I need you to arrange a meeting between me and your ex-husband."

"Mitt? What does he have to do with this?"

"I can't say yet. I'm following a hunch."

"He wasn't involved in Ella's disappearance. Sean said he has a watertight alibi."

Kelli held up her hand. "I know it sounds crazy, but I need to see him personally. To be sure about something I remembered from that night."

Aric's green eyes widened. "And you think...?"

"I can't say any more. Truthfully, I feel like I'm losing my mind. I can't get this idea out of my head. But, I need your help. You have an 'in' with Harker. If he's innocent, I'll move on."

"All right. I'll call him."

"Use a friend's comm-unit. Or a neighbor's. Just to be safe. Tell him that Kati Carter will be your liaison. I have a fake ID just so you know. I've enrolled in one of his virtual classes, so he should recognize my name."

"I'll go over to my neighbor's house as soon as you leave."

"Perfect. I wrote out a script for you to follow." Kelli dug it out of her jeans pocket. "Don't answer any of his questions. Set up the meeting. Then get off the phone."

"Okay."

"And remember, not a word to Sean. Please. I couldn't bear it if..."

"You can count on me." Aric squeezed her arm. "Thank you for all you're doing to find our daughter."

Chapter 8

Kelli chose a low-cut, cream silk blouse and tight black leather skirt. Funny that she'd kept it from her SARC undercover days. She'd worn the same skirt and a similar top when she helped arrest the corrupt leader of SARC. Only Director Barkley had shredded the original silk blouse. *Pervert.*

This time, Kelli added stiletto heels and some high-dollar bling—a necklace made from the now infamous Angel Gold. She bypassed perfume. Her nose had to remain undistracted by other scents.

Not that perfume or another other odor could mask

the overpowering incense. However, once it was burned, it transformed into a pleasant fragrance. If Mitchell Harker had burned all his, something of the scent might linger. She hoped.

After smoothing down her skirt, she checked the length in the mirror. Sufficiently short.

According to reports, Harker was a womanizer. With her outfit, Kelli would have no trouble distracting him from the real reason for her visit. If she read him right, she needed all the accouterments to get him to buy the package.

"This'll be fun." She spoke to her reflection as she rechecked every detail of her appearance. She closed her eyes, mentally preparing for what lay ahead. One deep breath centered her. Her new persona slipped over her. *Easy peasy.* She had fooled Director Pervert Barkley for a whole year. A few hours with Aric's ex would be cake.

"I'm so pleased to meet you in person, Dr. Harker." She spoke aloud, settling on a southern accent. For some reason, that felt right. And though he'd never earned a doctorate, the little bump to his status wouldn't hurt.

True to her word, Aric had arranged the interview. Harker was anxious to find out what Kati Carter was bringing him from his ex-wife. The meeting was scheduled for one o'clock at his home.

Perfect.

Now if only she could get there without being intercepted by Jayd. Over the last week to ten days, she noticed the absence of her trusty follower. Occasionally, he had been replaced by someone a bit less cautious. More than once, Kelli had shaken her head at the blatant lack of discretion. Or maybe USF didn't care anymore?

"Please let it not be Jayd today." Not only was he an expert at tailing, he always seemed to anticipate her moves.

After stuffing the heels and jewelry into a gym bag, she slipped sweats pants and top over her outfit. In no time she was ready. She peered out the door, noting with relief that Jayd wasn't her follower today. The guy behind the wheel of his terrain car was parked very visibly at a unit across from hers. He gawked at her. A lunch-drone had just delivered a meal, the large disc still hovering at the side of his vehicle.

"What is USF coming to?" She wagged her head.

On a whim, Kelli waved to him as she got into her aero-car, and waited until the drone buzzed away before driving off. She kept below the speed limit, making sure she didn't lose the noob in the traffic. Just in case he wasn't the only tail, she watched her side and rear computer displays. But apparently he was her only follower.

When Kelli arrived at the gym, she headed to her personal trainer, Jorge.

"Hey." He eyed her appreciatively. "Y'wore makeup for our workout? Wow."

"I need a huge favor." Kelli didn't waste time on pleasantries, but stepped close to him. "Listen, this creepy wannabe-boyfriend is trying to worm his way into my life. He followed me here and—"

"I'll take care of the dweeb right now."

"No, don't do that. Please!" Kelli grabbed his wrist.

"He works with me and recently got promoted. If you do anything, I know he'll find a way to fire me."

"Man, that's tough."

She smiled, squeezing his arm in appreciation. "Not that I doubt you could easily handle him, ya know. I promise when I move to another division, I'll let you punch out his lights."

"Love to do that for you, Kel."

"For now I need to show him he can't run my life. Could you call a cab? Have it come to the back door to pick me up? I'd be ever so grateful."

"Can do." It wasn't long before Jorge was back.

Kelli smiled in genuine relief. "I'm sorry I can't stay. But I'll definitely pay you for your time."

"Anything for my favorite customer."

"Are you the one Aric sent?" The man who came down the wide staircase tended to the heavy side, clearly from a life of indulgence. Mitchell Harker's face was a little pasty, the skin under his chin inclining toward looseness. His virtual form for his classes was quite a bit trimmer, by at least twenty pounds. Someone obviously retouched the holo. Quite a bit.

"Kati Carter. How d'ya do." Kelli smiled, assessing him from his tailored suit to his shoes. Were those hand-made Leonardo's? Seriously? They cost a couple thousand, easily. Expensive gold watch. What Harker carried around on his body was worth more than her monthly salary. The unusual ring he wore caught her attention. She dragged her gaze back to his face as he moved closer.

His housekeeper stood respectfully to one side. She'd let Kelli in both sets of doors after she'd verified ID.

As a precaution, Kelli advised the taxi driver to wait for her outside the massive gates. The hefty advance she'd given him convinced him to turn off the cab's engine. A glance over her shoulder revealed he was catching up on news and probably trying to imagine the size of the tip she'd promised.

Kelli coyly chewed her lower lip as she endured Harker's once over. Without looking at the housekeeper, he dismissed her with a wave of his hand. His gaze remained fastened on Kelli while the servant closed the doors and withdrew.

So far, so good.

"Miss uh, Carter is it?"

"Oh, please. Call me Kati." She effortlessly maintained her southern drawl.

Harker inclined his head.

In less than a minute, she summed him up. Self-indulgent. User-type. Arrogant. Blinded by his own importance.

No wonder Aric had dumped him.

Kelli presented her most dazzling smile. "Thank you for agreeing to meet me on such short notice."

"Anything for Aric."

I'll bet.

"You have a beautiful home. Better'n any others I've ever seen. Even the ones down south. Level six? Seven?"

"Eight."

Kelli pressed her hand to her neck as though overcome. It caused Harker's eyes to flicker to her low neckline. *Perfect.* "I mean, where'd you get all these artifacts?" She pointed to an exotic collection of statues prominently displayed in the foyer. They appeared to be from Keelias IV, the naked forms almost obscene.

"Here and there."

She widened her eyes. "I guess you really are a world traveler."

"Well actually, worlds. I've traveled to several."

"You mean you've gotten these from other planets?"

"A few." He shifted from one foot to the other and frowned. "Aric said you had something for me?"

"Oh, yeah." She rummaged in her oversized purse as she continued to chatter. "I wish I could travel. I moved up from Atlanta to New Washington, but never went anywhere else." She sighed as though in exasperation. "I know I brought it with me."

She had to get into another part of the house. The foyer was too well ventilated. The faint odors of lemon and a cleaning solution lingered in the air.

"I know it's in here somewhere." She paused in her digging. Only if necessary would she give him that precious locket. But she had to keep him distracted. "I really need to tell you, Dr. Harker, what a huge fan I am of yours. You're such a big celebrity and all. I even signed up for one of your virtual classes. Even though I don't understand half of what you say. It's so fascinating."

"You're one of my students?"

"For sure. I never miss a class. I can't wait for next

semester to sign up for two." She let her fingers drape across her neckline. "That story you told about those cannibals on Phineas VI? It was so real. I couldn't sleep a wink for a whole week. And your description about their feasts? Scared the pants right off me."

He grinned, his loosening shoulders indicating that he was beginning to relax. "You mean Phineas V. There is no six in that system."

"Oh, I forgot. It *was* five. Gosh, you know so much." Kelli fanned herself with her hand and leaned toward him as though swooning.

He looked at his watch. "Listen. I needed to leave for a meeting in a few minutes, but I really don't want to go. How about you come into my study? I've got some artifacts in there you might enjoy."

"Really?" She hoped she gushed just right. "I'd love that. More than anything."

"Let me make a call first." He pulled out his comm-unit.

"Mind if I use the little girl's room real quick?"

Holding the CU to his ear, he waved the general direction for her to go.

Kelli headed through a door and into a massive great room. A small bathroom was tucked discreetly around one corner. After glancing over her shoulder, she confirmed Harker was still occupied, back toward her. She veered left, hurrying to check other doors. All the while, she kept inhaling, trying to find that elusive scent she was sure she'd find.

Nothing.

"Ms. Carter? Kati?"

"Here." She pasted a vacuous look on her face. "I

got turned around."

"The bathroom's right there." Brow lowered, Harker pointed.

"Oh." Kelli giggled. "I swear I sometimes get lost in my own apartment. I'll be right out."

He was waiting outside the door when she exited.

"Can I see those artifacts now?" She swept her hair off one shoulder.

He didn't look as eager as before.

She smoothed her skirt, letting her fingers linger at the hem. "I have to tell you a secret. My favorite stories are the ones about alien love rituals. Especially when they dance together before..." She stopped, forcing a blush as she lowered her eyes. "It sounded so beautiful."

"The Bead Dance?"

"Yes." She met his gaze, shyly. "That's the one. They dance with those special beads."

"I have some. Want to see them?"

"I'd love that."

He led her back through the great room, then across the foyer to the other side of the house. His study was huge, stuffed with countless treasures from multiple worlds. Some illegally obtained? Her gaze lit on a miniature sarcophagus with elaborate scrollwork. A child's? She couldn't begin to guess where he'd obtained that but suspected the humanoids hadn't voluntarily donated a likely sacred item. And was that a floating head from Sumatria? The mummified skull danced above the miniature grav disc. Definitely taboo.

A multicolored rug cushioned her steps, covering most of the marble flooring. A glance down confirmed it was hand-woven sponge grass. Priceless. Countless glass cases were stuffed with gems, coins, beads, and carvings too numerous to take in.

"Wow, you got a lot of stuff. You really went to all those worlds personally?" His website said he traveled, but she wanted to make sure.

"I'm a *collector*. Not a buyer." His voice dripped with derision.

Kelli followed him to one display case, oohing over the beads. Then she pretended interest in another case, then the next, all the while looking for something that might hold the Xerxian incense. It had to be there. Some cases appeared sealed. What if she missed the jar because of that?

All the while she chattered about his class, throwing out enough information for him to confirm or add details. Kelli didn't know how much longer she could keep it up. After several minutes, Harker seemed to grow impatient of playing tour guide.

He obviously wanted to play something else, proven by his fingers touching hers, or his hand resting on her arm. A couple times he hinted that he had other artifacts, upstairs. When his hand lingered on her elbow, she knew she was nearly out of time. She toyed with the idea of acquiescing in the hope that he might have incense on the second floor. How far could she safely take this charade? She couldn't let it get out of control, and possibly cause problems for Sean and Aric.

Stuck on a corner shelf, a speckled, brown container caught her eye.

It can't be. From her college memories, the pottery

looked exactly like her professor's.

"Listen, Kati." Harker put his arm around her waist. "This has been fun, but—"

"Oh, what a pretty jar." She beelined to it. "Where'd this come from?"

"I can't remember." His tone flattened. When she reached for it, he said, "Don't! Don't touch it."

She pressed her hands together under her chin like a child dying to be naughty. "What's in it? Dried blood? Ground up bones?"

"Just a nasty perfume. That's all."

"Perfume? I love perfume."

"You wouldn't like this one. Believe me."

"Couldn't I take one teensy whiff?"

"No. Let's go see those artifacts. Upstairs." Harker latched on her arm.

It was now or never.

Kelli *accidentally* bumped it. The pottery crashed to the floor, shattering on the marble.

Pungent odor instantly permeated the room, one of concentrated vinegar, overripe citrus and hot tar. Raw Xerxian ritual incense.

"Oh, that is awful." Kelli covered her mouth and nose as she backed out of the room.

Letting out a string of curses, Harker bellowed for his housekeeper. Several of the staff came running. He barked orders and shut the study door behind them. From experience, Kelli knew it was too late to contain the odor. No doubt the scent encroached on the rest of the house.

Time to exit.

"I think—I think I'm going to be sick." She grabbed

her stomach and groaned.

"Don't you dare." Harker swore again.

She swooned against the front door. "I'm sorry, Dr. Harker. My hand bumped the jar. I didn't mean—"

"It doesn't matter now. You'd better go." He radiated hostility.

So much for the Bead Dance.

Clutching the doorframe, Kelli moaned.

"Goodbye, Ms. Carter." He opened the door and shoved her into the vestibule. She was barely out the first set of doors when he slammed them behind her.

Outside, she maintained the charade, acting as though she still fought nausea in case Harker was watching. She staggered to her waiting taxi. After climbing into the back seat, she told the driver to return her to the gym.

He glanced at her in the rearview mirror. "Sure thing."

Grimly proud, Kelli settled into the seat.

According to her research, Mitchell Harker had never been to Xerxes IX, or even the outpost. He could be a liar when he claimed that he'd personally acquired all his artifacts.

Or not.

How could she forget the contempt with which he'd spoken? *"I'm a collector, not a buyer."*

The man who had tried to kill her had spent enough time deep in Xerxes IX for their sacred incense to saturate his skin. Though Harker didn't bear the scent, he was now tied to the planet. According to her research, Xerxians didn't sell their incense. The only way to get it was to participate in one of their rituals.

Her would-be killer must have been in a temple and stolen the jar for Harker. How else could he have gotten it?

Though a long shot, her instincts told her she was on the right track. It all fit.

Harker was responsible for Ella's kidnapping. That's why there'd been no ransom demand. He never intended to return Ella. His biological daughter was merely another possession. A prized artifact. Kelli would bet her life on that.

The clincher, though, had been Harker's ring. Though she'd only gotten a glimpse of the one worn by her attacker, they were similar enough to cement their connection.

She smirked. Guess those sessions with the USF psychiatrist paid off after all. A warm, fuzzy feeling had definitely stirred in her.

As she leaned back against the seat, she congratulated herself on one of her better performances. The best part was she'd retained Ella's locket. As she stared out the taxi's window, she chuckled silently. As soon as she got home, she'd take a long hot shower to wash away Harker's pawing.

The driver sneezed twice. His gaze met hers in the mirror. "Sheesh, lady, what'd you step in?"

She lifted her chin. "You really *don't* want to know."

"What'd'ya mean you *lost* her?" Jayd couldn't keep his voice from rising at the nincompoop before him.

"She arrived at the gym but never came out. I finally went in and checked, but she was gone." The agent shuffled his feet. "The staff wasn't helpful at all. Wouldn't tell me a thing."

"Of course not. She *pays* them." Jayd bit off what he wanted to call him. *Probie.*

"I could check again."

Jayd snorted with derision. "And where is her car?"

"Still in the parking lot."

"At the gym?"

"Yeah. Of course."

"Unless she came back and got it after you left." Jayd threw up his hands.

"Uh, guess I hadn't thought of that."

"I guess you hadn't."

"Should I go back?"

"What's the point? You're off this assignment until you review your training. Specifically, how to conduct surveillance." Jayd shook his head. "Go on, get outa here." He pushed back his office chair so forcefully it banged against the wall. The agent scrambled to leave.

Jayd should have tailed her himself, but he'd been distracted by a c-mail Kelli received that day. Only that morning, USF's director had ordered him to read her c-mails, tap her phone, and maintain a twenty-four-hour watch. Intergalaxia's fault, no doubt. Had they found new evidence? As soon as he could, he'd corner his Inter-G contact and find out why the sudden change.

While combing through dozens of messages, Jayd ran across one sent that morning. Aric had written her new friend a short, cryptic message. "It's still a go."

What was? What were those two women up to? If he hadn't been so busy setting up the additional surveillance, he would have followed Kelli himself. Instead, he'd relied on that moron, on loan from another team.

He rubbed his forehead, not sure if it was the headache or lack of sleep that was getting to him. Probably both.

What should he do? Confront Kelli or Aric? Set up a meeting for the three of them? If he could play the women off each other, he could glean information more successfully. Both were intelligent. They'd know why he wanted to see them and would be extremely cautious.

Most importantly, he didn't want Sean involved. It seemed everyone in USF was preparing for the upcoming tribunal. Or *inquisition*, as Jayd called it. Kelli was going to end up the scapegoat.

Then again, since she was going to be sacrificed, why worry what she and Aric had been doing? How much worse could it get?

He glanced at his wall chrono. It was well past seven. He should head home and get some sleep. Monday was when Kelli's life would begin to fall apart. Jayd mentally counted. In five days she would receive a formal summons.

Once that happened, she would be cut off from everyone and everything at USF. Even he wouldn't be able to see her or talk to her. She would be barred from entering the building.

After the tribunal, Jayd had a sinking feeling that she would be led away in handcuffs. Next time he saw her, she'd be wearing an orange jumpsuit and a halo neckband.

Assuming she wasn't shipped offworld to some horrid detention planet, how often could he visit her? Would she even want to see him?

Chapter 9

Nine years.

Kelli stopped before the doors of the massive building, grip tightening around the strap of her shoulder bag. Nearly a decade earlier, her father had left her an electronic key in his will. She'd never bothered to find out what was inside the safety deposit box. Had not been interested. Until now.

If he'd left her even a little bit of money, she'd be grateful. A trip to Xerxes IX might get expensive, especially if she had to sneak off Earth without Inter-G knowing. Though Kelli had some savings, a little more would give her some buffer. Just in case.

Taking a deep breath, she pulled open the heavy door.

"May I help you?" A smartly dressed woman rose as Kelli reached the bottom steps of the bank's lowest floor.

"Yes. I'm here about a safety deposit box."

The woman handed her a stylo and pointed at a security screen. "Fill out the information please. All the highlighted squares."

Kelli wrote in numbers and other pertinent information. A scanner read her DNA.

"That's funny." The woman frowned over the information on her screen. "Your information isn't recorded."

"I know." Kelli retrieved the electronic key from her bag and held it up.

The woman stared at the sliver of metal. "I haven't seen a DNA key in years."

Of course not. She merely smiled. Daddy never trusted anything he couldn't touch. As long as Kelli had the key, it guaranteed that only she could access the box.

He'd always been a stickler for security.

"I'll be back in a moment." The woman disappeared into a side room and soon returned with a matching key. Together they walked into the vault.

For some reason, Kelli's heart rate increased. She clutched the cool metal that she had neglected at the bottom of her jewelry box.

This is silly. He's been dead for years.

Nevertheless, she glanced over her shoulder, expecting to see the ghost of her father follow her through the rows of safety deposit boxes. She shivered.

The woman inserted her electronic key and waited for Kelli to put in hers. "Take as much time as you need. There's a room behind you with a table and chair, if you wish."

"Thank you." She waited until she was alone before she pulled out the shallow box.

Yikes. It was heavy.

Arms shaking from more than the weight, Kelli took the box into the room and slid the door closed behind her. After sitting, she stared at the gray metal.

What would she find? After he'd died, she had wanted nothing from him. She was already established, had her own apartment and had refused any financial help from him for well over a year.

He'd left her a few items of furniture and knick-knacks, which she'd promptly donated to a charity. The will also revealed some minor assets and a key to this box. Nothing else.

What was inside? After taking a deep breath, she opened the box. And gaped.

Antique dollar bills filled the box, cushioning a plastic-wrapped gold brick.

"A Good Delivery bar?" Kelli gulped, unable to guess its current value.

One thing was certain. Her father was consistent. He'd always maintained that he didn't trust lawyers and the government. So he'd stashed his savings in a box. It explained why there was so little money in his will. And why he'd lived in a rented apartment for so many years. He'd sold his house and other property, then hidden the money here.

But what to do with the bills? She'd have to search for a collector who could convert the thousands of dollars into the more commonly used c.a.s.h.—coins, assets, securities and holdings. Though most people used digital money, her father had preferred the tangible dollars. It would be sweet if they were worth more than their face value.

Leaving the gold brick, Kelli took out a wad of bills and stuffed them into her purse.

For once in her life, she was grateful to her father.

How could she do this to Sean?

Guilt racked Aric as she surveyed the flora in her greenhouse without really seeing. Most of them were vegetables, some overladen with unharvested produce. Neglect marked every plant. But their lack of care didn't bother her as much as the secrets she withheld from her husband.

She should tell him about Kelli. About Mitt. About what Kelli was doing behind everyone's back.

This whole secret-keeping business was a painful reminder of Empusa III, when Sean had refused to tell her the whole truth about who he was and why he was there. The undisclosed information had nearly cost Aric her life. Ultimately, both their lives.

She lifted the stem of a drooping plant. "But I gave my word to Kelli." Speaking out loud helped assuage some of the self-reproach.

Her new friend needed someone to believe in her.

She certainly didn't need another betrayer in her life. From the many conversations they'd had over the last several weeks, Aric sensed the tall blonde was even more of a loner than she.

Sighing, she plucked a shriveled peapod from a nearby plant and tossed it into the recycling bucket. Shortly after the move into their new home, Sean had surprised her by putting in a greenhouse and garden—a way for her and Ella to bond after the years they'd been apart. They'd spent many happy hours digging in the dirt, examining worms and talking about insects. She smiled as she recalled Ella squealing with excitement when the first delicate leaves of a tomato plant pushed through the soil.

Lifting her gaze, Aric stared at the large corkboard above her workbench. Originally, Sean had put it there so she could chart the garden's progress. Now, a half dozen of Ella's drawings and assorted photos covered the cork. One was of Sean and their daughter, immediately after the adoption had been finalized. While he crouched at eye level, Ella smiled shyly into her new daddy's eyes.

Gulping, Aric fingered the worn edge, recalling how Sean had promised he would someday adopt her daughter. That dream had finally come true.

Only two pieces of paper in her corkboard collection were different. One was a handwritten note, scrawled by Jayd. *"I'll do all in my power to find her. God help me."*

The other had several hash marks on it—a visible reminder of how many days Ella had been missing.

Aric grasped a nearby pencil and drew a line

through another grouping of five. Her hand shook as she let the utensil drop from her fingers.

"Lord, please...please." She choked out the words as she slid to her knees on the rough dirt flooring. For once, tears didn't flood her face. Instead the relentless burning in her throat seared down to her heart and smoldered there.

What could she ask Him that she hadn't asked a million times already? For a long time, she knelt, finding no new wording for an old request.

She ground her forehead against the wide leg of the wooden worktable, searching for what to pray. "At least keep Kelli safe. And protect Sean from any repercussions."

Just recently, he told her how USF's director had taken him to task because he'd asked too many questions about Intergalaxia's investigation. The intransigent woman even threatened him with an "early retirement" or imprisonment if he continued to interfere.

Didn't they understand what an asset Sean could be if they would let him help? Had they forgotten why he'd been promoted in the first place? Because of him, Empusa III had been saved.

Inter-G and USF saw him merely as a grieving stepfather and had relegated him to the sidelines.

Aric pressed her clenched fists against the unyielding wood. "Stupid. So stupid."

A noise outside caught her ear. Was someone calling her name? It sounded like Sean, but couldn't be. He was at work.

"Aric!"

It *was* him. Though his voice sounded muffled by

distance, she heard a note of urgency.

She leaped to her feet and yanked open the greer-house's door. "I'm here." She rushed toward him as he ran across the yard. "What is it? Is there word about Ella?" When she reached him, she clutched his arm.

"No. I..." He paused to catch his breath.

"No news at all?"

"Sorry, no." He shook his head. "I called and you didn't answer. I searched the whole house and then came out here..."

"Oh, my comm-unit." Glancing back to the greer-house, she realized she hadn't brought it out with her. She patted her back pocket where she usually kept it. "I guess I left it in the house."

"It's on the counter. I thought..." Sean broke off, mouth flattening.

That she too had been kidnapped?

"I'm so sorry. I always have it with me. I don't know why..." She bit her lip as she realized why she might have forgotten her CU. Because she'd been so wrapped up in secrets? "I'm sorry. It'll never happen again."

"It's okay." Sean stroked her cheek. His hand lingered as worry eased from his face. "I'm just glad you're all right."

"I didn't mean for you to worry." Her heart pounded at his gentle touch and tender tone.

He should be irritated. Should berate her because he had most likely left the office in a hurry and driven like a madman to get home. All because she'd been too wrapped up in what Kelli was plotting.

"It must be after three." She glanced at the position

of the sun. "I hope this didn't cause you to miss something important at the office."

"Nah. Just a meeting." He made a face. "Nothing important."

"Really?"

Since his big promotion, it seemed like he worked constantly. Aric struggled with wanting him at the office so he could keep abreast of any news of Ella and wanting him with herself. But once he arrived home in the evenings, he was so preoccupied that he might as well be at work.

"You done out there?" Sean waved in the direction of the greenhouse.

"Yeah." She fell in step beside him as they headed toward the house. When he reached for her fingers, she caught her breath. How long had it been since they'd held hands? On impulse, she leaned her cheek against his shoulder as they walked. His grip tightened.

When they got inside, he released her hand to shut the door.

Without thinking, Aric picked up her CU. Nine missed calls, all from Sean. A short text from Kelli said she couldn't wait to share the news about "their project." Aric clenched the comm-unit as guilt slammed against her.

What had happened with Mitt? She and Kelli had not found time to get together and they dared not chat about that over the phone. Because of Sean's urgings, Aric had begun doing some professional writing about Empusa III and other planets with technologically immature humanoids. Working with SARC again was out of the question. They were headquartered in Seattle while she had settled permanently in New Washington.

But with Ella missing, Aric could barely put two sentences together, much less two thoughts.

When she looked up, she caught her husband's piercing gaze. At first she grew alarmed, thinking he might have seen Kelli's text and wanted to ask her what it meant. But no suspicion marked his face. Only relief. And love?

"Come here." He spoke softly, arms spread in invitation.

She didn't hesitate to bury herself in his embrace.

It had been ages since they'd held each other. Her fault. The pain in her soul consumed her until she couldn't stand his touch. Did she subconsciously blame him for Ella's kidnapping?

Dear Lord, I'm sorry if I made him think that.

How selfish to be so wrapped up in her own loss that she didn't consider how much Sean suffered. Twice as much, for both Ella and her.

She had to remedy that. Now. Without circumspection, she stood on tiptoes and pulled his head down until their lips met. She gave him a long, passionate kiss.

With her arms wrapped around his neck, she dared to ask, "Do you have to rush back to work?"

He pulled his head back to look into her eyes. Uncertainty flickered across his features.

Had she so wounded him with her coldness that he was afraid to hope?

"Because I was thinking." Her cheeks grew warm as she spoke. "If you had nothing else planned for this evening..."

His jaw flexed with emotion. She'd seen that look before, while she'd been desperately ill on Empusa III. It was the first day after her recovery. His expression had revealed the scope of his love.

"Nothing planned," he spoke in a husky voice. "You?"

I should tell him...

Ever so slowly, she shook her head, not only to answer his question, but to banish that nagging voice in her head. She had to keep her promise. More importantly, she had to protect her husband.

"I love you, Sean Reese. I'm sorry if I caused you to ever doubt that."

His mouth puckered, revealing the depth of his pain.

She trailed her fingertips lightly across his cheek. "If you'll let me, I'll prove my love. Right now."

Without a word, he scooped her into his arms and carried her up the stairs. Tonight she would show him that he mattered more than anyone else in the world. He needed that reassurance.

And so did she.

Sunday night. Why was he still at work? Apparently USF didn't believe in a forty-hour work week. Or fifty or sixty. Jayd would settle even for that. His insane schedule was beginning to wear him down.

But at least, he had everything in place as far as Kelli was concerned. Everything that Inter-G had demanded before he turned the case over to them. Surveillance, taps. Jayd didn't want to even think about the invasion of privacy. He'd surrendered all of Kelli's files to them as well. After tomorrow, he never wanted to talk to them again.

No one except Ryan. His buddy had tried to keep him abreast of what was going on behind the scenes. Why the sudden hostility toward Kelli? Apparently Inter-G had found a witness who claimed to know about a meeting between her and the dead waiter. Ryan hinted there were a few other things, things about which no one would tell him.

Of course not. That's because they had no concrete evidence.

It was all speculation. Inter-G had run out of people to persecute so they settled the blame on Kelli. She was the only one left.

Tomorrow, she'd get the summons to appear before a tribunal. No doubt, they'd rake her over the coals.

Weary to the core, Jayd rose. His office was a mess. His desk looked like a paper shredder had thrown a party. Funny how he still resorted to handwritten notes when he wanted to plan. He didn't bother straightening his desk. What did it matter?

He left his office and locked the door behind him. His gaze swept over the large open area, full of modular workstations but empty of personnel. Of course. He was the only idiot who didn't know when to leave like a normal person.

After punching the elevator button, he leaned his hand on the wall and sighed. The doors finally dinged open and he nearly ran into Kelli.

She looked taken aback. "Oh. I didn't think..."

"I'd be here?"

"*Anyone* would be here." After she stepped out, the doors of the elevator swooshed shut.

"Well you're right about that." His arm swept over the open space. "This place is a tomb."

"And you the living dead?"

"Pretty much." He resisted the urge to tease her. The impending summons weighed too heavily on his mind. "So what's up?"

"I came to study."

"Weren't you here last night too?"

She tilted her head to one side. "You're actually asking me if I was here? Like you don't know?"

Yeah, he did. But he enjoyed their banter. It was almost like old times, when he could lecture her because she was a junior agent on someone else's team.

When he could pretend he didn't care so much.

He cleared his throat. "I don't know everything. All the time."

"Ha." But she said it with a smile. And she didn't move away or act like she was in a hurry to escape from him.

"So, what's tonight's topic?"

She shrugged. "Oh, I don't know. Maybe something will come to me." Her eyes danced.

She's on to something. "C'mon. You can tell me."

She gave him a coy smile. "I was thinking of reviewing some religious practices. Alien ones, maybe."

He drew closer and rested a hand on her forehead. "You feeling all right? Running a fever?"

Allowing the touch, she chuckled.

He inhaled her perfume. Enjoyed the closeness.

"You worried that I'll stop being a poor, misguided pagan?"

Wow, she remembered his calling her that? He seemed to recall throwing that out once, when she'd mocked someone's beliefs.

It was his deepest desire she'd embrace Truth, but he didn't dare voice that. "No chance of that, Ms. Pagan Poster Child. I'm just concerned about your health."

She chuckled, apparently not offended by his name-calling. "I'm perfectly fine, thank you very much."

A wave of regret roiled through his stomach. She wouldn't be fine after tomorrow's summons.

Her eyes narrowed. "How about you? Looks like you've been working too hard."

Her fault. He didn't say it, though it was true.

"Haven't I been driving slowly enough for you to follow, Jayd?"

"Something like that."

I'm so sorry, Kelli. I wish I could stop what they're going to do.

Technically he wasn't supposed to know the details.

She tilted her head to one side. "You really should go home and get some sleep."

Her genuine concern touched him. He cast about for something to say. Anything. "After this week, things should slow down."

Was that the best he could do? Lame.

"What's that mean?" Her lips pursed. "Giving up on me? I been running you too hard?"

If only she knew.

He leaned his hand on the wall again. "Okay, yes you have. And where'd you learn to drive like that?"

"USF training." She laughed. "Finally paid off."

"Yes, it has." They stood inches from each other, comfortable for once. At least, Jayd was. She didn't edge away from him like he was diseased. What had changed? This wasn't their normal relationship—before the kidnapping.

Then it struck him. This was how she'd acted when he'd been her handler while she was deep undercover at SARC. She'd trusted him. Relied on him. During that year, she'd stopped being the idiot underling as he'd recognized her as a force to be reckoned with.

"Go home and get some sleep." Her voice came low as her gaze flickered to his lips. "I won't do anything wild and crazy tonight. After studying, I'll head directly to my apartment."

"Promise?"

"Yeah, I promise." She rested her palm on his chest as though to put a seal on her vow.

Jayd gulped, then stepped away before she could feel his heart kick into high gear. "No need to go to the library. You can use this workstation." He moved to an unassigned one and typed an access code into the imbedded keyboard. "There. All ready."

"Thank you." She sat, already engrossed in the screen. "Oh, can I get into the Accelerated Learning Program here?"

"ALP?" Her request surprised him. "Sure. Let me

get you deeper admittance." He leaned over, typing in additional commands and passwords. "You should be able to access the whole library now. Sub-dermal chips are in the top drawer if you really want to go crazy."

She looked up at him, blue eyes sparkling. "Thanks so much."

He nodded.

"One more thing. Um, random question." She smiled at him, innocently.

Look out. Here it comes.

"Yes?"

"Since Ella's kidnapping, have all transport ships coming to Earth been searched?"

He cocked an eyebrow. "That's classified."

"Yeah." She traced a delicate finger along the edge of the desk, then looked at him from under her lashes.

He recognized the ploy and wasn't sure if he should be annoyed or flattered. Deliberately he delayed his answer, letting her know that *he* knew what she was doing.

Of course she did. But it hadn't stopped her from trying.

He finally answered. "Yes, they have."

"And are still?"

"Still." He nodded.

She smiled, the shy gesture pure fiction. Oh, how talented she was.

Before she asked the next obvious question, he added, "There's a level two security alert at all air portals. Of course, we can't check all transports from the Xerxian outpost to other planets, but Inter-G has been trying." He leaned forward, planting a palm on the desk. "You know, my giving you this information could get me fired."

She sucked on her lower lip, moistening the skin. Her gaze again flickered to his mouth, then back to his eyes. "I won't tell." A soft smile slowly spread across her lips.

He straightened, uncertain if that was another ploy. Probably not. She hadn't asked for anything else. It bothered him more than the obvious wiles.

He cleared his throat. "Don't stay up too late."

"I'll try not to."

Jayd turned and strode to the elevator, trying to shake off how she affected him. Wouldn't work in a million years. Her perfume lingered in the small space.

Why was she so different tonight? Or was it him?

The elevator doors closed with Kelli still sitting at the computer, already engrossed. She might think him duped, but he'd used access codes that would leave an easy trail for him to follow. Tomorrow he'd find out exactly what she was anxious to learn from the library files.

Chapter 10

A pounding on her door ricocheted through her skull. With a groan, Kelli lifted her head. What time was it? Her bedroom chrono said 10:23 a.m. She flopped face down onto the pillow. Four hours of sleep wasn't enough. Not after last night's intensive study, the second in two days. Her brain still hurt.

Another knock, more insistent.

She slapped blindly at the comm—several times—without bothering to raise her half-buried face from the pillow. "What do you want?"

"Kelli Patricia Layne?"

Her head shot up. This sounded serious. She toggled visual to see who was at her door. One plainclothes and two uniformed men—*formies*—came into sight. She swore, then again pushed on the comm button. "Just a minute. I'll be right there."

She threw on a robe, knotted the belt tightly, and raked fingers through her hair. All the while, her mind raced for an explanation for why these men were at her door.

None of them were good.

Kelli straightened her shoulders and pushed the button to unlock the door panel. It slid open, allowing the brightness in the hallway to flood her darkened apartment. She squinted, assessing who they were and why they were here. Grim, impassive. The plainclothes guy was a courier. The formies were no-nonsense, hurt-you-in-a-second men. They all meant business.

One thing was obvious—her life as she knew it was about to end.

"Kelli Patricia Layne, you are hereby summoned to appear…"

Who cared what else he said? She knew the drill. The courier shoved an official document at her while she waited for handcuffs to appear. Why else were the *formies* here? She watched their faces as the courier droned on, but they didn't act as though preparing for an arrest.

Then she understood that they were there to make sure she got the summons. And protection for the courier? Why? Was she considered that dangerous?

After they left, she finally realized she was still standing at the door with nothing on but skimpy PJs and a silk robe. A noise at the end of the hallway caught her attention. A worker was replacing a light fixture. No, he was doing something else. She peered, suddenly realizing that he was installing a camera. And it pointed right at her apartment door.

They were watching her now. Not just Jayd. Intergalaxia.

She stepped back and slapped the panel button closed. With shaking fingers, she opened the summons, read it and the accompanying instructions.

She was to remain in the city.

She was to have no contact with any member of USF.

She was to have no contact with family members of USF.

She was to present herself at the inquiry exactly one week from today. The list of do's and don'ts went on.

Knees buckling, Kelli sank down on the sofa.

Had Jayd known last night when he'd let her access the USF library? He must have. Was that why he'd been so kind to her?

Her eyes burned. Why hadn't he warned her? He'd volunteered other information.

Perhaps he suspected she'd try to skip town. The noob who'd followed her a few days before would've been easy to lose. Kelli bolted up and stalked across her living room.

"Vi," she commanded the enviro-system, "open blinds, ten percent." The computer did as she bid. Kelli peered out to the aeropad outside the back door to her apartment.

No followers in sight. Obviously the 'C Team' had been replaced by the 'A Team.' She probably wouldn't see *them*. But they were there. Someone was probably recording her right now.

"Vi. Close blinds." She slumped against the wall as they slowly shut.

Mind racing, she let out a slow breath. What to do? After last night's research, she was certain she was on the right track. Harker's involvement in Ella's kidnapping was all but proven in her mind.

"I just need the evidence. That's all." As she paced, she crushed the document in her hands. Uncaring of the papers fluttering to the floor, she trod on them as she pondered all she suspected. If she came forward now, would Inter-G believe her? Unlikely.

Kelli clenched her fists, fingernails digging into her palms as she planted herself in the middle of her living room. What could she do? *They* had effectively gagged and bound her, leaving her no options. They wouldn't let her talk to Jayd, much less Aric and Sean. She couldn't lay out her suspicions, her research, her leads.

She whispered aloud in the darkened room. "But I know where Ella is."

"So what's the scoop?" Jayd slid into the chair opposite his Intergalaxia contact. Out of habit, he glanced around the coffee shop, assessing the other patrons. None of them were officials. No Inter-G. No one but Ryan, that is.

His buddy leaned closer. "For the last several days,

she's been laying pretty low." Ryan's eyes, too, darted to the people coming and going. He had reason to be nervous, like Jayd. They shouldn't even be talking to each other.

Playing like a regular ol' customer, Jayd took a sip of his coffee. "She staying in her apartment?"

"Nope. Been shopping. A lot. In a few days she's spent several hundred c.a.s.h."

He squinted at his friend. "You're kidding." Kelli shopping? That wasn't right.

"Yeah, buying lots of junk."

"Like what?"

"Clothing. Cosmetics. Give me a sec, I'll tell you what stores." Ryan tapped his comm-unit and named some obscure outlets as well as pawnshops. "She's apparently got this thing for alien accessories."

Jayd shifted in his seat. This did *not* sound like Kelli.

"You'd think she would pick something more professional for her court appearance, not..." Ryan threw several glances at a customer who took a seat not far from them.

Jayd, too, assessed the woman. Businesswoman. Pretending to be on a lunch break? New shoes. Expensive. Clothing expensive. Necklace very expensive. He glanced at her fingers. Single—no, married once. Ah, married pretending to be single. He could see where a wide wedding ring had been replaced by a thinner, nondescript band with a cheap stone.

The woman crossed her legs, already engrossed in an electronic book.

Not an agent.

She hadn't looked at them even once. After watching her for a moment longer, he scrutinized his friend. It finally dawned on him why Ryan was staring. He didn't radiate caution, but admiration.

Jayd cleared his throat. "Hey, bud, don't forget you're married."

"Nope, never." Ryan grinned before shifting his chair.

"Anything else I need to know?"

His friend looked again at his CU. "Yeah, uh, our friend still goes to the gym. And she made a couple stops at beauty salons."

Kelli was up to something. Jayd could feel it in his bones. "Any cameras inside?" He didn't need to spell out "in her apartment," mindful of the nearby patron.

"No. External only. That stupid Privacy Act of five years ago is playing havoc. We do have equipment in the hallway, aeropad and foyer, though."

"Think you could get me a copy of the pics?"

Ryan's eyes flickered. "Risky."

"Just a couple. So I can see what's going on."

"I'll do my best."

"Thanks."

His buddy glanced around, then leaned forward. "You know, things are looking worse and worse for her."

"What do you mean?"

"She recently gave us nine thousand reasons why she's guilty."

Jayd rested an elbow on the table. "What are you talking about?"

"Don't you know? Out of nowhere, nine thousand

in c.a.s.h. recently showed up in her bank account. Word is, she hanged herself."

Coffee forgotten, Jayd sat back.

"I thought you said she was smart." Ryan adjusted the lid on his coffee cup. "I'm not a betting man, but I'd say she received payment for her part in the deal. Can't believe she was stupid enough to put it in her account."

If that's what everyone believed, so would the judge. Jayd had no explanation where Kelli would have gotten the money. And yes, she was too smart for that. There must be a reasonable explanation.

"You still maintain she's innocent?"

"Yeah." Jayd rubbed his forehead with his fingers. "Although I have no idea how to explain the 9K."

"You're probably the only one that doesn't believe it's blood money."

"Wait a sec. Did it show up *before* she was served the summons?"

Ryan considered. "Yeah. But that only makes her appear more guilty in my book."

Yes, it did. As though Kelli thought the coast was clear. Jayd shook his head. "Hey, thanks for the intel. I owe ya."

"Yes, you do." His friend shook his hand as Jayd rose.

He nodded a farewell, then headed out of the shop after dumping the coffee.

What was Kelli doing? He wanted to head to her place and shake the information out of her. But he couldn't. His hands were tied. He had to stay away from her, not merely because he had orders to, but because he could help her best by being a character witness. An impartial one, supposedly.

But what about that money? Where had that come from? And what did she intend to do with it? Assuming, of course, that the judge didn't put a freeze on all her assets. Likely now.

Everything in him told him she planned something dangerous. What it was, he couldn't imagine. He vacillated between keeping the information to himself and sharing it with Sean. Better left unshared. Jayd wasn't even supposed to know what Kelli was up to, much less discuss her with anyone at USF. Especially his boss's boss.

The tightness between Kelli's shoulder blades expanded, blossoming until pain marched down her spine. Her head started to pound as the formal tribunal dragged through the morning and into the afternoon. From what she'd been told, the hearing would only be a couple hours long. And it was not supposed to be as formal as court.

Not true in her case.

Representatives from Intergalaxia lined one side of the room, facing Kelli from behind a polished table. The judge, a cross between a gargoyle and avenging angel, perched behind her bench at the head of the room, imposing and impassive. The audience—assorted guests from the celebratory reception—sat in rows. Because it was a closed hearing, only a few dozen were present. Only Kelli and a court-appointed "advisor" sat at a lone bare table along the fourth wall.

As succinctly as she could, she answered all the intrusive questions. Hour after hour they badgered her. Several times she shot glances at the judge who seemed to sleep with her eyes open. Was that a good sign or bad? Kelli could not present evidence or defend herself. Several times when she'd attempted to protest, her interrogators verbally slapped her down. And the judge did nothing.

Her gaze shot to the sea of faces in the audience. She saw only hostility, suspicion, disgust, even in those with whom she worked at USF. Only Jayd's stood out. He appeared contemplative. Worried. Several times he flashed her what might be a smile, but it looked more like a grimace.

She wouldn't look at Sean, especially as her relationship with him was questioned, dissected, sullied. The year she'd spent undercover with him at SARC was cast in a new light—as though she'd accepted the assignment not to expose the corrupt director, but to stalk Sean.

Mortification pummeled her into silence. She stared at the chipped polish on two fingernails, no doubt picked away because of stress.

Her advisor suddenly jabbed her ribs. "Stand up," he hissed.

Kelli shot to her feet, the chair scraping loudly on the glossy floor.

The judge spoke, voice as hard as chipped concrete. "Kelli Patricia Layne, in consideration of your exemplary service record with the Universal Security Forces..."

For what felt like minutes, the woman droned.

Kelli's ears began to buzz as the full import dawned on her in all the legalize jargon.

They think I was involved in Ella's kidnapping. They are treating me like I'm an accessory. Guilty until proven innocent.

"You have three days to get your affairs in order." The judge's gavel boomed.

Three days?

For endless moments she stood frozen, vaguely aware of her advisor scampering away. Voices exploded in the courtroom while across from her, Intergalaxia's representatives smiled in grim satisfaction.

She had to get out of there.

Before anyone could intercept her, she plowed through the rabble and stumbled through the heavy doors. She leaned against the railing in the foyer, still unable to process what had happened. Her chest squeezed impossibly tight. She couldn't get a full breath. The hum of voices, echoing footsteps, muted ding of the elevator sounded abnormally loud as she gripped the polished wooden cap of the railing.

She fumbled for her purse and pulled out tissue to dab perspiration off her upper lip.

How could they believe she was guilty? Why did they? Had they forgotten she was nearly killed?

"Kelli!"

When she heard Jayd's voice, she turned. The heavy door of the courtroom banged shut behind him, then immediately opened.

"Jayden, wait." A man grabbed his arm and talked low in his ear. The stranger glanced at her as they spoke.

"Stay away from her." Kelli could imagine the whispered advice. *"Avoid her—for your own good."*

She agreed. Jayd needed to keep as far from her as possible. He'd end up losing his job. He'd only hurt himself.

Before he could extricate himself from his companion, Kelli slipped into the crowd. She rushed down the steps and out the back of the building. For a few blocks, she strode without thinking about where she was going. Soon she noticed someone was following her. A couple of somebodies.

Intergalaxia, of course.

They expected her to run. Or make sure she didn't get far.

How could she have been so foolish to think the circumstantial evidence against her would be dismissed? She should have seen all the warning signs.

I'm on my own now.

When she reached the nearby park, she perched on a bench as though enjoying the warmth of the sun. She had to act low-key. Predictable. That was the only way to fool the A Team. As far as they were concerned, she was cornered. She had three days before the ax fell.

Thoughts rapidly clicked through her mind.

Her bank accounts would be off limits. They may have even frozen them by now. Thankfully, she hadn't taken all the money out of the safety deposit box. The collector who'd purchased the bills had insisted on a direct deposit of c.a.s.h. In retrospect, it was a stupid to have allowed that. Who cared that the highly respected collector had given her the best value? The electronic trail had acted as a neon sign, proclaiming her guilt.

She had no choice but to pawn the gold brick—and somewhere not so reputable. Now she was glad she'd checked several possible sources. No doubt she'd take quite a hit, but it had to be done.

Everything else was in place. She had submitted to the Accelerated Learning Program, even while she slept. For that, at least, she could be grateful to Jayd. She'd not had a chance to return the sub-dermal chip and now no longer planned to. The learning and the chip were vital for her plan to work.

She rose, setting her jaw with determination. In less than seventy-two hours, she intended to become a fugitive.

Kelli looked at herself in the mirror and laughed at the black hair and bluish-green skin. Though she'd seen few Xerxians up close and personal, she had no doubt she could pass for one.

"Thank the stars I'm…" She broke off what she was going to say, much more leery about casually invoking a deity. If there was a God, she didn't want to make Him mad by thanking something other than Him. But she didn't quite feel comfortable directly giving Him credit.

"I'm grateful that I'm tall." *There*. That seemed a safer thing to say.

Xerxian females averaged over six feet. At five-ten, Kelli would be considered a little short, but not abnormal for a young adult. She smoothed the tinted makeup on her chin, then realized she'd forgotten to apply a pale pink to her lips. The final effect was interesting.

"Hey, Dad, thanks for paying for that cosmetology course." She glanced toward the ceiling as though he could hear her. "It wasn't worthless, after all." Too bad she didn't have a derma-booth. It would have made tinting her skin a snap. However, smuggling small jars to Xerxes IX under the nose of Inter-G presented less of a challenge.

Focusing on her mission helped quell the doubts that continually battered her. Was she doing the right thing? Or was she out of her mind?

She clenched her fist. "At least I'm doing *some*thing. What difference does it make if I rot in prison four years for not trying or six for trying?"

Again, she dragged her mind back to the task at hand. Xerxes. Right.

What about clothing? On Earth, Xerxians likely didn't wear their traditional garb of flowing robes over a light tunic and pants, but what *did* they wear? She couldn't risk looking online to find those who dwelled on Earth. No doubt all her communications were being monitored.

She practiced striding around her living room with that particular gait she'd seen in the educational pics. Women walked with their shoulders back, head high, arms swinging. Because Xerxes IX was a matriarchal society, she must remember to meet others' gazes confidently. Men were supposed to be the first to look away. Easy.

Next she practiced saying a few Xerxian lines.

"Greetings, friend. I am honored. Where is the nearest temple?"

The Xer language was full of unique clicks which she'd been practicing since she'd first accessed the Accelerated Learning Program. Nothing would be as helpful as actually speaking to a native when she arrived on the planet, but for now, the drills helped. Good thing she'd scored high in linguistics. The imbedded sub-dermal chip behind her ear would assist her, not only with translation but with all things Xerxian.

Satisfied with her rehearsal, she removed the wig and washed off the green. Before she skipped town, she would apply the permanent stuff—for her hair, skin and lips. The skin dye would last about two weeks before fading. But that would be enough time to get someplace private where she could reapply it. Dark contacts would have to suffice to disguise her blue eyes until she got implants at the Xerxian outpost. *If* she made it to the space station. In light of her new status, that was a big if.

She hid the wig amongst her newly acquired assortment and threw the makeup in a drawer full of the cosmetics she'd bought over the last few days. Enough stuff to distract if someone searched her place. So far, no cameras were in her apartment. She checked and double checked, each time she left and returned. That didn't mean they weren't following her every move though. Depending on who was in charge of surveillance and how closely they watched.

Did they obey all aspects of the Privacy Act? Doubtful.

After grabbing her bag, she headed out for an early morning appointment at the gym. She trained hard, working to get rid of detrimental adrenaline in her system. She needed to sleep tonight. Not pace the floor for all hours. After the workout and a quick shower, she approached her trainer, Jorge.

He grinned, obviously pleased she sought him out again.

"Had any more trouble from the wanna-be boyfriend?" he asked.

"Yeah. He is worse."

His grin faded. "What's up?"

"He's not just stalking me, but I think he figured out a way to read my mail."

"Let me pay him a visit. Please." Jorge ground a bunched fist against his palm.

Kelli placed a hand on his arm. "Not yet, but soon. I promise. But listen, I need a *huge* favor."

"Anything, Kel."

She pressed her lips together, genuinely concerned that he might mess this up. Or worse, that some authorities may have talked to him already. "I need this note hand delivered. But if you can't, just mail it." She pulled out an envelope addressed to Aric. It was a big risk, but she owed it to her friend.

"On paper?" He glanced down. "Fancy neighborhood."

"Yeah, sweet gal. Married though. Sorry."

He laughed. "I won't be able to deliver this until after two-thirty when I get off."

"That would be great." She sought to word her next request. "I have training appointments set up for the next several weeks, but if I don't make a few, don't get alarmed, okay? I might buzz over to my sister's house in Colorado Springs for a week or so."

"Good idea. Get a break from that goon."

"Exactly. But when I get back, I'll buy you a drink."

He surprised her by demurring. "Technically we're not supposed to fraternize with customers."

"Well, then I'll buy you a water." She waved in the direction of free bottles clustered in a barrel.

He laughed. "Works for me."

"Thanks a ton." She knuckle-bumped him and left.

Next stop was a salon that specialized in hair extensions. She paid extra to have two technicians work with her. The process still took a couple hours, but when they were done, they had transformed her blonde locks until they reached past her shoulders. She verified it felt real, could be dyed and it would last several months. Though the technicians fussed, Kelli had them clip it up. She didn't want to draw attention to the change in length.

By the time she reached her apartment, she was ready to put the next part of her plan in action. She headed to the foyer to get the weekly advertisements from her mailbox, walking unsteadily.

"Hey, Ms. Kelli." The security guard beamed in genuine pleasure.

"Hi." She spoke in a soft voice, clutching her stomach.

"Something wrong?" Genuinely concerned, the older man rose. He was such a sweet guy.

"I think I got some bad food. Maybe the flu. You'd better stay away." Kelli licked her lips several times as though fighting nausea.

"Head hurt?"

"Yeah. A little. And it's getting worse." She squinted at the light coming through the main doors as though it pained her eyes. Deliberately, she dropped her key card as she fought to insert it in her mailbox's slot.

The security guard's voice reached her across the foyer. "You need to head to bed and stay there. Drink plenty of water. Order a vita-pak."

"Sounds like a great idea. Could you hold my mail and any deliveries for a few days?"

"You got it, Ms. Kelli. You take care, hear?"

"Thanks." She clutched her mail and leaned against the wall, as though gathering strength before heading to the elevator.

All the while, the older man watched her, brow furrowed. *Perfect.* When she didn't show up outside her apartment for a few days, he would tell everyone who was interested she had the flu. If they scanned her apartment, they would "see" a life-size mannequin under a heating blanket stretched out in bed. All levels of her enviro-systems would be cranked up, disguising the fact she was gone.

She hoped they fell for the ruse. For a little while, anyway.

Chapter 11

In the privacy of his office, Jayd watched the earliest recordings of Kelli going in and out of her apartment. He played them on his comm-unit, choosing a fourteen-inch virtual screen so he wouldn't miss anything. At first glance, she appeared to do normal, everyday things. For a normal and everyday kind of person. Which she was not. He watched them multiple times. What was missing? Then it hit him. None of the bags she carried contained groceries. Not one food item.

"She's going somewhere." His heart hammered at

the implications. If she left town, she would be a fugitive. Was she planning to run? It made no sense.

His CU rang, the number flashing on the big screen. Was it Aric? She rarely called him.

"Aric? What's up?"

"Jayd." She sounded breathless. "Can you come by the house?"

He glanced at the clock. "I have a meeting in fifteen minutes and—"

"Please. We must talk right away. It's about…about…"

Sean? Ella? Kelli?

The fact she wouldn't say alarmed him. She was afraid their call was being monitored.

For good reason.

"I'll be there in forty, forty-five." He secured his office before heading to his assistant's desk.

"Sir?"

He kept his voice low. "Find out where the chief is."

"Chief Reese?"

He nodded, gaze darting about the room to see if their conversation was being overheard. It would be better if Sean didn't know anything about this.

Jen made a couple calls. She'd picked up on the need to be casual, talking conversationally to the persons on the other end. Smart gal. As usual.

She hung up. "He's in a meeting, sir. Looks like it'll last another hour. At least."

"Thanks. I need to step out for a few. Reschedule my meetings for later. No, make that tomorrow."

Jen nodded. "Anything I can help with?"

"Not yet. I need to take care of something. Be back soon."

When he landed his car on the pad in front of the Reese home, Aric ran to meet him.

He held up his hand, not so much in greeting as to keep her from talking out in the open. "Wait. Let's go downstairs."

Though Jayd wasn't sure what Aric needed to tell him, he wasn't taking any chances.

Once the door to the silent room sealed, he nodded to her.

"Thanks so much for coming." Her face paled as though afraid someone might still hear. "I had to tell someone. Just not Sean. Not until I talked to you." She pulled a letter out of her pocket and handed it to him.

"I'm sorry I can't give details, but I need to leave town. I have a lead that I must follow. It may be nothing, but I have to find out for sure. Miss you lots. PS I will return the locket as soon as I can."

Even though the letter wasn't signed, Kelli had sent it. She had a lead? Obviously about Ella. And what was this about a locket?

"A guy hand-delivered this a little while ago." Aric's fingers clenched and unclenched. "She said she was leaving town. Isn't that illegal? I mean, with the tribunal and all."

He merely nodded.

"I was going to call Sean, but..." She gulped. "I thought maybe I should talk to you first. I'm really worried, Jayd."

She wasn't merely worried. She was frightened.

Locking her with his gaze, he spoke slowly. "I want

you to tell me everything you and Kelli have been up to. And I mean *everything*."

Events happened so quickly after that, Jayd felt like life sped into hyper-drive. One moment he was at Aric's home, and the next standing in a half-empty parking garage with Ryan, getting the latest pics on Kelli. His buddy wasn't too happy about the meeting, but Jayd couldn't tell him what was the matter.

As he played the CU's recording, Ryan looked over his shoulder. "Nothing happened this morning. Just the routine. Heard a rumor she has the flu."

I doubt that.

"Oh, there was a glitch in the electrical system in Layne's apartment for a few minutes. This afternoon. Nothing serious. Our cameras are on a different power source, so we didn't lose any footage."

Jayd watched the clip several times on the small rectangle, not daring to pull up a larger, virtual screen. On Kelli's floor, the lights flickered in the hallway, then people started coming out of their apartments, apparently to find out what was wrong. Deep shadow covered the end of the corridor where Kelli's apartment was located. People milled around. Some headed down the stairs since the elevator doors wouldn't open.

"We did a sweep of her apartment," Ryan continued. "She's still in bed."

Half listening, Jayd squinted at the small screen. A tall, dark-haired woman walked down with the crowd, a bag slung over her shoulder.

"Who's she?" He backed up the clip and played it again.

"Dunno. Not a regular. Visitor?"

Jayd had not seen her before. "Is that green skin?" He peered. "Or the light playing tricks?"

His friend looked. They replayed it yet again. "I think you're right. Xerxian? Man I would've liked to have met her."

"Me too." Jayd spoke grimly, certain they would have no footage of this woman entering the building.

Kelli!

"So what's going on?" Ryan asked.

He flicked off the CU. "Nothing. Bad food, I think, making me jumpy."

His friend's eyes narrowed.

"No, I mean it." Jayd displayed his most innocent smile. "You ever get itchy palms? But nothing happens?"

"Sometimes."

He turned, looking around the parking garage. "I swear I'm seeing Inter-G everywhere I go. It's getting to me."

"And you should." His friend grinned. "We're trained to be ghosts. When you get tired of USF, I could put in a good word for you."

"Thanks."

He turned, but paused when Ryan added, "Don't worry about our little friend. This'll be over soon. Tomorrow, right?"

"Yep. Thanks again for meeting with me on such short notice."

"No problem. Hang in there, buddy." Ryan clapped him on the shoulder.

Jayd climbed into his car. What was Kelli was up to? The clock was ticking. He couldn't involve Sean, so he called his assistant. Since he planned to push the speed limit, he put the car into manual drive.

"Jen, find out how many transport ships are scheduled to depart in the next twelve hours for offworld destinations. No, make that only to the Xerxian outpost. I'll hold."

She finally responded, using the military time he liked. "Two. Seventeen-thirty and zero hundred hours. Nothing tomorrow until ten."

"Can you pull up the manifest of passengers on the first flight?" As he merged into traffic, he estimated he should make the terminal in time. Not that he was planning on going anywhere. But he had to check.

"Eighteen people have reservations."

"What are their names?" He pushed his way through the freeway traffic.

As she read the list, Jayd recognized none of them. It was a long shot, but he'd hoped Kelli might be listed under a known pseudonym.

"Read the list for the other flight. And Darvis II." It was the only other planet that had a sizable population of Xerxians.

Still nothing recognizable.

"Ok, thanks," he said to his assistant when she was done. "One more thing. I'd appreciate it if you didn't volunteer information, but if someone asks about me, answer them. Understand? I don't want you to lie."

"Yes, sir."

He ended the call. Rush hour had begun in earnest. The number of vehicles was unbelievable. Summer tourist season had apparently arrived as well, making his trip all the more difficult. Jayd reached the terminal later than he'd planned so he left his car at the curb, holding up his badge as security charged toward him. When they waved an acknowledgement, he sprinted inside.

More delays. The VIP line through security appeared a mile long. He pushed his way through, incurring the wrath of those who thought they had more privileges. Finally, he shoved his way to the front, holding up his badge.

"I'm carrying no weapon," he volunteered. Since it would only slow him down, he'd secured it in the car's vault. However, that seemed to make no difference to the security agent who took forever reading his badge and matching his ID. Jayd clenched his teeth. His protest would only hinder him more.

Finally, the agent let him pass as his CU rang. It was his assistant.

"Sir, I wanted to let you know there was an additional passenger on the five-thirty. It just showed up. He or she bought a ticket a half hour ago."

"Name?"

She stumbled over the pronunciation. "Frecknard Kel'ari. Or something like that."

Didn't sound familiar. "Spell it."

She did.

"What nationality? Or race?"

"Just a minute."

He heard her typing as he jogged toward the gate.

"Looks like Frecknard's a female. Twenty-four. Oh, she's Xerxian."

"So, that's her last name. Don't Terran-born Xerxians use their last names first?"

"I think so."

He muttered the first name a couple times. Kel'ari. Kel—Kelli? He swore, then was mad at himself for doing so. "Thanks for your help."

Running headlong through the concourse, he leaped over luggage and pushed people out of the way. Breathless, he arrived at the gate's counter, barreling through two men and ignoring their protests. It took a minute to catch his breath, but he took out his badge again to silence everyone around him.

"The—the ship?" he panted.

"Just departed, sir. I'm sorry." The ticket agent glanced down at her screen. "But there's another at midnight. We still have a few seats left."

Jayd hesitated a second before taking the plunge. "Hold one for me." He could always cancel.

After giving his name, he moved away from the desk. One more thing to check and he needed more than just his CU. He located the security office. After identifying himself, he used one of their portals to access the reservation database profiles.

It took a few minutes, but when the image of the last-minute passenger came up, Jayd found himself staring at a green-skinned, black-haired Kelli.

He clenched his teeth. "Are you out of your mind?"

When a nearby security officer glanced his way, Jayd held up his hand in an apology. "Sorry. Having a bad day."

The man grinned and nodded.

Turning back to the screen, Jayd hunkered down in his seat. What should he do? What harebrained scheme was she pursuing? In minutes, he assessed every course of action. For starters, not alert USF or Sean. Definitely not Intergalaxia.

That left only one thing. He had to protect Kelli from her own stupidity and salvage the situation as best he could. That meant intercept her, preferably before she got to Xerxes IX.

Once he found her, he would drag her back to Earth by her long, fake-black hair.

Chapter 12

Kelli gripped the handhold of the sub-rail as it reached the terminal. Around her, numerous Xerxians, as well as humans, rose in anticipation of arriving at Xerxes IX's capital city. In the window, she caught sight of her reflection. For the first time she didn't start in shock, finally acclimated to seeing greenish skin and dark hair. Her black eyes, looking like huge pupils, stared back at her. Yesterday's implants looked completely natural. Without them, her blue eyes would have been a dead giveaway that she was not Xerxian. And passing as a native was critical for this mission to succeed.

"Please stand away from the doors." Though the computer voice instructed in the Xer language, thanks to her sub-dermal chip, Kelli heard the overlapping English, or Common as it was known here. However, she understood more and more of the language.

She flung her single bag over her shoulder and exited the sub-rail, allowing herself to linger in the small, unpretentious terminal. Surprisingly, her fellow passengers didn't rush to baggage claim or out the doors to the building, but sauntered toward their destinations. Missing were the inevitable shops and high security checkpoints common to other stations. The place really looked like a large hangar. Life here was devoid of a lot of the technology she took for granted on Earth.

So far, the social aspect of the Accelerated Learning Program had not yet activated. That would change the second she stepped out of Xer Prime's one and only terminal. For now, it felt good to walk, stretching her legs and deeply inhaling the moist warm air. She'd had her fill of numerous days of travel, countless gates and stations.

Suddenly disoriented, Kelli paused outside the building. Not only the people, but the sun, foliage and even atmosphere felt different. Though the shrubs and trees were green, they had a little too much yellow. The sky was cerulean, the sun more orange.

The ALP kicked in full bore, bombarding Kelli's mind with information.

Xerxes IX ambient year round temperature is…

No air travel permitted in strictly controlled airspace…

Known for its single sun and triple moons…

Oldest alien contact between Earth and…

The Terran-Xer Alliance was formed twenty-five stand-ard years ago after…

Her gaze, landing anywhere in the city, triggered a response. She paused at a landmark and closed her eyes, pretending to enjoy the fragrant flowers. *Ah.* Her mind finally silenced. When she opened her eyes, she stared at a sculpture, surrounded by an intricate metal fence. Foliage hedged in the statue, a woman with flowing robes and upraised arms. The walled-in mon-ument gave Kelli a little seclusion as she sat on a bench. Who was this again? The ALP supplied the an-swer.

Xerxes IX's current First Chancellor—as Terrans call the female ruler—resides in Xer Prime on the Great Plateau. It is the only city accessible from space which…

The ALP filled in other details, but at least it was one topic and not twenty. That subject exhausted, Kelli dared to look around. Slowly her brain acclimated. Once the information was disseminated, the program moved on to the next point. When she felt ready, she rose and continued her trek toward the heart of the city.

The further she walked, the more Xer Prime began to feel like old-world Europe with the narrow, cobble-stone streets, milling crowds, and vendors hawking their wares. Everything became more comfortable, more familiar with each step. The strangeness of miss-ing technology faded. The more she relaxed, the more she enjoyed the quiet pedestrian traffic minus the roar of aero-cars and mass transit. Life was slower, more contemplative here.

Kelli peered at the different symbols on the various shops, her mind gathering the info and identifying them with the help of ALP—restaurant, clothing shop, weaver, jeweler. The smell of that pervasive ritual incense hung in the air, tainting everything. The raw, acrid scent vied with the pleasant, burnt form. Though her nose itched, the odor no longer repelled her.

The ALP picked up the buzz of many languages and translated so she heard everything in English. Well, nearly everything.

"Fresh gazmandashi. Get your fresh gazmandashi here," yelled a hawker who stood before several large baskets.

Fruit, the programming told her when her gaze settled on the chartreuse orbs the size of softballs. *Safe for human consumption. No cooking or peeling necessary. Discard seeds.*

Having already acquired Xer cash at the outpost, Kelli purchased some. She bit into one, the juice running down her hand. The flavors of citrus and bananas with a hint of ginger burst in her mouth.

Delicious! She tapped her chin twice, the Xerxian equivalent of a thumb's up.

The hawker beamed, then continued to invite the crowds to sample his wares.

She walked up and down several streets, glad for the exercise. All the while, the sub-dermal chip kept her informed of sensory experiences. Every new bit of information her mind absorbed increased her knowledge. And confidence. Every Xer phrase reinforced her language base. Under her breath, she would repeat what she heard. The ALP would correct her pronunciation until she got it right.

Finally, she chose an out-of-the-way hotel. One that looked like it accommodated humans as well as Xerxians.

"Welcome to our establishment." The proprietor spread his hands and bowed.

Kelli did the same. "Common language? I can understand Xer but not speak it very well."

"I educate in C'mommen well. Although I am new to our great city and this humble abode."

"I need a room for two nights."

"Ah, I have one only remaind-ed." He reverted back to Xer. "However, I recommend at least four nights. The festival arrives in a few days. No rooms to be had in all the city."

She assessed him. Was he being sincere? "Very well. I'll take four."

"A wise decision. Designation, please?"

Designation: Xerxians usually use titles, not names, which are reserved for intimate friends or family members. It would be improper to give a stranger your name.

She thought a moment. "First Traveler."

"Ah, a fine title for the most beautiful of women."

"Flatterer." Kelli knew that by Xer standards she was rather plain. Her face wasn't long enough, her nose too short, her forehead not wide enough. Yep, plain. Maybe ugly?

He, on the other hand, was a typical Xer male, averaging five and a half feet, broad-shouldered, stocky. His black hair was close cropped. Not unattractive, but definitely not her type.

His black eyes twinkled. "You do me honor."

The Xer male is pleased by your stare. He responded by flirting. A laugh would be a neutral rejoinder. Flattening your hand, palm down, would be an invitation for more. If you are displeased, turn your head away and cast your eyes downward.

Men were the same throughout the universe. Kelli chose to chuckle.

Her room waited on the fourth floor. The Terran type bed and adjoining bathroom made her feel right at home. Terrace doors opened to a balcony, which she checked as a possible escape route. The outside of the hotel was like every other Xer building in the city—comprised of flat white stones, fixed by a gray, concrete-like material. Kelli tested the abundant finger holds, confident she could easily climb up or down the wall in an emergency.

After securing the room and showering, she fell instantly asleep.

For two days, she wandered the city, reinforcing many aspects of the learning program. Kelli also made some discreet inquiries about a human male traveling with a little girl, but nothing came up. The people she spoke to would glance at her, make some sort of assessment, but give no information. Why? Her programming gave no explanation for their reticence.

Xer Prime was the capital situated on the Great Plateau, the gateway to the rest of the world. She gambled that Ella was with one or possibly two men and that they were still on this planet. Somewhere. Had they traveled deeper into the interior? Unlikely. Xerxes IX was matriarchal, with strict social rules about male and female interactions. The best place for the kidnappers to remain inconspicuous would be to stay in the very metropolitan capital. Though not as free as the offworld outpost, the city still made allowances for the multi-alien population. Traveling to other cities would be difficult for them, although possible. That would involve traveling across the plains to reach the other plateaus. Risky.

However, after hours of searching and seeking information, Kelli began to doubt herself.

As the city grew more festive in preparation for their holiday, she found her optimism flagging. What had possessed her to come here? How could she have imagined that she alone would solve the disappearance of Ella? *What arrogance.* And now, because she'd missed her court date, she was a full-blown fugitive.

By late morning, she found she'd strolled so far that she'd reached the edge of the Great Plateau upon which Xer Prime was built. She pressed her forehead to the bars of the tall guardrail, gazing over the cliffs to the plains far below.

What should she do? To return to Earth would mean imprisonment. What would they give her? Five years? More? The other option was to stay on Xerxes, but *they* would eventually find her.

"No," she spoke aloud as she gripped the cool metal bars. "I will not give up."

The kidnappers *had* to have come to Xerxes IX. She went over her line of reasoning. They *were* here. She would find them.

The sound of chanting reached her ears. Turning, she noted a nearby building.

Xerxian temple. Accessing religious practices, the program told her. The ALP was surprisingly slow. Finally, it said, *Xerxians serve a single deity. No other information available.*

No other information? Why not? On practically every other subject she'd accessed, the ALP gave a ton of details. Interesting that this topic was limited. Perhaps religious discussions with outsiders were taboo?

She hadn't yet been in a temple although the city was full of them. They were x-shaped buildings, with doors open to the four points of a compass. Apparently the buildings were never locked, allowing access to the population all twenty-five hours a day. This particular one was on the very edge of the plateau. It was smaller and looked older, more neglected.

Kelli strolled toward the building. Since her quest had begun with the Xerxian incense, this seemed the next logical place to check. No matter how uncomfortable religion made her feel.

Pausing inside the doorway, she allowed her eyes to adjust to the gloom. Rows of seats with kneelers filled the room, a single aisle from each doorway leading to the center of the building. A beam of light spotlighted something in the middle. She walked forward, taking in information.

No statues. No candles. No religiously garbed personnel. No fetishes of any kind. And this was a temple? She drew closer to the center, squinting to see what sat at the middle. Five rows back, she stopped.

Nothing. Nothing there but a round, metallic table.

An altar? Underneath it was a small brazier with burning coals. Gazing upward, she realized the building was open at the top, with multiple mirrors placed strategically to capture the light of their daytime star. A focused beam of light pooled on the altar. But the surface was bare.

She glanced around. Perhaps there was some room where they brought out religious artifacts for holy days? No evidence supported her assumption. As she stood puzzling, a woman approached her.

"I am Second Watchman. Do you wish to make an offering?"

"Um, yes." Kelli fumbled for her coin purse. "How much?"

The woman appeared taken aback. Offended? "We take no money. You are not from our world?" Her dark eyes assessed Kelli.

"No, I'm sorry." She reverted to Common, hoping the woman would understand. "I was raised on Earth by humans. My mother died when I was young. My father traveled much."

"Ah." Her expression transformed to mild pity. "If you wish, you may make an offering. But we accept only worship."

Offering? Worship? What did that mean? Kelli frantically accessed the program, but it remained silent.

The woman smiled in sympathy. "Lay aside your outer robe, sister. I will instruct."

After taking off the long garb, Kelli smoothed down her plain tunic and pants. She followed the woman to a door opposite the one she'd entered. Several people worked nearby, wiping down chairs and washing walls.

The woman handed Kelli a broom. "Work as long as you like. Any offering is pleasing to God and a benefit to us all."

It took all of her training not to burst out laughing. Seriously? They wanted her to be a scrubwoman? That was their idea of worship?

Instead, she bowed, speaking in Xer. "You do me honor."

After the woman walked away, Kelli started sweeping. Several times she pressed her lips together to squelch her humor. Too bad she couldn't call Aric. Kelli imagined how she would tell her friend the joke.

"A field agent walks into a bar—no, I mean an alien temple..."

Then what? "After traveling light years to reach Xerxes IX, she uses her high-level training to clean a floor for a God she doesn't even believe in."

After she had time to think about it, cleaning was preferable to any other option. Kelli couldn't imagine bowing down to some idol and professing a lifelong poverty vow. Or something else equally as weird.

No one gave her any more directions, so she cleaned one wing of the x-shaped building and moved to the next. Several times the other workers would spontaneously burst into a chant-type song. The alien tune sent shivers down her spine. The simple words were strangely moving.

"Praise God. Praise Him. Praise God for our world. Praise Him in the heavens. Praise Him in the highest of heavens."

Loathe to leave for some reason, Kelli stayed until

she swept the entire building. The woman who'd originally given the task had apparently departed. When Kelli returned the broom to the other workers, she was invited to partake in some modest refreshments. A cool juice and soft, buttery bread renewed her energy. And gave her shoulders a chance to rest. But what was most interesting was the women's chatter. They spoke of their everyday lives, their husbands, their children, all subjects about which the ALP was limited.

She merely listened after telling them in halting Xerxian the same information she'd given the first woman. They smiled in sympathy, but appeared to accept her as one of them. When the break was over, Kelli stayed and cleaned more. By late afternoon, the building was almost spotless. Only a few worshippers remained now. They took their cleaning supplies to a small shed outside. Several bid farewell at this point, leaving only two women besides Kelli.

She stood awkwardly, not knowing what to do now. Not wanting to go.

"Must you leave too?" one woman asked her.

In an instant, Kelli made up her mind. "Not yet."

The Xerxian smiled. "Then come with us."

What were they planning? It didn't take long to find out as they thrust a soft cloth into her hands. Ah, more cleaning. She should have known.

This time, though, they headed to the center of the room where the huge altar sat on a raised platform. The two women paused before the altar, then knelt and started polishing the elaborate, metallic legs. Kelli mimicked their actions. Several glances in their direction told her this cleaning job was a little different from the rest of the temple. They labored in silence, yet their mouths moved as though they were praying.

It was hard work. Exposure to the elements through the open ceiling had dulled the metal with layers of dust and grime. That wasn't the hardest part though. The surface of the altar was blackened and pitted with countless incense offerings. Not the raw form, with its almost repulsive pungency but the sweeter, burnt form. Kelli rubbed the top until her arms ached. But the work filled her with a strange peace.

Second Watchman, the one who'd originally given the sweeping task, returned and pitched in. As the daylight waned, someone turned on lights. Apparently they were all going to stick it out to the end. Well, Kelli was no quitter either.

Finally, *finally*, the altar was polished to the women's satisfaction. Kelli leaned her head back, trying to ease a kink from her shoulders. Wordlessly, the women put the supplies in the shed and donned their outer robes.

Second Watchman grabbed her arm, preventing her from leaving.

Now what?

"You must not go so soon," she said.

Soon? Kelli nearly yelled, *Are you kidding?* She wanted to remind the Xerxian that she'd been there nearly the whole day. She was tired and cranky. And more than a little hungry.

"Come." The woman tugged on her sleeve.

Feet dragging, she followed the women back inside. They were halfway up one aisle when someone snapped off the lights. The temple was instantly plunged into darkness…except for the center. The riveting sight made her gasp. She froze, unable to take another step.

The altar, illuminated by countless stars, glowed in the blackness of the room. Like light sprang forth from inside. Chills ran through her body.

The memory of the recurring nightmare slammed into her. Terror reached icy fingers into her core. Then she fought to calm herself. The sight was similar to her dream, but not the same. Though Kelli was surrounded by darkness, an oasis of light lay ahead of her. The cool, inviting glow could not be overcome by the darkness. It was a refuge in the blackness of her nightmare.

Second Watchman remained by her side, silent, gauging her reaction. When Kelli glanced at her, the woman motioned with her hand to approach the altar. Slowly, with more trepidation than she'd felt all day, she followed. The others joined them.

"For the benefit of our sister, I will explain," the woman said. She removed a mottled, brown jar from the folds of her robes. Kelli instantly recognized the incense holder before the woman opened it and the pungent scent filled the air.

"Take three pinches and place them on the altar. You may say a prayer of thanksgiving or petition, then burn the incense. It is a pleasing aroma to the one true God."

Gulping, Kelli did as instructed. The others followed suit. After she placed the incense on the altar, her mind remained blank. She didn't believe in God. What could she thank Him for? What could she ask Him, since He was fictional and could not answer?

A petition—unbidden and reckless—came to her mind.

If You are real God, please give me a clue about where Ella is.

That would have to do. She dared ask nothing more.

Second Watchman handed her a burning wick. Kelli lowered the tip to the incense. It slowly caught fire, then smoldered. A sweet aroma filled her nostrils. Something deep within squeezed tightly as she closed her eyes. The fragrance seemed to invade every cell of her body.

No heavenly voice spoke to her. No flash of light or miracle occurred, yet Kelli was filled with inexplicable peace. She didn't want the feeling to end. Even after the incense was consumed, she remained unmoving. Eyes still closed, she allowed herself to be transfixed by the foreign, yet wonderful emotion. Could this be her new safe place? She thought of her meetings with the counselor and knew this is where she could mentally rest. The echoing stillness, the soothing sensation wrapped a serenity about her that was undeniable.

I will never forget this.

When she opened her eyes, she discovered the two other women had already burned their incense and departed, leaving her and Second Watchman.

She also realized that her cheeks were wet with tears. Stunned, she swiped them away.

The other woman did not seem surprised or embarrassed by her display of emotion. Nodding, she smiled softly. "You have worshipped with all your soul today. Please let me honor you."

Before she could respond, the Xerxian stepped closer and clipped an earring on her earlobe. Instinctively Kelli fingered the dangling charm. What did the jewelry signify?

"Wear it as you begin your new life here on our homeworld. It is a symbol of honor. All true worshippers will know of your sacrifice today."

Without another word, she turned and walked away.

Trembling with pent up emotion, Kelli clutched the edge of the altar. Tears again burned her eyes, yet she didn't understand why. Many moments passed before she was able to leave the now-empty temple.

After she traversed the dark aisle, she turned to look one more time at the glowing altar. It was then she realized that the woman had left the small pottery container. Sitting in the middle of the surface, the incense waited for the next worshipper.

The significance slammed into her mind.

Mitchell Harker had told her the truth when he said he was a collector, not a buyer. The scumbag had one of his henchmen sneak into some temple in the middle of the night and steal a jar of incense. That was the only way it could end up in his study.

Kelli sucked in a deep breath. All uncertainty about her course of action evaporated. She was on the right track.

Without a doubt, the answer to Ella's disappearance lay somewhere on Xerxes IX.

Chapter 13

The next morning the festival, which was a celebration of First Chancellor's birthday, was in full swing by the time Kelli joined the throngs of people. She wore a multi-hued outer robe to the party, like everyone else. Rainbow-clad throngs lined the main thoroughfare, waiting for the parade to begin. She laughed as children threw wads of colorful confetti at each other, even running across the street to shower those on the other side. High up, looped banners of blue and gold fluttered on the buildings, catching the breeze and ballooning. People laughed and shouted to their friends while hawkers roamed, selling delectable goodies out of their shouldered baskets. On the rooftops, crowds lined the buildings, firing off volley after volley of confetti with hand-held popguns. Someone started singing the Xerxian anthem. Hundreds soon joined the few voices.

The singing changed to cheering as the parade made its appearance at the end of the street. Kelli strained to see, along with everyone around her. They all had to wait though, until the procession grew closer.

A wide-wheeled cart, bedecked with flowers, came into view. Two Xerxians sat on secured chairs on the raised platform. Many pedestrians accompanied the humble vehicle.

"The First Chancellor! The Royal Consort!" murmured the crowds.

Kelli turned a surprised gaze to the couple who sat on humble thrones, waving greetings. Usually parades started with lesser officials, building to a climax when the main event came into view. Not so, here. She observed no soldiers or servants. Spectators along the street took hold of the harnesses to pull the cart while others followed behind, pushing. The volunteers changed frequently, giving all who desired a chance to honor their rulers.

Inevitably, someone began singing a birthday song, joined by everyone who knew the music and words. Kelli looked at the sea of faces, noting mostly were Xerxian, but many alien races had joined the festival as well.

After the rulers passed, other government officials,

men and women, followed on foot. They were greeted with almost as much enthusiasm as the chancellor and her husband. Many waved at the crowds, all smiled. Time passed but the procession didn't let up. As it continued, the crowd thinned a little, especially as the day warmed. Kelli's stomach growled in protest. In her haste to join the revelry, she'd forgotten to eat.

As the end of the parade came in sight, she sighed in relief. Soon she could satiate her growing hunger.

"Emaa!" A child on a balcony directly above Kelli yelled to someone in the parade.

She glanced up, grinning at the child's exuberance. How old was she? Six? Seven? The mother laughed and waved furiously as she continued walking down the street. Finally, the end of the parade passed, the mother throwing one more glimpse at her child who was still yelling from the third floor balcony, "Mama, mama!"

As Kelli watched, the woman's expression subtly changed. She slowed, her face betraying concern, then alarm.

Kelli again looked up, noting how the little girl had climbed the railing to get a better view. She teetered as she stood, straightening to wave to her mother. The next moment, she lost her balance.

The mother screamed.

The girl grabbed at a nearby banner. Her hands held for a few seconds. Body twisting, she slipped. Her foot caught in the railing, keeping her from plunging down three stories. She had only seconds before she would succumb to the pull of gravity. One hand lost its grip. The girl's arm thrashed to grab hold of the banner again.

Without thinking, Kelli stripped her outer robe and kicked off her slippers. Gaze locked upward, she evaluated the situation. A crowd amassed below, arms held upward as though to catch the child should she fall.

That could be fatal.

Silence rippled through the crowd whereas only moments before revelry had flooded the streets.

The next second changed everything.

The girl's foot disengaged from the railing and she plummeted downward. She shrieked, grabbing another ballooning banner. Abruptly her downward passage ceased. Horrified, Kelli saw why. The girl's body was caught by the silky loop, which had billowed in the breeze. The material had broken her fall, but, as she slipped further, it slid over her torso and neck, re-twisting. The tightening strand was slowly strangling the child.

Kelli had only seconds before the child's own weight killed her.

Leaping onto the side of the building, she grabbed for handholds in the stone. Breath coming hard, she gained the first floor balcony. Kelli sprang off the railing, clambering upward, her heart pounding from the adrenaline and exertion. Muscles protested, fingers screamed in pain. *Almost there.*

The girl's legs flailed. A gurgling sound floated down. Hurry!

Kelli reached her, but she couldn't maintain her hold and lift the child at the same time. Grasping another nearby banner, she tested its strength and used it to keep from falling. She raised the child a few inches, keeping the girl from being strangled.

The young Xerxian slumped in her arms, already unconscious.

"No, no!" Kelli grunted from the effort of supporting her, unable to lift her much further. "Someone...!"

Time crawled by in agonizing slowness. Kelli strained to hold the child up. Muscles quivered from exertion. How much longer could she do this?

Miraculously, arms appeared from above. A woman had clambered down from above, a banner tied about her waist. The climber reached them. "Give her to me."

Not until Kelli was sure the girl and climber were secure did she release her hold. She looked up. A couple people had fastened a banner on the third floor balcony and had used it to lower the rescuer. They raised the girl and woman upwards and out of sight.

Silence gripped the group above and below.

Arms shaking, Kelli grappled for finger holds. As she climbed back down, someone yelled from above, "The child lives!"

The crowd burst into cheering.

Kelli slipped, falling the last seven feet and landing on her bad ankle. Xerxians around her were still cheering. Limping to her robe, she donned it, grabbed her slippers, and escaped into the crowds.

Kelli was in her room only a short while when someone knocked. Alarmed, she hesitated to answer.

"It is I, the proprietor," said a male voice from behind the door.

Still, she hesitated. Was it proper for her, an unattached female, to open her bedroom door? Sometimes the ALP remained silent at critical moments.

She unlatched the door and peered through the crack. The innkeeper bowed. "Your presence has been requested."

"But—well, I was about to lie down and rest."

He waved his hand dismissively. "Not possible. This is more important." When she started to protest, he added, "You will soon see. Come."

After slipping on her outer robe, she reluctantly followed.

Below, three imposing women waited. They all wore the blue and gold of the chancellery.

All bowed. One spoke. "We request your presence."

Kelli threw the innkeeper a look of alarm, but he only nodded in encouragement, face beaming. She didn't think she had much choice anyway. Following the speaker, Kelli noted the other two fell in line behind her.

They passed through alleys and crossed streets until they reached a plain stone building, obviously a home. One female ushered her inside and into an inner room. There, a woman rose to greet her.

The child's mother.

The highly acclaimed Xer weaving was evident in the official's clothing. Her outer robe appeared golden, while her tunic and pants underneath was of the deepest blue. Filigree combs contained her long black hair.

However, the metal would not be considered precious by Earth's standards. Xerxes IX boasted of no wealth, no precious gems.

"I am Fourth Chancellor." Eyes unreadable, face impassive, she came forward and pressed her cheeks to Kelli's. She grasped her hands, bowed over them and finally spoke, "You gave back the life of my only daughter. I am forever in your debt."

It took Kelli a second to find her voice. "Forgive me, I speak Xer poorly."

"It is no impediment," the woman said in flawless English. "You understand me?"

"Yes."

"But you are not from our world?"

"I was born on Earth. My mother died while I was a child. I was raised by others since my father traveled much." Even now, the bitterness of the truth pained her.

How many boarding schools had she attended? Over the years, she'd lost track.

She refocused, allowing this Xerxian to draw her own conclusions like the others had. Her story would explain her appearance and ignorance of their ways.

The woman's eyes narrowed. "Why did you risk your life? For a child who is not your own?

Her fingers strayed to her throat, the memory of her own near-strangulation too recent. Ella!

"I could not stand by and do nothing."

"It is not the usual path for one not raised on Xerxes."

Uncomfortable with the praise, Kelli ducked her head. She'd not thought of the consequences. She'd only acted. In retrospect, it had been a stupid move. The rescue had drawn a spotlight to herself when she had wished to remain neutral. Anonymous.

Fourth Chancellor placed three fingers to her chest, head bowed. "I am deeply grateful."

"Is your daughter all right?"

"She will recover fully, I'm told. Now, she is resting."

"I'm really glad…" The words came out in a rush. Kelli's breath stuck in her throat, cutting off the rest of what she was going to say.

"Please, make yourself comfortable." The woman indicated a chair, overflowing with cushions. It had been the place she had occupied when Kelli entered the room. Without hesitation, she took the seat.

A man and woman entered, carrying steaming cups.

"A drink to celebrate and rejoice."

An honorary tea ceremony, her programming kicked in, filling in details about who should start, who should drink first.

Fourth Chancellor raised the ceramic cup and held it on graceful fingertips, before passing it to Kelli. She in turn, bowed her head slightly, but waited for the other woman to take her own demitasse. Simultaneously, they sipped the brew. Kelli found it sweet and fruity, very pleasant on her Terran tongue.

"What brings you to Xerxes, First Traveler?"

She gulped. The woman didn't beat around the bush. The fact that she knew Kelli's designation, and probably everything else about her alter ego, alerted her that this woman wasn't to be trifled with.

After debating a moment, she took the plunge. "I seek a little girl and a man. Humans. About sixty standard days ago, she was stolen from her parents. I came to Xerxes to find them."

The woman was careful not to alter her expression. "And this man, he was the one who took this girl?"

Kelli nodded.

"What are their designations?"

She hesitated. What would be the proper response? "Ella is the name of the girl. I do not know the man's name or what designation he uses."

The chancellor's mouth tightened.

Kelli knew the woman must be outraged, yet she was still cautious. She had only Kelli's word for what had happened. The official was wise to not take her at face value, even if she did look like a Xerxian.

"And yet no representative from Earth has come to seek her?"

She chewed her lip. How much information she could share? The more she told, the greater the danger to herself. And possibly to Ella. "A search on Earth has been ongoing. But no one believes she is here on Xerxes IX."

"No one but you."

Kelli nodded. "I arrived alone, hoping to find them. Or at least some clue of where they may have gone." She added in a low voice, "I am disobeying my government by coming here to search."

As soon as she realized she said *my*, not *Earth's*, she bit her lip. Foolish mistake!

"You, then, are considered Terran? Your parents relinquished their residency?"

Perhaps it wasn't an unforgivable slip. In the early days, many Xerxians had traveled to Earth to live there, giving up their citizenship to Xerxes IX. Kelli let the woman draw that conclusion.

"I am Terran." As much as she would like to spill everything, she could see how it could be used against her. This woman was Fourth Chancellor. Kelli didn't know for certain how the Xerxian government would respond if USF demanded her return.

Even though the chancellor could not know details, she obviously knew the implications of Kelli's presence. She probably knew as well, that she could not directly assist in the search.

The chancellor fixed her with a gaze. "You are an exceedingly brave woman."

She ducked her head, not feeling brave or anything commendable.

Having lost her mother at a young age, Kelli had grown up without any female companionship. She fought the overpowering longing to pour out her heart to this woman. Fourth Chancellor couldn't be that much older, but she seemed so much wiser than her age.

I wish I had an aunt, a sister, someone.

Kelli pressed an arm against her ribcage, the solitary feelings piercing her.

"This girl," the chancellor continued, "is related to you?"

She debated lying, but something prevented her. "No. But I feel she is…she is like a niece to me. I love her mother." Kelli struggled with the foreign emotions and the shocking confession. "Though I am an only child, the girl's mother is akin to a blood relative. I consider her my sister." She took a deep breath, overwhelmed by the simple truth. And her free admittance, despite its profoundness. "I would sacrifice everything for her."

And I have... for Sean, Aric and *Ella.*

"Ah, I see." The chancellor's smooth brow wrinkled. She suddenly rose. "We show our appreciation on this world by giving gifts. No, please remain seated." The woman walked to a nearby desk and picked up a small, carved box. She returned to Kelli's side and opened the lid.

She looked in, puzzled by the small metallic circle, which looked like a silver charm for a bracelet. The small disc had a symbol etched on it, three black lines overlaid by a circle of blue. A delicate chain was attached.

"It belongs on your earring," the woman explained. "Let me honor you by assisting."

Kelli removed the one she'd gotten just the day before and handed it to her.

The chancellor deftly added the second charm. "Thus it is placed." She clipped the earring on Kelli, but fastened the chain higher on her ear. "Come and see." She beckoned her to a mirror.

Kelli looked at her reflection, noting how the earring was fastened both on her lobe and the helix. The charms dangled and sparkled.

"Wear them with pride. You are marked with honor." She pressed her lips together before adding, "Though you may not have letters of introduction, your earring will be a better help in your quest."

Kelli placed three fingers against her chest and bowed. "You do me great honor."

"I have duties, and so must depart. My assistants will escort you back to your lodging."

"Thank you again."

The chancellor walked to the doorway. Before exiting, she had one last thing to say. "A human male and a girl might pass through this city without much attention. Even in the cliff villages. But not on the plains of our planet. Even if they were both Xerxian, their passage would excite the suspicion of all mothers. Go there. You might find the answers you seek."

Kelli sucked in a deep breath at the useful information. "Thank you."

The woman inclined her head. "May our great God grant you favor in your search."

Chapter 14

Kelli, Kelli, what have you done?

Jayd slumped against a wall in the courtyard, defeated. Nothing had gone right since the moment he'd left New Washington. Mechanical problems, last minute high-ranking delegates who commandeered his spacecraft, missed connections... He had reached Xerxes IX a day and a half after Kelli, not intercepted her like he'd hoped. His request to see a Xerxian official also had been delayed several times because of some citywide celebration.

And the results of his efforts? The Fourth Chancellor basically told him, "Thanks, but no thanks." As a representative of the Xerxian Council, she made it clear they would neither hunt nor deport Kelli. They would not lift a finger to help or hinder USF—and in particular him—in any way.

He shouldn't be surprised. Xerxians didn't like anyone tampering with the peace of their world. At least he didn't need to worry about them kicking him off the planet. Unless, of course, he broke their laws.

Sighing, he straightened and headed toward a café that advertised Terran dishes. A headache pounded, probably because of a lack of food and sleep. He finally located the restaurant and chose a seat in a corner because he didn't want to fraternize. With anyone.

After he ordered a meal, he slouched in his chair. How much worse could this situation with Kelli get?

The answers were immediate. And ones he didn't even want to consider.

Before he'd left New Washington, he'd disabled his CU's locator, but that had bought him only a little time. He had represented himself as an agent of Universal Security Forces in order to plead for Xerxian assistance. Following protocol, the Fourth Chancellor would send an official communiqué of regret to the Terran Embassy. They in turn would contact USF's director.

Once the director knew where he was, she would inform Intergalaxia. Everyone would know he was on Xerxes IX.

Great. Just great.

After Jayd's food arrived, the waiter chatted with him briefly. But Jayd wasn't in the mood to talk. He paid for his meal, including a handsome tip. After bowing several times, the server got the message and left him alone.

Jayd's morose thoughts again hounded him.

Inter-G wouldn't sit on their thumbs. If he could get to a long-distance communications terminal, he could verify what they would do, via Ryan. That is, if his friend would take a chance and even respond. First though, Jayd needed to check in with his assistant.

He wolfed down the rest of his food, then headed to the nearest space-comm hotspot. After forking out an exorbitant fee, he logged onto a social website under an assumed name—one prearranged with his assistant before he'd departed Earth. Jen's single message jumped off the screen.

Word is out. Exit ASAP. Multiple acquaintances on their way.

His forehead beaded with perspiration. USF already knew his location? How was that possible? He'd seen the Fourth Chancellor mere hours ago. No way she could have contacted the embassy already.

Jen used the word "exit." Obviously a reference to his return to Earth. Because she could no longer cover for him? USF must have found out he had used a defunct account to purchase his flight to Xerxes IX rather than his personal funds. And he thought he'd been so smart.

But what made his throat go dry was the last sentence. Jen said "acquaintances." If she'd said "friends," he would have assumed USF agents were on their way to intercept him.

No, her word choice had a much more ominous meaning—Intergalaxia agents. Ones who would shoot first, ask questions second. Jayd tried to swallow the ball of dust in his throat.

I'm a fugitive from the law as well.

No doubt they had orders to track him *and* Kelli down and return them to Earth. With or without the use of deadly force?

He had to find Kelli *now*. And do whatever necessary to save her from her own stupidity.

Not just hers now. His foolishness as well.

At last!

Kelli's heart sang from the news she'd learned. Finally, a solid lead. No longer did she merely speculate that Ella's trail led to Xerxes IX. She finally had proof.

The road's steep incline forced her to be prudent, tempering her impulse to skip with happiness. She paused and leaned against a low wall. Ever since her flying trapeze act two days before, her ankle had ached. The miles she'd walked since then hadn't helped either. But it didn't matter.

I know where Ella is.

After her meeting with Fourth Chancellor, Kelli had left Xer Prime and had descended to the sprawling towns below. These smaller, more rural hamlets were built into the cliffs, the buffer between the Great Plateau and the plains a thousand feet below. She could barely wrap her tongue around the various names that had different meanings for each section. The matriarchal society was much more strongly felt here. Kelli had no doubt that the plains villages would have the strictest enforcements of female rule.

Not that a man would feel threatened here. Xerxians were benevolent, but their society was peaceful and well ordered, ruled by self-law. Women traveled without fear, even at night. The crime rate was low, punishment swift and drastic. According to the ALP, crimes committed by men against women were extremely rare.

Kelli climbed on the stone wall and inhaled the dry, grassy fragrances riding on the updraft from the plains, far below the Great Plateau. This world was so peaceful.

"Thank you, thank you," she breathed aloud, not minding that her words could almost be considered a prayer.

Ankle rested, she descended the rest of the way from the small temple she'd visited. The Fourth Chancellor had been correct—the earring she wore opened countless doors.

And today, it paid off.

Kelli headed toward the town center and to the new hotel she'd found. She needed to be alone, to mentally sort through the implications of the information she'd received. Because it was near the noon hour, crowds of people swarmed the streets, visiting and sharing a repast together on tables set out on their balconies or porches.

As she neared her hotel, someone grabbed her arm.

"Don't make a scene. Just come with me." Jayd's voice fell low and menacing on her ear.

Too shocked to reply, Kelli allowed him to drag her in the opposite direction. Finally, she reined in her surprise sufficiently to speak in a calm tone. "You realize, of course, you're in a matriarchal society."

He merely grunted in reply.

"What you're doing right now is akin to assault. See the looks you're getting? Bad sign."

Several Xerxian women shot glares in Jayd's direction. He must have noticed too, because he slowed.

"Don't try anything, Kel. I've been chasing you for over a week and I'm not in the mood for jokes."

Coming to a standstill, she forced him to stop with her. Kelli remained at ease, supremely confident. Nothing could spoil her joy. She maintained her relaxed body posture and spoke slowly. "This is no joke. Believe me when I tell you that if I screamed right now, your life wouldn't be worth more than the bag you carry."

Gaze darting to several Xerxians, Jayd's shoulders and face tightened with tension.

"I am going to my hotel right now." She used a softer voice. "You're welcome to join me. I promise I won't try to escape. Well, won't as long as you're willing to listen and hear what I have to say."

His jaw jutted. "Seems I have little choice."

She allowed herself the luxury of a chuckle. "Oh, I'd say you have *no* choice."

His dark eyes flashed anger.

"Follow me, please." Humming a Xer tune, she sauntered away from him. She resisted the impulse to laugh aloud. For the first time ever, she had the upper hand where Jayden Song was concerned.

It felt so good.

Jayd rubbed his eyes, the sensation like grinding grit into them. The odd odor that clung to Kelli didn't help either. It smelled like she'd been standing too close to a bonfire, except something identifiable—like heated orange peels and balsa wood—permeated her clothing. In the enclosed space, the scent was nearly overwhelming.

His mind kept having trouble with the way she looked. Not that pale green skin and black hair weren't flattering. Kelli would look good no matter what. But somehow, they threw him off. He'd much rather berate the blond-haired, blue-eyed version of a subordinate agent.

After they entered her hotel room, he slammed the door behind them. "Do you realize what you've done? Missing your court date was unbelievably foolish."

"Please lower your voice." She locked the door.

"I cannot tell you how many times in the last week, I've wanted to kill you with my bare hands."

"That wouldn't be advisable. Xerxians really frown on murder." Kelli busied herself by shutting the wooden slats at the windows, blocking the possibility of curious lookers.

He spoke through clenched teeth. "I had to wait two days to see an official, sleep on the streets because of some stupid party, put up with rudeness—"

"I'm sure it's been tough." Kelli patted his arm as she walked by him to shut the other blinds.

Unable to fathom her serenity, Jayd growled. "This whole thing has been a huge pain in the…"

"Asteroid?" She turned to face him, smiling.

"This isn't a laughing matter, Kel. We are both up to our eyeballs in indictments. Warrants for our arrest are probably flying across space now. It's only a matter of time."

"I know."

Her flippant tone pushed him over the edge.

He grabbed her shoulders. "Not just for you, Kel. Me too. We're both going to end up prison because we skipped the tribunal. You don't walk away from that sort of thing."

Her mouth twitched. "Actually, we didn't walk. We flew."

He let out a hiss of exasperation. Energy spent, he slumped in a chair, head in his hands.

Wordlessly, she continued to secure the room.

If she wouldn't listen to reason, then he had no other choice but to incapacitate her and smuggle her off the planet. Somehow. But since learning how volatile Xerxian women were, he'd have to wait until dark.

He jerked upright when a glass of water appeared under his nose.

"Take it." Kelli grinned at him. "You look like you could use a drink."

Was it drugged? He wouldn't put it past her. No doubt after he was out, she'd sneak off.

She stifled a chuckle. "No, I didn't put anything in it."

Could she read his mind now? He resisted muttering invectives.

"Jayd, I swear there's nothing harmful in the water."

Still cautious, he pretended to take a sip before setting the glass on the nearby table.

If Kelli noticed, she didn't remark on it. "Are you ready to hear me out?"

"Sure." He crossed his arms.

Her amused expression faded to something more serious. She squatted down before him. "I know this probably feels like the end of the world to you, but can you try to lay aside your superior, senior agent attitude?"

Before he could make a sound of derision, she rested her hand on his forearm. "Please."

Was this another one of her ploys? Her posture, tone and touch melted him a fraction. Her playful smugness had vanished.

"I stumbled onto something back on Earth." Her fingers tightened on his arm. "It wasn't much, but I had to take a chance that it might be an actual lead. I knew Inter-G was going to crucify me at the tribunal. So what did I have to lose by coming here?"

"Aric told me you'd gone to see Harker."

She let her hand slip away. "I'm sorry she involved you. But now that you're here, I'm glad."

Was she really? Suspicion flooding him once more, he leaned back.

"This morning, I found out something. A concrete lead." Her dark eyes gleamed. "About two months ago, a man and a little girl passed through here. This society, if you didn't already know, has strict guidelines about their male and female interactions. It is considered strange for a man to be traveling alone with a girl, even if they're father and daughter."

Jayd straightened, intrigued in spite of himself.

"The man claimed his wife had passed away. He said he was taking his daughter to her aunt—his blood sister who would raise the little girl. So he hired a guide to travel with them. A woman. Which is entirely proper. Even necessary." Kelli slid backwards to sit on the edge of the bed across from him.

He leaned forward. "Go on."

"They headed down to the plains, but something happened while they were traveling. For some unknown reason, the guide abandoned them in the forest and returned home."

"How do you know all this?"

"The gossip channel." When he frowned, she smiled. "Long story, but a woman I spoke to this very morning is the *sister* of the guide. This guide just happened to be visiting here when the man and girl passed through. And he hired her."

"How do you know the girl is Ella?"

"According to my source, she spoke only Common. That's what they call English here. And the little girl was less than ten standard years of age."

"Then why didn't someone alert an official?"

"Again, it has to do with this society. Grief is considered an extremely private affair. This little girl cried and cried, calling out for her mother repeatedly. This confirmed the man's story. No one asked questions."

Jayd shook his head, still unconvinced. "You'd think someone would've raised a stink about two humans—"

"That's another point," Kelli interrupted, brow tightening. "They both appeared to be Xerxian. It's an easy thing for most humans to pull off. Well, obviously, if you take my current appearance into consideration. We are almost biologically identical. I think that's why Ella wasn't found on the outpost. They'd already altered her appearance. Since everyone was looking for a human child, they were able to pass through all the security checkpoints. I doubt anyone even questioned them when they left the space station."

He sat back, stunned. How could they—and Inter-G—have missed that? He pressed fingers to his chin. "Unbelievable."

"No. Diabolical."

Interesting choice of words. He assessed her. Gone was the playful flippancy from earlier. With narrowed eyes, she watched him. To determine if he believed her?

"Jayd..." Her face hardened. "They forced Ella to witness my near murder, they drugged her, and probably performed surgery on her—eye implants, like I have. Then they took her to a strange world where no one could understand her. No one would rescue her if she even cried for help."

"Who did, Kel? Who's responsible?"

"Mitchell Harker. I can't prove it, but I'm sure he's the scumbag behind this."

"But he's never been to Xerxes IX. I checked that myself."

"Correct. But his henchman was. Most likely my attacker."

"How do you know the two are connected?"

"The incense they use here. Harker had some in his house. I saw it. Again, it was a long shot, but I had to check it out."

"Okay, sorry. I'm not following." Jayd shook his head.

"Xerxians *never* sell this incense. It's sacred. The only way to get a hold of some is to physically *be* here. Since it wasn't Harker, then his associate probably set up everything for Ella's kidnapping. When I visited Harker, he bragged to me about being a collector, very insistent that he doesn't *buy* artifacts. When I saw the incense in his house, I concluded his associate gave him a sample."

"Why? What's with the incense?"

"I smelled it the night of the kidnapping. My attacker reeked of it. Again, a lot of big assumptions. But enough to convince me that Harker is behind the kidnapping."

"And that's why Sean and Aric never got a ransom note." Made sense.

"Exactly. Harker never intends to return Ella. Not because he cares for her, but because he is very possessive about what he believes is his. That fanaticism is all over his website. To him, Ella is merely another item to add to his collection." Her eyes burned.

He'd seen that look before. If she did not have dark implants, her eyes would be shooting blue daggers.

Jayd slapped his knees. "Okay. I'm convinced. Where do we go from here?"

Hope suffused her face. "You believe me?" Her lips parted, cheeks suffused with pink under the pale, blue-green dye. *Beautiful.*

Did he? Her line of reasoning was sound, even if her actions could be considered crazy. What did he have to lose if he hung around a few days longer to find out if she were right? He had to proceed carefully. If he acquiesced too quickly, she really would drug him and slip out of reach.

He answered slowly. "Let's just say you've given me enough evidence to pique my curiosity."

When she made a face, he added, "And if I recall, I once promised to help you find Ella."

Her eyes narrowed, the gesture not born of suspicion but gratefulness. "Yes, you did promise." Did her chin quiver ever so slightly?

For once he had nothing to say.

Her expression grew wistful. "Are you really going to help me?"

Baffled by her unexpected softness, all he could manage was a nod.

Letting out a breath, she smiled in genuine joy. She suddenly reached across the space between them and squeezed his hand.

That, alone, was reward enough.

Chapter 15

Kelli left Jayd sound asleep on her bed. Poor guy was exhausted. However, she couldn't help her chuckle when she imagined his spending a few nights on the street. Cruel, yes, but after all the trouble he'd caused her back on Earth, it was just desserts.

While he rested, she ran a few errands. For starters, she needed to explain Jayd's presence to the innkeeper. Kelli hadn't missed the frosty look when they'd arrived as she'd escorted Jayd to her room.

"I wish to register the man in my room," she said to the hotel's owner, a woman.

"Oh? You did not mention him when you checked

in." The proprietor's tone was clipped, forehead marked by a disapproving frown.

"I am sorry. My companion surprised me by arriving earlier than planned."

The woman's severe expression melted. "Ah, that explains it."

"I wish to pay for him. He will stay in my room."

"There is no fee for a Companion. I will send up additional bedding for him as soon as possible."

"May I pick it up later? He is resting after a long journey."

The woman smiled. "You are kind to treat him so."

Kelli wasn't sure what that meant, so she bowed.

As she turned away, the woman said, "Did he lose his earring?"

Again, Kelli wasn't certain how to answer.

The owner went on. "He should have received his symbol when you acquired him. You too should be wearing yours, proving your ownership."

Ownership? Kelli bit her lip, feeling like she'd inadvertently jumped out of the proverbial frying pan into the fire.

Pretending surprise, she reached up to her earring. "Oh, it's missing. I must have lost it."

"There is a shop on the next street that can replace your symbol. Tell them I sent you."

"Thank you. Thank you very much."

Three fingers to her chest, Kelli bowed.

As soon as she was far enough from the hotel, she slumped against a wall and chuckled. She *owned* Jayd? When he found out, he really was going to kill her.

"This should suit you perfectly." The shop owner held up matching charms. Kelli made a note of the symbols, which apparently advertised she was the proud owner of an unattached male slave. The ancient term of "indentured servant" was probably the closest description Earth had of the relationship. Once Kelli accessed the ALP concerning "Companions," she learned more. However, it was another topic about which the program had little information.

"May I?" The shopkeeper fastened the symbol to her earring, then chose an appropriate man's earring for Jayd. It too bore a charm like hers. He smiled. "You must be proud to own a Companion."

"Yes, I am. Thank you." After she paid him, she stepped out of the shop into the growing dusk.

Sighing, she reflected on the irony of the phrase—she *owned* Jayd. Usually when they met at USF's gym, he usually "owned" her. She wouldn't even try to count how many times he'd pinned her when they'd wrestled.

Payback would never be so sweet.

She purchased food for their dinner, then picked up other supplies for their trip across the plains, including preserved food, water skins, pocket knives and bedrolls. It wouldn't hurt to be prepared. When she reached the door to her hotel room, she noticed that the innkeeper had placed a bundle of bedding by the room.

With care, Kelli crept in.

"I was wondering if you were going to return."

Jayd's voice came out of the darkness. He snapped on the bedside lamp. "Or if I was going to have to hunt you down again."

Kelli squinted in the sudden light, waiting for her eyes to adjust. Hair tousled, Jayd reclined in bed. But he looked more rested than earlier.

Truth be told, she liked having him on her team. And not merely because she got to be the leader in their Xerxian band.

"Brought some dinner." After Kelli set the things down on the table, she retrieved the bedding outside the door. "And some blankets and such."

"They look nice and cushy." He smiled at the bundle. "You'll be much more comfortable sleeping on the floor tonight with them."

"Ha! These are for you, compliments of our innkeeper."

"I'm very comfortable on the bed, thank you very much."

"That is where I intend to sleep tonight, mister."

"I'm already here. I see no reason to move."

She placed a fist at her hip. "You'll have to wrestle me for it first."

He grinned slowly. "Win or lose, it's bound to be fun."

Her cheeks burned. Kelli opened her mouth to say something more, then snapped it shut. Instead, she turned to their dinner. In silence, she divided what she'd purchased into two portions before sitting.

Finally she had a comeback. "I shouldn't have let you sleep."

"Too late. Damage is done." He slid off the bed and

joined her at the small table.

His indomitable humor had definitely returned. Hang him.

She broke off a piece of butter bread and shoved it into her mouth.

"Mind if I pray?" Jayd asked.

Nearly choking, Kelli hastily swallowed. "Go ahead." She quickly squeezed her eyes shut and locked her fingers together in case he got the bright idea they should hold hands.

He took so long to start she was sure that had been his intent. Even so, she kept her head ducked.

"Thank You, Father, for Your love and grace," Jayd's soft tenor washed over her. "Thank You for watching over Kelli and keeping her safe. Thank You as well for Your provision. We pray for Your direction and strength for us in the days ahead. Amen."

"Amen." Ack! Why had she said that?

Jayd shot her a questioning look.

No way would she tell him about her "God experiences," if that's what they really were. To hide her confusion, she shoved another piece of bread into her mouth.

"Hungry?"

"Starving." She spoke with her mouth half full.

He slowly tore off a piece from the loaf and thoughtfully chewed. "So, what's your plan?"

Before answering, she swallowed the dry mass in her mouth. "Find that guide, verify details, track the kidnappers." She retrieved an unused glass from the sink, then pointed to his half-empty drink. "Refill?"

"Sure. Thanks."

She filled both with water. "How much do you know of the Xerxian geography?"

"Not much, I'm afraid." He looked sheepish. "I hadn't time to prep."

"Well thank your lucky—rather, be grateful I did."

Kelli set a fresh glass in front of him. "Above this hamlet, where Xer Prime is located, is what they call the Great Plateau. There are a few lesser plateaus with cities built on them. I'm guessing our kidnapper was heading to another one of them. To distance himself from the capital."

Jayd scratched his cheek. "Why not fly?"

"Strictly forbidden. The Xerxians are fanatical about maintaining their culture. The shuttles from the space station to their capital city are the only aircraft allowed on the entire planet. Their airspace is protected by treaty. A ship entering their atmosphere is considered an act of war."

"Which could be advantageous for us."

"As long as you don't mind all the walking we're going to do." She smiled.

"So our man was heading toward another plateau city?"

"That's my guess. Oh, let me show you something." She again rose to retrieve a map she'd purchased.

Jayd made a space on the table for it.

"We're here." Kelli pointed to a spot below the Great Plateau on Xer Prime. "There are several cliff towns perched around the column. Xer Secundo, the next largest plateau, lies to the south, about a five-day journey by foot. He likely headed there, but I think we'd be wise to first find the guide and confirm the story and their destination."

"And Secundo is as metropolitan as Xer Prime? So he and Ella could blend in with the population?"

"Exactly. But in order to get there, they needed that female guide. She is here." Kelli pointed to a town southeast, a two or more days' journey. "The Plains have even greater societal restriction. This planet is a perfect hiding spot in one way, but a huge detriment in another. For a man and child." Kelli folded up the map and tossed it on the bed before continuing her dinner.

"You know—no you wouldn't—there was a woman on the outpost at the time of Ella's kidnapping who was mysteriously injured. I'll bet she is somehow connected."

Kelli pondered the news. "It's possible. With all the planning they'd done, it would make sense that Harker had a female lined up to help with the kidnapping."

"So that they could travel unhindered?"

"Exactly." Kelli took a sip of water. "What happened to her?"

"Broken collarbone. Inter-G questioned her, so I have no idea how that went. But from what I heard, she had some lame excuse for how she was injured. They let her go, of course."

"Stupid. But that explains perfectly why they had to hire a guide."

Jayd nodded. "So this guy would hole up for how long? And then what?"

"Don't know. Till it's safe to move Ella to Earth perhaps?" Kelli split a ripe gazmandashi and gave half to Jayd.

"Harker should be strung up by his thumbs. What a creep."

"You don't know the half of it." Her shoulders twitched at the memory of his touch.

Jayd's eyes narrowed.

No doubt he had interrogated Aric and learned everything about the meeting with Harker. Kelli was certain he'd guessed what had happened during the interview. Harker's profile was littered with scandals and paternity suits. Jayd would know what kind of man he was.

She met his gaze squarely. "I wasn't intimate with him, in case you're wondering."

"I didn't ask."

"Yes, you did. Or rather your eyes did."

He pursed his lips, contemplating her words. Finally, he said, "I'm glad you weren't."

"Some things even I wouldn't do, Jayd."

"I believe you."

Unable to bear the intensity in his eyes, she looked away.

He held his glass up as though examining the water. "We're going to need to move quickly. I have no doubt USF, or Intergalaxia, has already contacted the Xerxian government about us being here."

"You said you saw an official. What was the result of the meeting?"

"The chancellor said the Xerxian Council preferred not to get involved in our domestic quarrels. A couple days ago, I was acting on my own. It'll be a different matter when Intergalaxia contacts them directly."

Kelli nodded. "As you know, Xerxes IX doesn't

have an army. Or police."

"My guess is Inter-G will send operatives to retrieve us. Once they get permission from the Xerxian authorities."

"I doubt the government will allow more than a few in." Kelli pressed her palms to the table as she leaned forward. "This is a tightly ordered society. They don't like conflicts—especially those originating from other races. And they don't like single men running roughshod over their planet."

"I got in."

"But you were still in Xer Prime, the most permissive place. Once we get further into the interior, it'll be a different matter."

"You get all this from the ALP? I know you went through the Xerxes program."

"I figured you would." She smiled. "But some of that information is inaccurate. A lot of it applies to the space station or Xer Prime, but not on the plains below."

"Like what in particular?"

"The only way down from the plateau to the plains is via the Great Lift. Before you can take the lift, you have to pass through a checkpoint with a high-level security sweep. All alien equipment—electronic equipment, that is—will have to be surrendered."

"You mean I have to give up my CU?"

Kelli chuckled at his forlorn tone. "Don't worry. They'll return it. Once we head back to Xer Prime."

"What about your sub-dermal chip?"

She pretended innocence. "What makes you think I still have it?"

"Oh, come on. I know you're brilliant, but I doubt you could've learned everything in that short amount of time."

Brilliant? The compliment warmed her. "Thanks for letting me borrow one. You didn't get into trouble, did you?"

He pulled on his earlobe. "Actually, no one else knows."

"Seriously?"

He bent the rules for her?

When he didn't answer, she dropped the subject. "Well, it's gotta go too. I can't chance being identified as Terran. And I'm pretty certain the scan would pick up those items. Only a translator earbud is allowed."

"Good. I get to keep mine." A look of speculation flashed across his face. "But that also means anyone who's following us won't have a technological advantage."

"Exactly. I've seen the checkpoint. Nobody gets around it. Travel is by foot or carrier beast." She rose and cleaned off the table. "I have an extra tunic and pants that might work for you. That is, until we can buy you something else. Clothing is unisex. We can't alter your appearance enough to be a benefit to us, unfortunately."

"I'm going to be conspicuous wherever I go."

He not only had his Asian features, but his height. At six feet, Jayd would literally stand out in a crowd. Xerxian men could be up to seven inches shorter.

"We'll make the best of it." He too rose.

"Oh, um, there's something I need to tell you." Kelli traced her finger along the edge of the table, debating how much she should confess. "You'll be traveling as my Companion."

His eyes narrowed. Clearly he'd picked up something suspicious in her tone. "And what's that supposed to mean?"

"You're my purchased slave."

She expected some biting retort, but instead, he grinned. "This doesn't involve whips and chains, does it?"

Kelli picked up a pillow and flung it at him. "If you get out of line, it might. But for starters, *you* sleep on the floor."

Jayd was staring at her. Again.

As Kelli re-dyed her hair, she could feel his gaze tunneling into the back of her head. Though he pretended to study the map as he sat on his bedding, she knew it was all an act. She wished she could send him into the town to sightsee, but that was no longer possible. With his Companion designation, complete with an earring, he couldn't go roaming around by himself.

Besides, if she asked him, he would find some excuse to refuse. He might pretend like he was on board with her in the search for Ella, but could she be certain?

When it came to Jayd, nothing was sure.

However, the re-dying of not only her hair but body, had to be done. Once they headed down the Great Lift to the plains below, she would not have a chance to take care of this vital task. But this small hotel room offered no privacy. Down the hall, a tiny water closet would not provide adequate space or seclusion.

With her back to Jayd, she retouched her hair roots, eyebrows and lashes, using the in-room sink and mirror. Neither one of them talked. The longer the quiet, the more self-conscious she became.

Finally, part one was done. Hair still damp, Kelli clipped it up. Now she had to redo her skin tint. That would prove a little more awkward. She sat on the opposite side of the bed from Jayd as she hiked up her loose pants and smoothed the cream over her feet and legs.

"How often do you have to do that?"

She answered without looking his direction. "A week. Ten days max." Though the package boasted of lasting two weeks, she'd noticed how the color had already faded.

He took a moment before answering. "Good thing you're taking care of it here, then."

"Exactly." She verified he was still sitting on the floor. "Mind turning around for a few?"

His eyes flickered, just once, before he swiveled to face the wall. He didn't hesitate, didn't joke, didn't say a word. What was he thinking? Where was his usual biting humor?

After Kelli stripped off her outer clothing, she wrapped a towel around her torso, leaving arms, shoulders and legs bare. She again sat on the bed. "Thanks."

The rustling behind her proved he resumed his earlier posture.

She quickly worked the cream into her skin. On

previous missions, she'd shared rooms with colleagues—both male and female. No problem. This was
different. Was it because of something in Jayd's eyes?
Now that he was no longer angry at her, his expression
held an emotion that she couldn't place. And was
afraid of delving into.

"You missed a few spots." His voice sounded like
he was leaning over her shoulder.

She started. How had he moved without making
noise? He stood at the foot of the bed.

"Let me help." He reached for the cream.

She leaned forward. "I got it."

"No, you don't." Jayd's fingers brushed hers as
they both grabbed the jar.

Not willing to wrestle for it, Kelli pulled away.

"Stand up a sec."

"Why?"

"So I can reach the places on your back. I don't
think you want…" His brow lowered.

What was he about to say? No way was she going
to hazard a guess.

Acquiescing, she gripped the sink, more to steady
herself than anything else. In the mirror she watched
while he scooped out a handful of cream and saw her
expression betray her turmoil.

Try as she might, Kelli could not ease the small furrow between her eyebrows or the rigidity of her
mouth. When he caressed her shoulder, she stiffened.
The cool cream warmed as he spread it over her skin.
Tingles skipped down her spine. Kelli closed her eyes,
unable to watch. Or witness the growing unease on her
own face. She willed herself to breathe normally.

Willed herself to relax taut arms as she clutched the sink as though a lifeline to sanity. His touch disappeared. His fingertips again spread the cream.

Closing her eyes had been a mistake. Her nerves went crazy trying to anticipate where he would touch next.

While he worked, Jayd acted perfectly at ease. Face tight with concentration, he apparently relished doing a thorough job, even making sure the skin dye went up into the hairline at the nape of her neck.

"There." A smile of satisfaction tugged at his lips.

"Thanks." She cleared the frog out of her throat. "Make sure you wash your hands right away." She stepped aside so he could get to the sink. The small room didn't have much space for the two of them. Her thigh bumped against the bedside table. It, and Jayd, hemmed her in.

He washed his hands twice. "Done for now?"

"No. I have to re-dye my face too." She expected him to retreat to his bedroll, but he merely backed away a step. In a hurry now, she slathered the cream on her face and neck.

"Done." She slapped the lid back on the jar.

"Uh, not quite." He moved closer. "Let me."

With a gentle finger, he tilted her head so he could smooth the cream into the folds of one ear, then the other. Jayd scrutinized her face until her cheeks grew hot. "Hold really still." He gently dabbed a spot by her eye, then one on her jawline. "One…more…place." He leaned in, smoothing the dye along her lower lip. "There. That should do it."

They were inches apart. Never had she felt so flustered. Or so baffled.

Was she attracted to him? *Seriously?* Her gaze lingered on his mouth.

Do I dare kiss him? What would it be like?

His Adam's apple bobbed while his dark eyes glittered. Was *he* attracted to *her?* His breath brushed her cheek and neck.

The memory of *that* night slammed her.

"Dear God, please..." Though she couldn't remember the exact words, she would never forget the desperation in his voice as he called her back from the grave. His arms about her. The strong beat of his heart under her cheek as she had pressed into his embrace.

He saved my life.

And now, she stood mere inches from him. Wanting something. For the longest time, they stood unmoving. Waiting. Waiting for...?

The jar of cream, teetering on the edge of the sink, suddenly clattered as it slipped into the basin.

Jolted from a dream, Kelli backed away. The hard edge of the nightstand again pressed into her leg.

What was she doing? *Inviting* his advances? Was she out of her mind?

This was Jayd. A man she could not trust. He'd betrayed her. She could never forget that.

While he retrieved the jar and tightened the cap, she busied herself looking for her lip dye. Again, Jayd cleaned his hands. After he finished and had moved back to his bedroll, she washed the excessive dye from her palms.

She really should put the cream on her whole body, but there was no way she could do that. Not here. Not now. When she glanced at Jayd, he was lying with his back to her. Quickly, she applied the pink dye to her lips, then used the colorless activator spray to seal the dye on her body. She waited impatiently until it dried. Finally!

After yanking on a tunic, Kelli turned out the lights and crawled into bed. For what felt like an eternity she stared at the dark ceiling, squelching the deep sighs that threatened again and again.

"Good night, Kel." Jayd's quiet voice cut through the stillness of the room.

She didn't answer, letting him think she was already asleep.

No doubt he knew she wasn't.

Chapter 16

As soon as she stirred, Jayd woke. Gray light filtered through the slats of the shutters. Even without checking his CU, he knew daybreak was at least an hour away. Kelli fidgeted and sighed. Because she didn't want to rise quite yet? Or was she thinking of last night?

Even while he'd slept, he couldn't put her out of his mind. Why hadn't she berated him? Or told him to mind his business while she'd re-dyed her skin? He'd grown so used to her bristling like a *kotse* that he didn't know how he should react to this amiable Kelli.

Admit it. You like it.

Okay, he did. He looked forward to working with her, even if he had to play the part of a subordinate. Perhaps he'd misjudged her leadership abilities. This was as good a time to evaluate them as any.

She soon rose. While it was still dark, they slipped out of the hotel and headed to the checkpoint at the Great Lift. As per her instructions, he followed her, walking a foot behind as was befitting a servant. He kept his head down and never met the gaze of another woman. Not only that, he carried all their baggage.

His new earring felt odd, the charm bobbing against his neck. Though few people lingered in the streets at this early hour, he did notice that his earring was one of the first things women checked. The glances were subtle, but were there nevertheless. The next inevitable look went to Kelli, a knowing smile on their faces. Should he puff up or feel crushed by his new, although temporary, status on Xerxes IX?

He hoped he wouldn't have to include everything in his report. That is, if he ever got to present his account to USF at all. After his abrupt departure from Earth, with no approval and no communication with his boss or even Sean, his actions would most likely be viewed as aiding and abetting Kelli. He too must now be considered a fugitive.

Too late to worry about that now.

They reached the checkpoint as the sun peered over the horizon with a bleary red eye. A stern matron gave them a bin to surrender forbidden equipment. They were prepared, already having placed their items and leftover dyes in a plain cloth sack. They also stashed his Terran clothing. To identify herself on their return,

Kelli gave the matron an interesting name. First Traveler? From what he could tell, she spoke almost flawless Xer. She probably didn't need a translator. Jayd's bud was pressed deeply into his ear canal.

They passed through a high level field that scanned them for contraband equipment. Once cleared, they began the descent on the Great Lift to the shadowy plains below, well over a thousand feet. Other travelers made the passage with them, along with an assortment of farm animals and carts. The lift could easily hold fifty people. From all appearances, the mechanism ran continually from early morning until late night. On the way down they passed another lift going up, full of those heading to the cliff towns or Xer Prime to sell their wares.

They finally reached the bottom. A village was a short distance from the lift, already abuzz with activity for the day.

Several clothing shops were open. As they entered the first one, Jayd didn't miss the sly smile the female shopkeeper threw in Kelli's direction. Hating to be at a disadvantage, he regretted not going through the accelerated learning like she had. As the designated slave, he put the extra clothing into their sacks, noting the finely woven material. Kelli instructed him to don a voluminous outer robe of azure-colored fabric, complete with a hood.

"We need to make one stop before hitting the trail." She pointed to the town's temple. "It'll be only an hour."

"Are you kidding?"

"Trust me."

Uncertain what to expect, Jayd shrugged and followed. He paused inside the building, squinting in the gloom. Odd place. Nothing in it but chairs and an altar. Kelli walked confidently to the center where an old woman was sweeping.

"Is it permitted?" She spoke in Xer as she pointed at Jayd.

The woman nodded. "You both do us honor."

Kelli held out her hands for the broom, which the woman gladly surrendered. Puzzled, Jayd watched as his colleague came toward him. "Put our bags here. They'll be safe."

He did as she bade.

"Here ya go." She pressed the broom into his hands.

"What am I supposed to do with this?"

She planted a fist on her hip and cocked an eyebrow.

Not ride it, apparently.

He made a face. "You're not serious. Are you?"

"Just do it." She glanced over her shoulder. "And don't give me any more lip. You're protesting way too much for a slave."

Tempted to say more, he clamped his lips shut when he saw the old woman glaring at him. Though she appeared as ancient and tall as a weather-beaten scarecrow, he ascertained she could put him in his place. Quickly. And painfully.

Kelli pointed. "Start there. Sweep this section of the temple."

"Aye-aye, Capt'n."

A smirk tugged at her mouth.

At first he thought she was going to sit and watch him work, but he was wrong. She located a cloth and joined the crone who polished the altar. The three of them where the only ones in the building.

This was too weird.

Intent on getting done as soon as possible, Jayd swept vigorously. Across the room, Kelli quietly chatted with the old woman. Was this the so-called gossip channel she'd mentioned earlier? If so, what were they talking about? His curiosity grew. And admiration for this very resourceful special agent.

Of course, he should trust her. Kelli never did anything on a whim or without purpose. Once she fixed her mind on something, she wouldn't give up. He finished the one section and brought the broom toward her.

"We are nearly done. You can leave that by the chair." She held a burning wick.

"Now what?" He looked around. The old woman had left.

She reached for a gray-brown jar on the center of the altar. "We offer a petition."

"What?" He couldn't believe his ears.

"Shh!" She took three pinches of the pungent incense and placed them on the altar. "You can do it too. Men are allowed."

"Um...I'll pass."

Still holding the wick, Kelli did nothing for the longest time, eyes closed. Was she praying? Impossible. Finally, she held the red-hot tip to the incense. It burst into flame.

Jayd grunted in surprise as sweet aroma filled the

air. When she leaned forward to inhale the smoke, he stared.

What had come over her? This was a woman known for her scorn of religion or anything sacred. Last night, when he had prayed aloud before their meal, he'd only done it to goad her. Now she was offering up an invocation in an alien temple? He wasn't certain if he should tease her or warn her about worshiping false gods. Instead, he kept his mouth shut.

Kelli placed the wick back into a holder under the altar. "Ready to go?"

He shook himself. "Always."

They made good time, staying on the well-trodden trails. Abundant road signs pointed the way to the next towns and plateaus. The byways were traveler-friendly with plenty of watering troughs and enclosed "privacy" stops. People they passed nodded their greeting, but didn't ask them who they were or where they were going.

Though they traveled at a brisk walk, Jayd began to enjoy the scenery. Xerxes' daytime sun had risen, detailing the landscape. It looked remarkably like the African plains of Earth, if he discounted the rusty colored soil. Trees and brush were sparse, although plentiful grasses of many kinds spread over the fields. He noted the browns and greens, somewhat similar to Earth's and could almost pretend he was on a safari, *sans* the big game animals. He saw only a few small, dog-like creatures at a distance. Even with the physical exertion, the trip was delightfully peaceful.

Their pace slowed after a few hours. A long empty road disappeared into the distance. Since they'd left the small village, Kelli had retreated into silence. Though he tried to engage her in conversation a couple times, she'd been reticent. What was she mad about now? He wondered what he'd done. *This* time.

He hitched the travel bag higher on his shoulder. "By the way, thank you."

Kelli glanced at him out of the corner of her eye. "For?"

"For following your heart. Even though it may cost your future in the long run."

She opened her mouth—probably to give him a smart aleck reply—then apparently changed her mind. They walked on in silence for a little while. She sighed.

Help her to open her heart to me, Lord. There's so much I want to say.

"I think I'm getting soft." She brushed her long black hair from her face.

He waited before prodding. "How so?"

"Chasing a hunch. Throwing away everything for a girl I barely know." She shook her head as though astounded at herself.

Because Ella was Sean's daughter? He kept that to himself. "I'd say that makes you more human."

She let out a sound of derision. "I don't know if that's a compliment."

"It is. And I meant it as a sincere one."

Her brow lowered, still not convinced.

Stopping on the road, he dropped his bag and waited for her to face him. "Can we clear the air between us? One minute, we're getting along great, and the next I feel like I should sleep with one eye open."

Her chin rose a notch, mouth flattening into a stubborn line.

"Okay, I'll start." Jayd took the plunge. "You wanna talk about the rumors flying around USF about you and Sean?"

Kelli dropped her baggage and planted a fist at one hip. "Yeah, let's talk about that."

"You may not believe me, but I told no one about your feelings for Sean. Not even him. I didn't even include it in my report."

"You recorded it."

He debated how much to say.

As he hesitated, her shoulders tightened and her eyes flashed. "How many people did you show it to? Did they all have a good laugh?"

"I showed it only to my superior. And he got the edited version."

"Really." Disbelief rippled through the word.

"I deleted our discussion about Sean." He crossed his arms, still fighting guilt about hiding all the facts from his superior. And so much more.

The night Jayd had saved her life, he'd seen her attacker fleeing the scene. In that split second, he'd chosen to rescue her. Not Ella. Time and again, he'd wrestled with his decision. Why wasn't important. He'd failed his duty as a senior agent of USF.

Worse, he'd hidden the truth from everyone. Including his best friend.

Kelli struck a pose. "So how'd they find out about Sean?"

"Isn't it possible others noticed your moping around during the reception?"

"I didn't mope."

He raised his eyebrows.

"Okay, so I was a little—a little…" She appeared to search frantically for a word in the sky and the birds that fluttered overhead. "A little *petulant* that night."

"It was written all over you, Kel. A blind man could've seen it."

Face clouding, she surprised him by ducking her head. "Was I really that bad?"

He spread his hands. "Please believe me. I didn't say a word. I would never have betrayed your feelings."

Her mouth remained a stubborn slash. She wasn't ready to be friends yet. "Then what about hounding me when we got back to Earth?"

"You mean my following you?"

"And searching my apartment."

And he'd thought he'd been so careful. "You knew?"

"Of course I knew. I'm trained to know."

He repressed his smile. "I made sure I didn't leave any evidence."

"And I made sure that I'd know if anyone came into my apartment."

He didn't ask how. "The director personally ordered me to turn in reports about you every day. *Detailed* reports. They took hours to prepare. If my supervisor thought I'd left anything out, he dragged me into the office and interrogated me. You know what a pain he is."

Her expression softened a little.

"I was just doing my job, Kel."

She glanced away, then back. "Do you always have

to follow orders?"

He waved a hand at their surroundings. "Obviously not. I wouldn't be here if I did."

She grinned. "Okay, okay. Point taken."

"Anything else we need to clear up?

"The tribunal." Her face again tightened. "The night I came to USF to study. You knew then, didn't you?"

It was his turn to look away. "Yes."

"Why didn't you tell me?" Recrimination rang in her tone.

If he could rewind time, he'd do it. Too late.

Why hadn't he? Was he so concerned about doing his job that he forgot to do what was right?

He swallowed his pride, answering slowly so that she couldn't miss his sincerity. "Because no matter what I did, when it came to you it always seemed the wrong choice." He met her gaze. "I'm sorry, Kel. You're right. I should have told you."

Surprise etched her expression. Because she couldn't believe he'd apologized?

He kept silent, allowing her to absorb the truth.

"Since we're being honest..." She paused, seeming to debate with herself. "I never thanked you for coming to my rescue. That night." She spoke with difficulty.

Had she guessed he'd followed her? That because he was worried about her, he'd kept her in sight? In retrospect, he wished he had been more diligent, but he'd worried that she would resent his presence. So he'd backed off.

Her expression of gratefulness was balm to his battered soul.

He kept his voice soft. "Best thing I ever did."

Do you know how much I care for you, Kelli?

Yes, he did care. Had for years.

When they were at odds with each other—which was the usual scenario—he could keep her at arms' length. With her at a safe distance, he could tease and provoke her. But now...

Now he wasn't so certain.

When Kelli smiled softly at him, he stuck out his hand. "Friends?"

Brow furrowing, she slowly slid her fingers against his. But instead of shaking her hand, he merely squeezed. She didn't pull away. Unwilling to let go, Jayd took in a slow deep breath. She gulped, eyes wide, gaze straying to his lips.

How I wish...

Wish what? He had no answer. He just wanted them to be friends.

Liar. He wanted more than that. Stupid, of course. They were spiritually on two different planes. She didn't even believe in God. And he shouldn't even be considering a relationship with her. Much less want one.

Relationship? No, his carnal nature rose up to challenge him. He wanted so much more.

Releasing her hand, he stepped back. "Someone's coming." He hoped his hoarse voice didn't betray the almost overwhelming temptation to forget all his high ideals.

As he retrieved their bundles, she appeared to snap out of her reverie. Again they walked in silence, picking up the pace for the time they'd lost.

They reached the next village in time for lunch. This place looked similar to the last one—white stone and adobe-like buildings of mostly one story, some two. However, this town was laid out a little differently. The main road led to the open middle, a hub of commerce, with lesser streets branching off like spokes on a wheel. Shops circled the outside of the core. A large, prominent fountain occupied the center of town. Its water geysered up by means of some hidden mechanism, spilling into split tiers where people could fill their hydro-flasks at the uppermost levels. The lowest were wide troughs, reserved for animals. Several children splashed in the shallow water at the base. Crowds of people congregated at the nearby restaurants, proving this was obviously the place to be at noontime.

While Kelli did all the talking and buying, he stood quietly to one side. This was a new role for him. And odd. He didn't like being so passive but he kept telling himself it was only a part to play. She chattered in Xer, amazing him with how quickly she'd picked up the language. Which was another reason for him to remain quiet. As she bargained for the best food at the best price, he merely listened.

She's incredible. After one purchase, she held up her hand for him to remain where he was while she went into a shop. Jayd stayed by the well, surrounded by people and domesticated animals. He was aware of the stares in his direction and overheard comments about what a fine specimen he was.

It took all his training not to laugh out loud. Did they think he was deaf? Or couldn't understand them?

Some women, especially, appeared enthralled as they articulated their admiration of his taupe skin and dark eyes. Though Xerxians also had black hair, his was a shiny blue-black, thanks to his Chinese heritage. His height and lean build drew the most comments. Xer males were short and stocky while Jayd towered over most men by six or more inches. He guessed he was a bit of a novelty as a Terran in the middle of an alien planet. After looking around, he realized he was the only non-greenie in the village.

One woman in particular was more vocal than the rest. She came within a couple yards of him.

"I wonder if he's for sale," she said to her friends. Emboldened by her, three others drew closer.

"You already have a Companion," one said. "You don't need another."

"I'd trade him in an instant for this one." The Xerxian fixed dark eyes on him. She was tall, at least six foot three. An Amazon. Beautifully proportioned. Everything a mythological female warrior should be.

When she drew nearer, he met her gaze. Was that the correct response? The next statement by one of her friends alerted Jayd that he'd erred.

"He likes you." The friend laughed. "See how he invites you with his eyes."

Shifting his gaze to the ground, he suppressed a growl.

"I would take him." The Amazon's voice grew husky. She stepped closer.

What should he do? The last thing he wanted was an intergalactic incident with an offended Xer female.

As they stood nearly toe-to-toe, he willed himself

not to look at her. She had definitely invaded his personal space.

"Stand away!" Kelli's voice rose above the hubbub of the crowd. Around her, people ceased talking.

Jayd shot her a glance. Did she mean him? No, she was staring hard at the Amazon.

The woman straightened, clearly assessing Kelli who appeared petite by comparison. Shoulders squared, the woman's mouth pursed and eyes grew hooded as she evaluated her smaller opponent.

Jaw jutting, Kelli strode with purpose toward the Amazon. It looked like *she* was going to cause the intergalactic incident.

Exhaling slowly, Jayd couldn't tear his gaze away.

She let her purchases drop to the ground as she stalked toward them. The next moment, he flinched as her hand shot out. She struck the Amazon squarely in the chest with the heel of her palm, knocking her backward a step.

Oh, crap.

They squared off, eyeball to eyeball, more or less with the height difference. Any second, Jayd expected them to come to blows.

A list of possible repercussions ran through his head, all of them bad. Should he intervene before the Amazon attacked Kelli? Or should he initiate a fight? But that was a huge *no-no* in this society. He pictured them hightailing it out of there, the whole town chasing them. A mob of waving pitchforks, brandished torches and raised fists flashed through his mind. That thought was followed by the inevitable consequences of incarceration, assuming they weren't lynched first.

He clenched his teeth, wishing Kelli would look at him and let him know what he should do.

Suddenly laughing, the Amazon stepped back. "I meant no offense, sister. I am merely jealous of your good fortune."

Immediately Kelli relaxed her stance. "No offense taken, my friend. You do me honor."

Jayd let out a long slow breath. No way in the universe would men have backed down. They would have come to blows, involving the whole town in a brawl.

After picking up Kelli's things, the Amazon handed them to her. "Peace to you on your travels."

Kelli bowed. Before heading to Jayd, she watched the woman stalk away. She spoke under her breath. "Let's get out of here."

Only when they were well away did Jayd burst into laughter.

"That wasn't funny." Brow tight, she marched away from the town.

"In retrospect, yes it was. I wish I had my CU to record that."

Kelli threw him a look that would have killed.

He caught up to her. "Were you worried she was going to wallop you?"

"Of course not." She glared at him. "I knew I could take her." When he didn't say anything, she said, "I *could* have."

"I don't doubt it. Much."

She fairly screeched to a halt. "I'm a trained field agent. The last couple months I've done some strength exercises. I've been working with professionals and even picked up some new street-fighting techniques."

"Yeah, but the Amazon had three friends. That's four to one. The odds were a bit steep."

She shrugged, still defiant. "I'd have managed."

"I know. And frankly, I wasn't as worried about you as my own skin."

"How so?"

"Four women? What would I do with them all?"

Her expression finally relaxed. Kelli chuckled. "No worries. You'd have been bored to death, carrying their packages all over town. And they would have made you stand around so others could *ooh* and *ah* over you."

"Good. I was concerned." He blew out his cheeks in exaggerated relief. "You may find it difficult to believe, but I'm not interested in polygamy. Besides, it's against my religion."

This time, she laughed out loud. "The ALP gave no help for that situation. I pretty much winged it back there."

"Obviously the right choice. You did great."

"Thanks." She blushed prettily. Then she pointed. "Let's stop there for lunch."

Off the road, they sat cross-legged under a shading tree while they ate. Jayd liked how she'd relaxed. It was good to have finally cleared the air between them. And have an adventure about which they could laugh in the future.

Assuming they didn't both end up in prison. Jayd pushed that unpleasant thought away.

After Kelli consulted her map and compass, she showed him they were on course. And making good time. Somehow, they started talking about their shared history, of people they knew who'd moved on to other jobs. Of those who'd gotten promotions and those who deserved them.

He dared bring up an old memory. "Do you recall the first time we met?"

"In the gym at USF. Just over five and a half years ago."

Interesting that she would recall the exact time. "Remember what happened?" He bit into some fruit.

"Yeah. I challenged you to a wresting match."

"Um-hmm. I was always curious why."

She paused before replying, brushing crumbs off her blue robe. "Because you were smirking. At me."

"Smirking?"

"Yeah, when I was sparring with my partner. I could see that you thought I was a greenhorn."

"Well, you were."

"That's beside the point."

"So you challenged me to prove what?"

"I don't know." She shrugged. "I lasted a few rounds before you pinned me."

"Yeah. Yeah, you did." He wasn't going to admit that he'd purposefully held back. In truth, he could've taken her out in the first three minutes. Or less.

But in the last five years, she'd improved greatly.

Eyes gleaming, she tossed her head in challenge. "You up for a rematch?"

"Last night I told you I was. Any time."

Her cheeks flamed dark red, evident even under the green skin. "You weren't serious, though."

"Of course I was serious."

Not good. He might have stepped over the line

with her. A visible wall of resistance flared through her body. What used to be the right way to deal with her—teasing, mocking, sarcasm—again proved to no longer work.

Before their conversation spiraled out of control, he added, "But I'd rather save my energy for the thug who hurt you."

Her jaw tightened. "I get dibs."

"You'll have to get to him first. Before me."

Instead of arguing with him, she gazed at him with a speculative look. "I have a bigger reason to thump him. Why do you want him so badly?"

Why do I? It took Jayd a second to analyze his own motivation. It finally dawned on him, striking at the heart of his being.

Because he nearly killed the woman I love.

His world rocked, off balance as the full force hit. Yes, he did love Kelli. Somewhere along the line, "caring" for her had morphed into love. And now that he finally admitted it to himself, he couldn't find an adequate lie to replace it.

Clenching his teeth, he fought to hide the truth, but no doubt it was written all over his face. For once in his life he felt powerless to hide his true feelings. The longer his tongue remained locked in his head, the more furious he became with himself.

He shot to his feet and shoved his uneaten lunch into a bag. "Let's go. We have a job to do."

Slowly, Kelli rose. The whole time she gathered their things, he was aware of her gaze straying to him.

He shouldn't have laid himself open like that. Why didn't she argue with him like she usually did? He could deal with her hostility, her resistance. This new side of her kept throwing him off. Caused him to let down his guard.

Jayd had to back off. Keep some distance for sanity's sake.

Don't forget she's in love with Sean.

By throwing away her career to find his stepdaughter, Kelli once again proved her feelings for him. Even married, Sean stood in the way.

No, that wasn't completely true. Someone much more important blocked Jayd. One who demanded unswerving loyalty and trust.

God.

As Jayd tramped down the dusty road, he sensed he would someday have to make a choice. Pursue Kelli and indulge in all the pleasures a relationship could offer? Or follow his conscience and obey the Lord?

Chapter 17

The afternoon waned with ominous clouds gathering along the horizon. The roads emptied with no village or villagers in sight. Kelli hunched her shoulders, unease growing as steadily as the ache in her ankle. Who was out there? Waiting for them? Invisible eyes seemed to follow as she kicked up the dust on the trail.

Perhaps picking up on her apprehension, Jayd glanced behind. "Should we keep walking?"

"We'll have to stop somewhere."

He pointed. "Your ankle bothering you?"

"Not much." She lifted her chin. "If it wasn't going to be dark soon, I could walk another twenty miles."

His grin proved her bravado hadn't fooled him.

For several more moments they trudged along.

Jayd cleared his throat. "I forgot to ask. What's the wildlife like around here?"

"Nothing big and scary. The predators are pretty small. And they usually go after other animals. No humanoid predation."

"That's good to know."

She noticed how his gaze darted about. "Don't tell me you're afraid of camping."

"Not of camping, no." He surveyed the area again. "Just what goes along with camping. Usually."

She started to chuckle. "Bugs? Snakes? Spiders?"

He hunkered his shoulders. "I don't think it's funny."

She couldn't suppress her humor. The longer she chuckled, the funnier it became. Under his breath, he muttered all sorts of invectives against her.

Jayd? Fearful of creepy crawlies? If she told anyone, they'd never believe it. How had he coped with USF's rigorous survival training, complete with forests and jungles as well as living off the land?

"I thought you…" She couldn't finish her sentence because she'd started sputtering again.

"Yeah, yeah." His tone could dry out the Sahara.

Finally, she could laugh no more. Wiping her eyes, she hacked as though to rid herself of humor. For now. She borrowed his phrase from the night of the reception. "Don't worry, Jayd. Your secret's safe with me."

"Oh, I feel a lot better now."

"I had no idea."

"Good. I've worked hard to keep it that way. For

years."

They walked on in silence.

"Tell you what." Kelli gestured for him to hand her one of the bundles. "We'll walk until it gets dark, stop and eat. Then find a place to rest."

"Sounds good to me."

But as the sun sank below the horizon, Kelli noticed a glow ahead.

"A town?" Jayd asked.

"I don't think so. We have another day of travel."

The brightness on the skyline continued to grow, especially as dusk fell. When they crested a hill, she finally understood what she was seeing. Instinctively, she and Jayd crouched.

The area looked similar to a campground on Earth, surrounded by a fence, with a huge bonfire in the middle. More than a dozen humanoids had spread bedrolls inside the fenced area. Livestock clustered in small pens around them.

"What do you think?" Kelli kept her tone low.

Jayd's eyes narrowed. "Though I like the idea of being in a more protected area, I don't favor being that close to other Xerxians. And whoever else might be there."

She nodded. "I concur." Joining the group would provide benefits, but definite risks as well. "We can try to go around them..."

"There's a ravine to our right. And I think I hear trickling water. What do you think of stopping there for the night?"

"Let's do it."

They backed away from the group and cut off the

road. When they reached the ravine, they found a safe place to climb down. Small rocks clattered as they slid down the embankment.

Kelli brushed off her hands. "I hope no one comes to investigate."

"I think we're far enough away. But look at it this way. No one can sneak up on us either."

"Good point."

They found a level camping spot, under an over-hanging rock formation. Pleased with their find, she reasoned they could remain hidden while seeing any-one's approach.

Before the evening darkened further, they sat and ate dinner.

"If you don't mind," she said when they were done, "I'm going to take advantage of the water to bathe."

"Go for it. I'll do the same when you're finished."

Grabbing a bar of soap, she found a tunic to use as a towel. Kelli moved around the curving ravine, out of sight of Jayd and the road. She dunked herself in the shallow water, enjoying being dirt-free. The unscented soap didn't lather much in the chilly water, but it re-moved the gritty dust. Soon she returned to Jayd who had set up camp.

She was sitting on her bedroll, rubbing her ankle when he returned from his bath. Carrying his tunic, he wore only pants. In the dim light, his hair appeared damp. Water glistened on his skin, highlighting the lean muscles of his chest.

He sat near her on his bedding. "That bothering you?"

She hated to admit it. "A little." That slide down the rocky slope had played havoc with her.

"Here, let me."

Before she could protest, he'd lifted her ankle and expertly assessed it. "You have some inflammation here. And here."

She hissed as he pressed sore spots.

"Sorry. This should alleviate it." Expertly, he massaged the skin, his strong thumbs rubbing upward.

It hurt at first, but after a few minutes, the pain eased.

He glanced up. "You reinjure it recently?"

"Yes. My first days here. I jumped down too great of a height."

"Ah. That would do it." But he didn't ask for details.

She sighed.

"Helping?" His fingertips smoothed across her skin.

"Oh, yeah."

However, Kelli realized the sensations she now felt were definitely more uncomfortable. Zings of pleasure traveled up her leg. When he massaged the bottom of her foot, the tingling blazed all the way to her scalp.

"That's good enough." She tried to pull away.

"No it's not." He grabbed hold more firmly. "Don't be a ninny. You need to be able to walk without pain. I can't carry our bundles plus you. For more than a few miles anyway."

True. She quit resisting. Her ankle had to be in top shape for their long trek on the morrow. Jayd was a professional. His aid was intended to be impersonal.

She needed to get over her reticence about the contact. Like the night he had helped her with the dye. That had meant nothing. This meant nothing. Apparently she alone had a problem. Not him.

However, the more pleasant the sensations, the more she tensed. He didn't appear aroused by the touch. But she definitely was. More than once she had to rein in her imagination.

Get a hold of yourself.

She was glad he didn't chat. No way could she have answered him coherently.

Time and again her gaze was drawn to his face, tight with concentration. Jayd was intent on relieving her discomfort. Why was he always more concerned for her than himself? He was so different than other men she'd known. They always talked and talked about how much they wanted to be with her. How much they "loved" her. Jayd merely showed his concern. Numerous times and in countless ways.

Like his conduct *that* night. He'd never left her side. When she had grown hysterical, he cradled her in his arms. She would never forget how it felt, to lean on his chest. An elusive memory sharpened—his lips brushing her hair. His gentle hand caressing her bare shoulder. The reassuring thump of his heart, beating steadily against her cheek.

She tried to bolster herself with antagonism. That used to always work. Not now.

As dusk deepened, her detachment grew. Detachment from the old Kelli and Jayd to this new relationship that had begun the moment he'd arrived on Xerxes. Why had he followed her? Why had he risked his future? She understood her reasons for throwing away her career, but why had he?

When they had talked about the man who'd attacked her, Jayd had betrayed emotion that she'd convinced herself she'd only imagined. Did he really care for her—as more than a colleague? The very fact that he didn't gush with lovey-dovey talk endeared her to him.

What sort of man was Jayd? She found herself dying to find out.

"There." He finally released her foot. "I'd recommend you soak it in the water for a bit. Should take down more of the swelling."

She fought for an even tone. "Thanks." She rose. "How about I take first watch? I'll wake you in a couple hours."

"Works for me. Good night." Without another word, he turned on his side.

Kelli had no doubt he'd fallen instantly asleep. How did he do that? Did all males have an "off" switch somewhere that allowed them to shut down their minds? Men!

Jayd had the oddest dream.

One moment, he was curled on the hard Xerxian soil, silently praying. The next, he sat in the living room of his parents' house. The whole family had gathered, including his sisters, their spouses and kids. Everyone talked at once. But he couldn't focus on what anyone was saying. The conversation suddenly grew muted as though the volume turned down.

Jayd's wife walked through the middle of the spacious room, but no one paid attention to her.

"Liu?" He stared as she moved in slow motion.

Part of him knew she had died. He remembered seeing her body, laid out at the morgue. By the time he'd arrived that one horrible day, they'd washed away the blood from the multiple gunshot wounds. He would never forget the ghastly gray of her skin, eyes permanently sealed.

Black hair pinned, Liu sauntered through the crowded living room. She wore her red wedding dress, which was embroidered with elaborate flower motifs. When she reached the front door, she walked through without acknowledging him.

Don't go. He thought he said it, but no words escaped. She was in danger.

Fear pounding through him, he chased after her. He ran through dim hallways. In the distance he saw a flash of red material. But his wife wasn't standing in the distance. It was Kelli, hair dyed black, eyes closed. A dark line marred her throat.

Jayd heard himself begging God to save her. Not merely her soul, but her life as well. When he reached out, his fingers brushed cold skin. Her face appeared pasty.

As he gathered her into his arms—crying over her—her eyes fluttered open. She touched his face. And smiled.

In the serenity of the night, Kelli sighed deeply, repeatedly. The hum of some night creature—mammal? amphibian?—plunged her into a surreal dream-like state. When the triple moons of Xerxes floated into the sky, their light painted the landforms with gold and purple. The breathtaking view amplified her disconnectedness from reality. She was in a time warp where every movement in the universe ceased. Stars hung, twinkling quietly in slow motion. The night breeze stilled, waiting with bated breath. Worlds wound down and halted in their orbits.

Despite the surrounding beauty, Kelli's gaze was drawn to the man beside her. Again and again, she squeezed her eyes shut, confounded by her feelings for him.

What about Sean? Somehow he had faded out of the emotional picture. Not merely because he was off limits, but because she realized she'd never really known him. The time they'd spent together, undercover at SARC, had been purely fictional. Now that Kelli had seen him at USF, and when he was with his wife and daughter, the old Sean melted away. She couldn't deny his aloofness. His gaze contained a polite acknowledgement like it did with all other USF agents. Nothing more.

But Jayd...

On this alien planet, with no distractions, out of their normal mode of life, she finally noticed him. The man, Jayden Song. Gone was his biting humor and mocking demeanor. He didn't challenge every one of her decisions or question her motives. He didn't act like a senior agent. She didn't feel like an idiot underling.

It was more than that.

As was his habit, he still watched her, but now she detected an expression she'd never before seen. Something that had always been there? But perhaps she'd been too defensive to notice.

Kelli reflected on her suspicion that he loved her. But "love" seemed too sappy a word. She'd spent time with many men who claimed to be "in love" with her. No, Jayd was different. Was it commitment she sensed in him? That seemed a stronger, more pure emotion. *Commitment* spoke of a steady faithfulness that would stick through the difficult as well as easy times.

He was unlike any other man she'd known. Or allowed to get close.

In his sleep, he mumbled something, then rolled on his back. His arm flopped out toward her, resting on the ground between them. A mute invitation?

His relaxed hand beckoned to her. A gentle, nonthreatening enticement. One that left the decision completely up to her.

Totally her imagination. He was asleep!

Yet once that thought entered her head, it wouldn't leave her alone. She *was* attracted to him.

The idea badgered her, wearing her down. Her whole body betrayed her, fighting against her mind. Her heart joined in, pinning her in a half Nelson and forcing her to concede. She couldn't win this wrestling match. She didn't want to.

I want...

Before considering the consequences, Kelli crawled next to him and settled against his side. It felt so good, so right—to share his warmth and feel the pulse in his bicep against her cheek. Jayd sighed in his sleep, his muscle growing taut under her head. In his unconscious state, he bent his elbow and rested his arm against her back.

She inhaled slowly, enjoying the nearness. Relishing the embrace even if he wasn't fully awake. *That night* flashed through her mind again—his arms about her, holding her as she had fought her way from the abyss of death.

Snuggling closer, she smoothed the tunic over the increasingly erratic beat of his heart.

"What...?" His whisper alerted her that he was awakening. What would he do?

Hand resting on his chest, she raised her head. His eyes blinked open, then focused on her. She could hear his slow intake of breath. While he became fully conscious, Kelli waited, but he didn't protest or push her away. In the shimmering light of the moons, she could see his eyes widen and fix on her. He must know why she was lying beside him.

After scooting closer, she boldly leaned in to kiss him. He lay passive a moment, then his arm suddenly tightened, crushing her against himself. Kelli's heart leaped as his lips came alive under hers. One kiss melded into the next and the next, growing more passionate by the second. His whole body grew taut as he raised himself to meet her embrace. Breath grew ragged.

A roaring need filled her senses. *He wants this. I want this.* Kelli tugged at his shirt, sliding her hands underneath to caress his skin. She moaned as his lips touched her neck and his breath roared in her ears. Her pulse pounded through her.

"I want you," she whispered. "Please. Oh, God…"

He suddenly jerked back as though the name broke a spell. Panting hard, he stared at her. He leapt to his feet and backed away, hand out as though to ward her off.

"What is…?" Jayd shook his head and took another step back. "What—what am I doing." It wasn't a question, but a statement. His tone rang with self-recrimination.

Sitting up, Kelli straightened her tunic. "What's wrong?"

He opened his mouth, but merely shook his head. Finally, he said, "I—I can't do this."

"But I thought…"

I thought you loved me. Pride imprisoned the words.

"I'm sorry. Truly." Running both hands through his hair, he looked around as though he had no idea where he was.

He didn't want her. How could she have been so stupid? How could she have so misunderstood…?

Drawing up her legs to her chest, she wrapped her arms about her knees. Her throat hurt so much she could hardly breathe. Each inhale burned, each exhale made her gasp for more air.

Don't cry. Don't let him see you cry.

She pressed her forehead to her knees, unable to stop the dam from breaking. With superhuman effort, she suffocated the sound of her tears. An agony of minutes crawled by while she hid them, but she didn't know how much longer she could suppress the urgent and imminent storm.

"I'm sorry, Kelli. I'm so sorry." Jayd's whisper reached her. Gravel ground under his feet as he strode away.

When she was sure he was out of earshot, Kelli flopped over and buried her face against the bedding. A sob, coming from the recesses of her soul, ripped through her.

Chapter 18

Heat shimmered in the distance in the early afternoon. As Jayd adjusted the bag's strap, he glanced at the silent woman beside him. Though the evidence of her tears had faded, the grim line by her mouth was a constant reminder of how he'd wounded her.

You know I didn't mean to, Lord. I would never willingly hurt Kelli.

In the hours since they'd broken camp, she'd barely spoken. Several attempts to engage her in conversation had failed.

He cleared his throat. "About last night."

"Hmm?" Without slowing, Kelli marched ahead.

He hurried his pace. And dodged a direct state-ment. "Your ankle. I hope I didn't hurt it when—"

"It's fine."

Did she understand that he was talking about more than her ankle? Her jaw thrust, warning him to drop the subject. Best to revert to default mode. Pick up the pieces and move on. Or better yet, pretend last night had never happened.

He scratched his neck. "So, how long do you plan to *not* talk to me?"

She swept back the hair that clung to her damp forehead. "It's not that I'm not talking. I just don't have anything to say."

Right. The enmity between them was so thick he could slice it.

He sighed and looked to the road in front of them. Okay. The damage had been done. He could see no way to rectify the situation.

Yet, how could he have resisted her? How could he have not responded to her kisses? Her caresses?

Impossible. He wasn't made of stone.

However, the moment he realized she was lying next to him, he should have pulled away. Instead, he had remained passive.

He shouldn't have kissed her. Or returned her em-brace.

Instead, he had lied to himself. In his half-aware state, he convinced himself he could stop at any time.

A few more minutes, his heart had demanded. *Just a few more.*

Kelli was right. Silence was the only sanity.

When they arrived at their destination, relief swept

over him. The village where the guide lived was a welcome sight. The sooner they found her, the sooner they could be on their way. Then off this rock.

And far away from Kelli who tempted him day and night by her mere presence.

As was her habit, she went to the temple. However, this place was well tended. No cleaning needed. The altar, though, could always use polishing. The burn marks of constant use marred the surface. This time, Jayd also grabbed a polishing cloth and bent his attention to the time-consuming task. As he worked, Kelli spoke in a low voice to another worshipper, presumably to discover the whereabouts of the guide.

When the work was done, he took several pinches of incense as he'd seen Kelli do numerous times. He picked up a burning wick, hoping that he wasn't inadvertently giving homage to a false god.

He closed his eyes. What should he pray?

God, help me explain to Kelli why I pulled away. Help me find the right words. Please, Lord, help her understand. And give me strength to do what is right.

He lowered the wick to the incense, again amazed at the soothing smell when it burst into flames. A symbol perhaps of prayer being a fragrant aroma to God?

When he raised his eyes, he noted Kelli watching him. Her pained expression quickly disappeared. Once she appeared to recover, she beckoned him to follow. When they reached the doorway of the temple, she said in a low voice, "Our guide isn't in town."

He let out a sigh of frustration.

"She is about a half-day's journey from here. And is expected back tomorrow evening or the next day.

Should we wait? Or move on?"

Everything in him said to keep moving, but he was weary of the walking and of the oppressive silence between them.

"How about we rest here tonight, then head out in the morning. Meet her halfway?"

Kelli nodded. "We can restock our food supply."

"And give your ankle a breather too."

Her cheeks grew greenish pink. "It's much better today. That's not even a factor."

He debated arguing. "You're the best judge of that."

For some reason, she remained standing in the doorway opposite him, as though unwilling to get on with the needed errands of finding a room for the night or purchasing food. Her gaze darted to the altar, to the market place beyond, to the floor.

"About last night—"

"My fault," he interrupted. "I shouldn't have—"

"No, it's *mine*. I take full responsibility." Her cheeks grew dark red, even under the dye. "I took advantage of you while you slept. It was unprofessional." She chewed the inside of her lower lip.

"I wasn't passive. It was every bit my fault."

"No, Jayd. You aren't to blame. I…" Growing rigid, Kelli suddenly clutched his arm.

He squinted into the brightness where she stared. "What is it?"

"That couple." She backed away from the opening, positioning herself so that she would be half hidden behind the doorframe. "See them?"

Jayd too, instinctively moved out of sight. At first

he couldn't locate those of whom she spoke. Then he saw a man and woman. They appeared Xerxian.

"Something about them is off." Kelli's voice fell low on his ear.

He agreed. They didn't belong. The evidence was subtle, but undeniable. The way they walked, the way they scanned the crowd, their bearing. Everything about them said *dangerous*.

Kelli continued to watch. "They aren't Xerxian."

"You sure?"

"Positive."

He wouldn't argue. She'd prepped much more than he.

Her gaze flicked to him, then back outside. "Anyone you know?"

Jayd stared hard at them. "No. And I'm betting not USF."

She swore.

How had agents gotten to Xerxes IX so quickly? His mind flicked back to the message from Jen. Obviously, the intel about "acquaintances" had reached him later than he realized.

If they were from Intergalaxia as he suspected, they would be more treacherous, definitely more unpredictable than USF agents.

"I don't see any indication of weapons," he said. "Do you?"

"No. Maybe only knives?"

He gripped her arm. "How strict are the Xerxians about off worlders? Do you think they surrendered their weapons and equipment like we did?"

Under his fingers, the muscles of her forearm tightened, then loosened. "The ALP repeated how adamant the Xerxians are about protecting the plains. But I think we'd be stupid to assume these agents don't have some technological advantage."

"I agree."

"What should we do?" Kelli finally turned to him, eyes creased with worry. "We can't stay here tonight."

"If we move onto the next town, they'll follow. Get us in the open and…" Although Jayd didn't know their specific orders, he had no doubt it boded ill for him and Kelli.

Her expression told him she thought the same thing.

"We have to take them out." He stated the obvious.

Kelli pressed her fingers to her mouth. "No. In good conscience, I can't kill them. They're agents. Like us. Just doing their job."

"Then we should march over and surrender ourselves to them."

"Impossible! We are so close to finding Ella. I can't give up now."

"Then what do you suggest?" Jayd crossed his arms. The fact that she was unwilling to kill them proved something subtle had happened in her thinking. She used to be the "get-it-done-by-any-means" operative. But something had changed since her arrival on Xerxes.

Something good.

Again peering at the couple, Kelli's lips pursed.

"You know," Jayd said, "they might not know what you look like." When she appeared puzzled, he explained how he had altered her Xerxian ID in the profiling database.

Kelli's eyes widened. "You're kidding."

"No." He grinned sheepishly. "That was when I was convinced I could single-handedly haul you back to Earth. And save both our bacon."

"Haul me?" She smirked. "I would've paid money to see you try."

"I'm sure."

Her expression faded, tightening into concentration. "We might be able to use that to our advantage." After a minute, she said, "I have an idea. If I do something wacko, please don't interfere."

"I'll try not to."

"Mind being the bait?"

"Love to."

Her brow clouded. "It could be dangerous. If they have orders to kill on sight."

"You said Xerxians frown on murder. I'll assume these agents know that too."

"It wouldn't be murder if they have permission from the High Council."

"Then I'm willing to gamble they won't kill me in the middle of a busy town square. In front of children."

Her lower lip caught in her teeth a second. "I hope you're right."

"What do you want me to do?"

"Wander into the town square and find a comfortable place to watch the show. Obviously keep an eye on them. I'll make my move in a few minutes after you settle."

He spread his hands. "And that's it?"

"I don't know exactly how this will play out. Be

prepared to disappear. We can meet up at the ravine if needed."

"You're the boss." Stepping closer, he deliberately came within inches of her. Jayd rested his hand on her waist. Would she pull away? She didn't. "You'll watch my back?"

Her gaze strayed to his lips and returned to his eyes. "As best I can." Her words came out in a whisper.

"Okay, then. Here goes." He nodded before strolling out of the temple into the town center. The townspeople all but ignored him. Several times, he'd seen first hand how the scent of incense heavy on clothing was a mark of honor. Every time Kelli finished her temple ritual, the Xerxians gave them space, a mute respect that lasted well after the fragrance dissipated.

Avoiding eye contact with the agents, Jayd casually filled his water pouch from the fountain in the center. He moved slowly as though he hadn't a care in the world. Xerxians would see it as contemplative. However, he was more interested in how the agents saw it. He made sure he didn't turn his back to the operatives, keeping a surreptitious eye on them.

All the while, they watched him. And Kelli, he hoped, observed them all.

Sighing loudly, he took a seat near a restaurant, in the shade of the building. Slowly he leaned back, pulling his hood up as though covering his eyes from the blazing sun so he could pray. Or doze.

Through the thin layer of material, he watched the couple move closer. Maintaining a safe distance, they shot several glances at each other as though deciding what to do. Their heads came together briefly, then the woman wandered away from her companion. To locate Kelli? He lost sight of the agent in the crowd.

He'd give it ten minutes. Then he would have to figure out a way to get back to Kelli without one or both of them on his heels. It might involve hurting the agents. As little as possible.

After glancing around, the man edged nearer. Tensing, Jayd prepared himself for anything. The agent strolled toward the restaurant and studied the posted menu, as though contemplating a meal. Someone else also stepped up to read the menu, standing close to the man.

With a start, Jayd realized it was Kelli. What was she doing? Why was she putting herself so blatantly in danger? Sliding his feet under the chair, he prepared to vault himself at the man if needed.

She suddenly screamed.

Chair crashing, Jayd shot to his feet.

"You dare touch me." Her Xerxian words pierced the sudden stillness of the town square. She slapped the agent's face, the sound like a thunderclap. "Vile *jeffira*."

Whatever she'd called him, Jayd's translator couldn't convert the word. Or wouldn't.

If he had any thoughts about her needing protection, they vanished the next second. A crowd immediately closed around them. Anger crackled in the air like static electricity. In moments, a mob surrounded Kelli and the agent who shrunk back like a trapped animal.

"I didn't—look, you're wrong." The man spoke in English.

Big mistake.

"I swear I didn't touch her." His hands raised in defense. Or surrender.

"You lie." Kelli's voice contained the right amount of contempt, her Xer flawless. "I am dishonored." She dropped her face into her hands while a single sob escaped.

"He wears no symbol," someone in the crowd said, spurring the growing outrage.

"No symbol?" The words were repeated, indignation spiraling out of control.

A woman, clearly one of authority, spoke up and hushed the crowd. "Who vouches for this male?" She looked around.

No one answered.

"Will anyone vouch for him?"

Someone had better answer quickly. The man clearly was in trouble.

Finally, a woman raised her voice. "I do. I vouch for him." Her words were passable Xer.

As the crowd parted, the female operative stepped forward.

"What have you to say about his actions?"

"I beg to speak to you in private." The woman spoke in a low voice, still in Xer.

"The crime was public. Therefore what you have to say will be in public as well."

The woman's jaw jutted. "If my companion says he didn't touch the woman, then he didn't."

"You dare cast aspersions on an honored member of our community?" The town leader drew herself up. "How do you explain his, and your, lack of symbols?"

"We are not of this world. We seek—"

"Yet you come here and presume upon our hospitality? And break our laws? There will be retribution."

Several Amazons grabbed the arms of the two agents.

"Time to go." Kelli appeared at Jayd's side and tugged at his sleeve.

He almost felt sorry for the pair. The look of panic on their faces said it all. Do nothing and they faced some unknown punishment. Fight to escape and they would cause an intergalactic incident.

When they were well away from the town, Jayd said, "That was brilliant."

"You think so?" She flashed him a smile.

"I know so." He blew out a breath of relief. "Glad you're on my side."

"Glad you're on mine."

They kept up a brisk pace, putting as much distance as they could between them and the town.

"What're they going to do to him?" Jayd panted after they'd sped-walked a few miles.

"He might be flogged. After all, he dishonored a female." Her mouth pulled to one side at the obvious lie.

"Poor fool."

Kelli slowed. "However, the incident might be dropped since I won't be present to testify. The Xerxians are fair people."

"Then what? So we gained a few hours? Guess it's better than nothing, but they'll still come after us."

"I don't think so. Those two have to reveal who they are. And why they appear to be Xerxian. *Why* they're here will make little difference to these towns-people at this point. Even if there is no proven crime, they made several capital errors."

"Such as?"

"Pretending to be Xerxian. I gather that is frowned upon. It would explain why the learning program is so quiet about some aspects of this society. Xerxians are very private people. The treaty ensures we respect their laws."

"Okay," he drew out the word. "So what'll happen to them?"

"I'm guessing they will be escorted back to Xer Prime and be 'invited' to depart."

Jayd chuckled. "As I said, brilliant."

Her eyes gleamed. "Yeah, not bad, I guess."

It was better than *not bad*. The morning's adventure at least got them talking to each other again.

He waited a few minutes before saying, "We would be foolish to assume they're the only two agents." His assistant's communiqué didn't specify how many operatives were sent.

Kelli's mouth settled in grim lines. "The thought did cross my mind."

"We're going to have to be more cautious."

She shot him a look, but merely nodded.

The next ones they encountered might not be as foolish. Or so easy to entrap.

Chapter 19

"Welcome. Welcome to my temporary home." The guide they'd been searching for invited them to sit in the dusk of the evening outside an isolated and modest cottage. A circle of benches surrounded a large fire pit. "You must be the ones my sister told me of."

Kelli glanced at Jayd. How had the woman known they were coming? No one had passed them on their trek to the nearby town where she lived.

"You needn't be surprised." The woman smiled. "We have our ways."

Kelli thought it impolite to ask. Sitting by the fire, she enjoyed the warmth. This remote village was along the side of a mountain. The evening was considerably cooler than the nights they'd spent at a lower elevation.

The guide was tall, extremely lithe and clearly used to an active lifestyle. Her face was lined with proof of many years of travel, yet her expression revealed a serene kindness that Kelli found appealing. She noted too that the woman had an earring that indicated her guide position—a bird symbol overlaying what appeared to be a sun and a single moon.

So was that how they communicated? By carrier birds?

"Your Companion may share the warmth." The woman graciously invited him closer.

"You do me honor." Kelli pressed three fingers to her chest and bowed. Though she nodded for Jayd to take a seat, he remained further back from the women out of respect. He had learned well.

The guide threw a stick into the fire. "My sister said you were not raised on our world?"

"That is correct." Kelli again repeated the story about her mother dying at a young age. Like others, she let the guide assume her parents had relinquished their Xerxian citizenship.

"Ah, that clarifies some things in my mind." The woman threw another branch into the roaring blaze. "Tell me what you wish to know."

Kelli moistened her lips. "I understand that about sixty standard days ago you escorted a man and young girl across the plains."

The woman's expression hardened. "I did."

"I am seeking that little girl. She was wrongfully taken."

"I suspected as much. However, at the time, the man's story seemed plausible."

"But that changed?"

The guide threw in another stick. The flames roared. "He claimed to be her father. Yet I saw no affection for the girl. And when…" Her jaw hardened.

"I am sorry this memory brings you grief." Kelli spread her hands.

The guide nodded. "He hurt her. He thought I didn't notice. But he struck her secretly. It was not the first time. I noticed other bruises."

Eyes burning, Kelli sucked in a deep breath.

"I see you hold her with deep affection." The guide met her gaze squarely.

"He is…" She hesitated to use the phrase, but it was true. And the highest Xer insult. "He is an abuser of females." She clenched her fist as she imagined the noose again tightening around her neck.

"How can I help?"

"I must find this young girl. I hoped you could tell me where they went."

"I left them on the plains. A day's journey from here. I could not stay with him any longer. I prayed for the child. But I could not help that father one more hour."

"He is not her father." Kelli spoke through clenched teeth.

"Oh, God of the heavens." The guide looked to the sky, eyes filling with tears. She pressed her fingers together as though in prayer. "I am sorry I helped him at all."

"You could not have known. He is an evil man.

Full of violence."

The guide met her gaze. "I must alert my leader. She must be told—"

"No, I beg you." Kelli held open her hands. "If he learns he is being followed, I don't know what he'll do to the child."

The woman's eyes widened. "Then what? I cannot stand by and do nothing."

"We will continue the search. I believe secrecy is the best way to protect this girl. And to rescue her."

She slowly nodded. "I see the wisdom in your plan." She pressed her lips together, apparently weighing the options.

Kelli took a breath, hoping she wasn't saying too much. "My companion and I are specially trained to deal with men of his character. We will find him and bring him to justice."

That decided it, apparently. The guide rose. "I will help you."

Kelli threw Jayd a look. "Our road may be dangerous. I could not ask you to risk your safety as well."

The woman smiled. "There is another way I can assist. Come." She led them around the back of her home. "I am a guide. I do many things in my profession." She drew closer to a small shed where small chirping sounds came. The guide laid her hand on the wooden door. "I also tend the carrier birds for several villages. This is how we communicate quickly across the plains."

Kelli smiled when her suspicions were confirmed.

"I will send messengers at first light and find where the man and girl have gone."

"Thank you." Relief welled up inside. She smiled at Jayd, hoping it expressed her joy. At long last!

"In the meantime," the guide continued, "I ask that you be my guests tonight. My cottage is humble, but you would honor me by taking my room. I will sleep by the fire."

Kelli squelched her protest. To refuse would be an insult. "You do us both honor." With her heart singing, she bowed deeply.

"Jayd? Are you awake?" Kelli's soft voice reached through the darkness while he lay on the cottage floor.

Since retiring to the single bedroom, they'd been quiet. The privacy this arrangement afforded both soothed and tortured him. For over an hour he had feigned sleep as he listened to her every sigh. Every creak of the bed.

Keeping his back to her, he disciplined himself to face the wall. Though she was out of sight, he could not forget she was behind him.

We're alone.

The memory of her lips continued to torment him. How she'd felt in his arms. The way her body had pressed against his. Her hands on his skin.

How easy it would be to capitulate to his desires.

"Jayd?"

He should continue to pretend he didn't hear her, the sanest thing to do.

No good. "What's the matter?"

Kelli stirred. "I can't sleep." She padded across the

floor and sat next to him.

He tensed. Though darkness filled the room, he could tell she was close. Her warmth radiated toward him.

Wary now, he sat up. Cold chilled his spine as he scooted back and pressed against the outside wall. "What's wrong? What's worrying you?"

She let out a breath, then took another. "God."

He couldn't have heard right. "What?"

"I said *God*. He is worrying me."

Knock me over with a feather…

"Promise you won't laugh, Jayd."

"Scout's honor."

"Please. No sarcasm either."

An element of urgency, almost desperation, rang in her voice.

"Okay." He spoke slowly, carefully. "No sarcasm."

For a few moments she didn't respond. He could tell she was wrestling with herself. Could tell by the rustle of clothing and the low sounds she made in her throat.

"You believe in God, right?"

Of course. But to admit that to Kelli was on par with *hari-kari.*

"Never mind. I know you do," she answered for him.

He remained mute.

"Ever since I've been on Xerxes… No, I should tell you what happened one of my first days here." She paused. "I met a woman in a temple who challenged me to ask God for something. And I did."

"What did you ask for?"

"A clue to help me find Ella."

He waited.

"Well, something happened that gave me an 'in' with the Xerxians. One thing let to another. And here we are."

"And you think they're not mere coincidences?"

"At first, I convinced myself it was because of my cleverness. Or ingenuity." She sniffed.

Tears? An unsteady breath met his ears.

"Now, I'm afraid to take credit."

He couldn't imagine her being frightened. Of anything. While undercover at SARC, she'd nearly single-handedly taken down one of the most corrupt men he knew. For her to admit fear about anything blew his mind.

She again sniffed. Waiting for his answer.

"Why afraid, Kel?"

"Because what if God *did* answer my prayer? I mean, I've prayed that same thing each time I've gone to a temple. And every day, we've learned something important. Something that leads us closer to Ella."

Still cautious, he said, "Then I guess you'd better thank Him for it."

Something scraped as she shifted. "I have."

"Are you admitting you believe in God?"

"I think so." She sucked in a huge breath, then released it. "Yes. I do. Now."

Wow. Really? He tamped down an urge to shout, "Hallelujah."

Thank You. Thank You, God!

"That doesn't mean I buy the whole Jesus and Bible package." Her sharp tone punctured his joy. "So don't launch into a sermon."

That's exactly what he'd planned to do. He clenched his teeth. Without the Savior, Kelli had embraced a mere fraction of the truth.

Sensing the conversation wasn't over, he waited.

What can I say, Lord? Please give me wisdom.

He stared into the black void where her face should be. "What else worries you, Kel?"

She took so long to answer that he wondered if she would.

Finally, she said, "I've had this recurring nightmare." She cleared her throat and rushed on. "I'm running in this black mist. I think I'm heading toward light. But the further I go, the darker it gets. And it closes in on me. Like—like the fog has fingers. I can't breathe. I can't get away. Then I wake up."

"And you think this nightmare has something to do with God?"

"Yes. No." She made a sound of frustration as she rose. "I don't know." Her footsteps padded away from him.

Jayd stood as well, feeling his way in the dark.

Inside, a rattle and a wooden creak sounded. The room flooded with light.

Kelli raised her face toward the moons, hands gripping the shutters. Light sculpted her features, illuminating her beauty. Her chest rose and fell as she gulped air. Never had she looked more desirable. Never had he loved her as much as now.

Did Kelli know how she affected him?

Transfixed, Jayd swallowed the hard lump in his throat. With an effort, he struggled to focus on her.

"Tell me," he said in a soft voice, "tell me more about your nightmare."

A trail of light followed a glistening tear as it slipped down her cheek. She turned to him. Without a word, she slipped into his arms. "Hold me, Jayd. Please." Her voice reverberated with suppressed fear. A deep tremor passed through her body.

How could he resist? Jayd wrapped his arms about her, trying to keep his imagination from leaping to other things. Impossible! His lungs felt overinflated. She trembled, her fingers restless against his chest.

"I worry that I'm running away from God." Kelli's voice grew muffled as she pressed her forehead to his shoulder. "What if that's why it gets blacker and blacker and I can't breathe?"

Unable to speak, he rubbed her back. It would be so easy tilt her head back and kiss her. Then tell her he'd made a mistake the other night. That he wanted to love her, fully. Right here, right now.

"I'm scared, Jayd. What if that isn't just a nightmare? What if I can never find my way out of the darkness?" She raised her head, allowing her hands to drop away from him as she pulled away.

Cool air rushed over him. With it came sanity. What was he thinking? To give in to desire would not only destroy her, but himself.

He stared out the window to the star-bedecked sky, fighting to get his mind and heart where they needed to be.

Help me, Lord.

In the quiet, an idea came to him.

"So, Kel, you admit God exists. But do you believe

He is personal?"

Head ducked, her body twitched as she visibly struggled to answer. "I don't know."

"You believe He cares for Ella. Do you think that's why He listened to your prayers?" When she said nothing, he added, "But what if He answered because He cares for you?"

She remained unmoving. Finally, her head shook. "I guess. Maybe." She raised her face. "But what does this have to do with my nightmare?"

He straightened. "Okay, say it's real. Say it proves you've been running away from God your whole life."

Her eyes grew wide, scared.

"Turn around. Run *to* Him. Ask God to reveal Truth."

She moved her shoulders as though frustrated. "How?"

"Invite Him. Invite Him to prove Himself to you, in a way that only He can. Ask Him to prove it *personally* to you."

She opened her mouth to reply, then shut it.

"Many people claim there is a God," he went on. "As a matter of fact, there's a verse that says even demons believe that. So your beliefs have to go further than merely acknowledging He exists."

Her shoulders hunched as she visibly shrank from Jayd. "Bible rhetoric. I told you—I don't believe those fairy tales."

"Fine." He spoke with as much seriousness as he could. "I dare you to ask Him. When God answers you, Kel—and I've no doubt He will—recognize that you'll have to make a choice. Continue to go your own way or surrender your will to His."

Brow furrowed, she stared at him. After what felt like minutes, she waved her hand in dismissal. "Okay, I'm done talking religion for the night. Let's go to bed."

Without another word, Kelli spun on her heel and settled on the wide cot. She scooted toward the opposite edge, hand resting on the space between them. Did he imagine it or was she inviting him to join her? In the dim light, he couldn't read her expression.

It didn't matter. He had to do what was right.

Clenching his fists, Jayd slowly backed away. After he settled on his bedroll, back again to her, he squeezed his eyes shut.

A sense of victory—for himself—washed over him.

Chapter 20

"So this is the progeny." Mitt Harker studied his daughter, disappointment flaring through him. From across the room, she huddled on a narrow pallet.

Like her mother, Ella was petite. However, she appeared rather mousey and tended toward skinniness. Probably because Aric's freakish mother had fed her nothing but health foods for the majority of her life. Not only that, the woman had isolated her on that ranch of hers in the middle of nowhere. Though the kid was seven, she seemed younger. Infantile. Repressed.

Pathetic.

Lonnie Krueger, his long-time friend, sat on a hard

wooden chair and planted his foot on the pallet's rough frame. The sparseness of the dwelling didn't appear to bother him. However, Mitt had learned years before that his friend was a man of simple tastes. Expensive ones, true. And definitely illegal. One of the reasons why they got along so well.

"You sure this whiny brat's yours?" Lonnie leaned back and balanced his chair on two legs.

"Oh, yes. DNA tests proved it." With his gaze still fixed on his daughter, Mitt took a seat on the only other chair. Ella continued to shrink away from them both, a thin blanket clutched to her chest.

Not that he expected any gush of daughterly emotion from her. But where was her backbone?

That would change. Once he resettled her in his new house, he'd toughen her up.

As though she'd heard his thoughts, she started to quietly snivel. He turned away.

Lonnie let the chair thump as it settled on all four legs. "So what's the plan?"

"Get that green goop off your skin. And return your eyes to normal. Those black ones are unsettling."

His friend grinned. "Sounds like a good start."

"Next I'll set you up in a cushy house, off this stinkin' planet." The odor of Xerxian incense gave Mitt a headache. The smell of that stuff was everywhere.

"Better and better."

"I have nearly everything arranged on Keelias IV."

Lonnie frowned. "Not Earth?"

"For now, too dangerous. But no worries." He grinned, knowing his buddy grew weary of his monkish existence. "You'll like it there. I'm lining up all sorts of distractions for you. And on Keelias, pretty much anything goes."

"Excellent."

"The place is nearly ready with all the high-tech toys you could wish."

Best part—it was a write-off for Mitt.

Lonnie slapped him on the back. "My kind of friend." His smile vanished as he glared at Ella who continued to whimper. "Shut up. Or else."

She pressed the blanket to her mouth, muffling her mewl.

"Internal security will be tight," Mitt continued. "You won't have to worry about watching the kid day and night." He glanced at his daughter. "I have only one condition—don't molest her."

"I haven't." His friend's lip curled. "You think I want a dozen hyper-hormonal Xerxians descending on this shack? I couldn't take them all out."

Mitt chuckled. "Should've trusted you'd never endanger this operation."

His friend smirked. "I'll continue guarding that treasure until you say otherwise."

"Good. The payoff will be worth it." Mitt rose. Already he had ideas how to use the girl to hurt Aric. His ex would pay for stealing what was rightfully his for all these years.

Lonnie slowly rose and stretched. "What's our time table?"

"We're stepping it up. We need to finish our business here. And soon."

"Why's that?"

"Intergalaxia hasn't apprehended those missing

operatives. Agent Song and..." Mitt waved his hand, "and whatever her name is. The one Barkley hates so much." He didn't add, *"The one you failed to kill."*

Despite that one error, Lonnie had followed orders perfectly. It wasn't his fault Barkley's men had flubbed everything else. The waiters hadn't drugged that female agent enough so Lonnie could easily dispatch her. Then they tried to double-cross him by taking Ella. Stupid mistake for them to believe Lonnie would be an easy mark.

It no longer mattered. Mitt got what he wanted and Barkley could rot in prison for all he cared. The ex-director of SARC wasn't even a consideration, especially since he was serving multiple life sentences.

"Think those missing agents might be here on Xerxes IX? Or at the space station?"

"Hard to say." Regardless, Mitt didn't plan to hang around and find out. "I'm arranging for a temporary house in Xer Prime—one that's better than this dump. Be a day or two before something decent is ready. We'll stay only long enough until we can make the move to Keelias IV."

"Can't wait."

Mitt nodded. "Be patient a little longer. The rewards will be incredible."

"You've always been a man of your word."

They shook hands and Mitt departed.

As he puffed up the steep street to Xer Prime, he grinned at his friend's comment. A man of his word? Not with the number of women Mitt had lied to over the years. Aric had been one of many. Unfortunately she had developed an annoying conscience while they were married. When she continually challenged his ethics, he was forced to dump her.

But this matter of their offspring—she should never have withheld Ella from him. That was unforgivable.

The trick would be to taunt her with enough hints that her daughter was alive. He had no doubt he could continue to outsmart Intergalaxia and even Aric's new super-spiffy USF husband. Letting Reese adopt Ella had been a stroke of genius. No one would believe that Mitt—the disinterested biological father—was the guilty party.

Too bad he couldn't bate her with what kind of world Ella would grow up in. He would love to wipe Aric's holier-than-thou expression from her face.

But even from a distance, payback would be immensely gratifying.

Sitting at the cottage's rough wooden table, Kelli stared into her tea. Why couldn't she shake this melancholy? Despite the conversation she and Jayd had the night before, uncertainty continued to nag her. And fear?

It was bad enough that Ella and her kidnappers had continued to elude her, but a bigger worry dogged Kelli. What if God wanted nothing to do with her? What if she continued to run in the darkness and He let her be permanently lost?

Rising, she paced as she waited to hear from the guide. Jayd had made himself scarce, leaving her alone to fidget and stew.

Taking her teacup, Kelli returned to the bedroom and leaned on the windowsill. Their midnight conversation haunted her. She thought admitting to believing in God would have elicited excitement from Jayd. Instead, his words had thrust worry deeper into her core.

Was God as cruel as she'd once believed? If He was as all-powerful as some said, then why had He let His Son be crucified?

"Are You really a God of love?" The breeze seemed to carry away her words. "How can I trust You?"

The door to the cottage banged open.

"We found them!" The guide's voice filled the cottage.

Leaving her tea on the windowsill, Kelli bolted to meet her. "Where? How far?"

"Have you a map?"

"Yes." She rushed back to the bedroom and rummaged through their possessions. In no time she returned, paper rattling as she unfolded the well-used chart.

Out of breath, Jayd appeared in the doorway. Had he heard their voices and run to hear the news?

"There." The guide pointed in triumph to a cliff town.

"Below Xer Prime." She stared at Jayd. "All this time…"

Impulsively, she hugged the guide. "Oh, I'm sorry. That's a Terran custom of happiness." She wasn't sure if she insulted the Xerxian or not.

The woman smiled. "It is a good one."

"Thank you so much for your help. We should get started right away." They had almost a three-day trek ahead of them to reach the Great Lift.

"Let me give you provisions for your trip."

"But you've already done so much."

"I insist. I am overjoyed that your journey will end successfully."

They quickly gathered their things. In no time, they were ready to depart.

Outside, the woman waited with a sack of food. "I will send word to my fellow guide to expect you. She will help you in whatever way you need."

"Thank you. Thank you again." Kelli could not bow low enough.

The woman surprised her by giving her a hug. "I share your happiness."

They set off. Before plunging down the hill, she waved once more to the guide.

"Whoa," Jayd said after they were beyond the village border. "At this pace, we'll get there by nightfall."

"Fine by me."

"We need to reserve some energy for what lies ahead."

She laughed. "I have more than enough!"

Her heart thrilled at the new information they'd gotten. So close. *So* close! The months of worry would soon pay off. She could taste success.

"Have you a plan once we find them?"

"Oh, yeah." She clenched her teeth. "Pummel the jerk who tried to kill me. Find Ella. Leave."

"Oh, good. I thought it was going to be a lot more complicated than that." His voice dripped with sarcasm.

She laughed again. Nothing, not even his biting

humor, would spoil her happiness.

"And we'll just walk off the planet once we get Ella?"

"Sure, Mr. Smarty." She bit her lip to hide her smirk.

"What are you not saying, Ms. Layne?"

Swinging around, she walked backwards in front of him. "That I have our escape route already planned out. It's a done deal, really. We snatch Ella, ride the shuttle to the outpost where I have a private ship already waiting."

"A private ship?" His surprise was comical. "You bought one?"

"No, silly. I rented it."

"How much did that cost? And where did you get the money?"

"I didn't steal it, if that's what you're implying." Withholding the truth, making him beg, was delicious. Kelli turned again to walk normally.

"I know what your USF salary is. There's no way you could've afforded that on your own." He clucked his tongue. "Okay, I give. You won."

She sighed happily. "I've waited a long time to hear you say that, Jayden Song."

"And you just did. Now tell me."

"My father's safety deposit box."

She again surprised him. Knew he had no idea what she was talking about.

"What was in it?"

"Money. *Loads* of it."

"I thought he passed away years ago. Why am I just now hearing about this?"

She felt as though a shadow passed over her. "He told me about the box before he died. I figured he'd stashed money in it. But I had no idea how much. Truthfully, I didn't even want to open it. And I didn't. Until recently."

Jayd appeared to absorb what she said. "That angry at him, hmm?"

"I hated him."

"For?"

She struggled to answer. "Since he insisted I get the best education, I spent most of my childhood in boarding schools. And while I was away, my mom died." She paused to swallow a couple times. Why did that bother her so much to admit it? "I didn't even know she was sick."

When he remained silent, she risked a glance at him. "Okay, go ahead and psychoanalyze me. I can take it."

"I'm just putting together what I've suspected for years. That's all."

She stopped in front of him, spreading her hands to keep him from walking on. "And that is?"

His eyes narrowed. "That all your life you've believed in God's existence. However, you think He's like your earthly father. That's why you've rejected Him all these years."

She'd been prepared for almost anything, except that. Instead of retorting, or punching him, she spun and walked away.

Was it true? If God was nothing like her father, then who was He? She had no frame of reference to figure that out.

Jayd wisely said nothing more. Good thing. She would have definitely punched him.

"We're being tailed." On the second day of their trip, Jayd jabbed a thumb at the empty road behind them. Correction, it might look empty, but he was certain it wasn't. A couple times he thought he caught a glimpse of someone who ducked out of sight.

"I wondered." Kelli glanced back. "I've had a creepy feeling all morning."

"Can we abandon the roads? Cut across to the next town?"

"Think that's wise?"

"We can lose 'em if we do." At least he hoped.

"With our compass and map, it should be no problem to stay on course."

Jayd nodded.

They found a perfect spot later in the morning as they trudged up a huge hill. A town perched in the distance. Once on the backside of the mound, they would be out of sight of their trackers for many minutes. One side of the road was lined with thick trees. Would their followers assume they had continued their way into town? Jayd hoped so. By the time they realized their error, he and Kelli would have a good head start. And maybe shake them?

"Let's do it. Now." Jayd hurried down the hill at breakneck speed, Kelli right behind him. With no one in sight, they plunged into the woods. He paused to cover their tracks, then they sprinted through the brush.

Both of them were panting hard by the time they stopped. Mutely, he signaled to wait a few minutes to catch their breath. When they were both ready, they took off again, jogging as long as possible. They pushed hard, not even talking. Kelli consulted their map and compass a few times to make certain they headed in the right direction.

"We'll lose a few hours. Traveling this way. Even jogging." She waved the map, clutched in her fist. "And the terrain gets rougher. In a few hours."

"It's safer this way." Jayd kept his voice low.

They paused to consume a light snack, hiding behind a large fallen tree. Every nerve in his body felt stretched tautly. *Someone* was out there. Someone who hadn't been fooled very long by their slipping into the woods. He could feel it. "Let's move."

Kelli shoved the rest of her fruit into her mouth and gulped. "Ready."

Again they covered any evidence of their passage.

After they were on their way for a little while, he said, "Let's not rest again until we have to."

"Agreed."

They pushed themselves the rest of the day, not stopping until nightfall. The forest grew too treacherous to continue traveling in the dark.

Kelli grabbed his sleeve, forcing him to stop.

Catching his breath, he waited for her to speak.

"Not far from here is a deep ravine. We risk breaking our necks. We have to stop."

He nodded, feeling like every sound they made reverberated in the woods. Drawing closer, he resorted to a whisper. "Anything dangerous living above?" He pointed upwards.

"No."

"Let's climb one tree. No, make that two. Split up. Keep your ears open." He was glad she didn't protest or argue. Did she sense the tension? The danger?

Kelli took one of the bundles.

"Tie it out of sight," Jayd breathed. "And make sure to lash yourself securely to a tree. Oh, trade your blue outer robe for the dark one."

She nodded. Though he was over-instructing her, he couldn't help it. After slinging the bag over her shoulders, Kelli located a huge tree. Jayd watched her dark silhouette ascend until she disappeared. Following her example, he shimmied up a nearby tree. Once he was high enough, he took his pocketknife and sliced off the hem of his robe to use as rope. First he secured his bag, then lashed himself to the trunk. He settled as comfortably as possible, telling himself that he needed to rest, if not sleep.

Squinting across the dark expanse, he looked for Kelli. Was that her form, balancing on a large branch? He wanted to call to her and tell her to sleep well, but prudence forbade it.

Sighing, he closed his eyes.

The next minute, he came to. Gray light filtered through heavy branches above. Had he really dozed through the night? He vaguely remembered waking several times, but always returned to sleep.

After untying himself and his bundle, he clambered down. Stiff muscles protested, but he ignored the discomfort. Time was wasting. He needed to get Kelli going as soon as possible. While Jayd stood at the base of his tree, a rustling sound made him freeze. A stealthy step was moving his direction.

Kelli? He remained still, listening.

There it was again.

Everything in him said something was wrong. To move. *Now.*

He shuffled to one side, intending to put the tree between him and the noise. A popping in the distance made him lunge sideways. Something bit into his forearm. Jayd flattened himself against the back of the tree, his heart wildly pumping.

Kelli! He wanted to shout a warning, but dared not. Whoever was out there would get her too.

His arm started to burn. In agonizing pain. Through a haze of torment, he saw a small dart protruding from his sleeve.

Chapter 21

A bursting sound, like a balloon popping, jerked Kelli from sleep. What was that? Disoriented, she remained motionless until she got her bearings. Was it morning already? She straightened, then grabbed for support as a wave of vertigo hit her. Oh, right. She had slept in a tree. As she stretched out one leg to relieve the stiffness, her and Jayd's exhausting flight rushed back at her. She struggled to untie the knot in the rope that secured her to the trunk. Taking care, she wrapped it about her waist. Instinctively she kept her movements slow and quiet.

Where was Jayd? She peered through the trees,

looking for him in the upper branches. He was nowhere to be seen.

The remembrance of that peculiar noise came back to her. What had she heard? She leaned forward and looked below. Morning light filtered to the dusky forest floor. Something caught her eye. Her blood ran cold as movement many yards away caught her eye. A gray form crept forward, advancing in her general direction. Kelli remained frozen, hardly daring to breathe. The person—it wasn't an animal—looked like he was carrying something. A weapon? He had to be an operative.

Jayd! Her mind screamed. Where was he?

The agent stopped and scanned the area, then looked up. Kelli pressed against the tree. Could he see her on the large branch? When she again heard his almost noiseless progress, Kelli again watched.

Something on the ground, many yards from her tree, fixed his gaze. She ducked her head to look. What she saw made her heart grow cold.

Jayd lay on the ground, flopped to one side. Unmoving.

No!

How…? Her mind slowed as the fear gripped her. Then it sped to an impossible speed. Even before contemplating the risk, she began to execute her plan. Emotion shut off. Survival kicked into high gear.

While his attention is fixed on Jayd, climb down. Now. Approach from the left. Use the large boulder as cover. Then the tree over there. Watch for fallen leaves. There are fewer on that side. Approach the attacker from his right.

Other details filled in, her mind gauging time and

distance without conscious thought. Before she realized it, she was halfway down the blind side of the tree.

The agent crouched, many feet from Jayd while Kelli mapped out her next move. Apparently the operative wasn't convinced it was safe to approach the sprawling form. She waited. When he moved, she did too. It was a *pas de deux* of death, with the man leading the dance's cadence. Each step allowed Kelli to draw closer. Finally, the agent reached Jayd, leaning to feel for a pulse.

Kelli sprang. Noiselessly.

The attacker turned. *Not a man.* With little effort, the woman deflected the incapacitating blow. Undeterred, Kelli attacked again.

Hurry. Another agent might be on his way.

The woman couldn't be much taller than five and a half feet, yet Kelli's height yielded no advantage. With lightning movements, the woman struck her torso in quick succession. In moments Kelli's aggression turned to defense. This operative was skilled. Tough. Kelli fell back a pace.

I cannot fail. She blocked, grappled. Determination thrummed in her ears. *Incapacitate her as fast as possible.* The woman's elbow glanced her jaw. For a moment, Kelli saw stars.

Breath came hard, grunts when she deflected blows. Resolve grew. She slowly pushed the woman down a slope. When Kelli slipped, the agent hit hard. Two punches to her side left her gasping. For a second, Kelli lowered her defenses. The agent used the opening to yank Kelli's collar. Her fist twisted. The tunic became a noose. She gagged.

No! Never again would she be strangled.

Kelli pretended to drop to one knee. Her other foot slid. The agent lost her balance. As soon as her grip loosened, Kelli swiveled. A jab with her elbow, punch to the chest, and the attacker fell back. Teetering, she clawed at air. Kelli saw her one second and the next, she disappeared over an edge. The woman didn't even cry out.

Panting hard, Kelli crouched. Was another agent nearby? Nothing could be heard but her stifled breathing. She rose and to peer into the dry ravine. Duskiness masked the bottom.

Thirteen feet below, the woman lay unmoving, leg bent at an impossible angle.

Two choices tore at Kelli. Go down or check on Jayd? Not a hard decision. Abandoning the woman, she ran up the hill.

Prudence urged her to slow when she realized another operative might be waiting. She crept back to where Jayd slumped, listening and watching. However, his prostrate form made her throw caution to the wind.

What difference did it make if something happened to her now? If he were dead…!

She couldn't think of that.

"Jayd. Please, please." Breath choked as she fumbled for his pulse. In relief, she stifled her cry. He was still alive. "Thank You, God."

She checked other vitals. Why was his heart rate so erratic? A quick body check revealed no wounds, no trauma. What had knocked him out? She tapped his shoulder hard and sharply spoke his name. No response. What had that agent done to him? Kelli had to find out.

Gently, she rolled him onto his back. Using his bag to prop up his knees, she carefully positioned his head to make him as comfortable as possible. Then she returned to their attacker.

The woman wasn't where she'd fallen. But she hadn't gone far. Groaning from exertion and pain, she pulled herself along the ravine floor. Kelli stepped in front of her after she determined the operative had no visible weapon. The woman might have a broken leg, but she wasn't going to give in easily. She thrashed to elude capture.

With ease Kelli subdued her and tied her hands. She patted her down to make certain the woman had no hidden weapons. Then she secured her to a sapling.

"Who are you?" Kelli didn't expect a response, and she didn't get one. "Where is your partner?" All the while, she crouched as she kept a lookout. "I asked you, where is your partner?"

Nothing. A grim determination settled over Kelli. Her course of action couldn't be helped. She rose and placed her foot on the woman's broken leg.

At the slightest contact, the agent gasped. Kelli hated to do it, but she had to know. She put a little more weight on the leg until the woman cried out. More pressure. More.

"I'm alone." The woman ground out the words in English, face white, body spasming.

Kelli lifted her foot, but she left it poised, ready to lean on it again. "Is your partner nearby?"

The woman shook her head.

"Is he in Xer Prime?"

"Don't know." The agent could barely speak.

"What did you do to Jayd? I won't ask again."

Panting, the agent threw her head back and grimaced. "Modified toxin. He'll wake. Soon."

Kelli could barely understand the jerky words. "I'll be back."

Again, she headed up the ravine's wall. After a quick check on Jayd, she climbed her tree and retrieved the other supplies. From it, she took the bedroll and a robe. She headed back to the woman. It took some time, but she tied the woman's two legs together, using the uninjured one as the anchor for a splint. One of Kelli's robes had to be sacrificed, the material turned into strips to use as more rope.

"What's your name?" Kelli asked. "First will do."

The woman clamped her mouth shut.

"Fine, I'll call you Connie." She recalled the name of a USF supervisor with whom she had once worked. As she tore the tunic into strips, she grunted. "She's stubborn too."

Finally, she was ready. After she positioned the woman's body on the bedroll, she secured her. Grunting, she heaved the agent up the ravine. The trip seemed to take forever. By the time they reached Jayd, Kelli dripped with perspiration.

After tying Connie to a nearby tree, she again checked him.

"Why won't he awaken?" She glanced back. The agent was staring at him as she lay propped on her side.

Glaring, Kelli rose and planted a fist at her hip.

Connie's eyes flickered to her, then back to him. "I have no idea."

"I don't have time for this." With deliberation, she stalked toward the woman.

The agent's eyes widened. "I told you, I don't know. I have no reason to lie. He should be awake by now."

Kelli evaluated the statements. Was it the truth?

"Where's your gear?" When she didn't answer, Kelli tilted her head as though staring down a naughty child.

"Behind me. Stashed in a hollow tree." Connie jerked her chin in the direction.

It didn't take long to locate the items. Kelli searched through the knapsack, hoping to find an anti-dote. Nothing. However, on the way back, she did find Connie's weapon, a crude air gun. It would explain the tranquilizer darts in the knapsack, probably over-looked by the Xerxian scan at the Great Lift.

Without a word, she retrieved the woman's canteen and held up Connie's head so she could drink. Though surprise etched her face, she didn't refuse.

"Hungry?" Kelli held up a nutrition bar.

The woman shook her head.

Squatting, Kelli ate her own food and debated what to do. She couldn't stay there. Both Jayd and Connie needed medical attention. She couldn't care for both, not with limited food and supplies. The woman said she was alone, but what if another agent was on his way? Kelli didn't relish the idea of torturing the wom-an for more information. It wouldn't change the fact that she needed to do something. Soon.

Kelli retrieved her map, then checked the position of the sun. It was still early morning. If she started out now, she could make it to the nearest road. A couple hours and she'd be back. But which invalid should she take?

Jayd was still unconscious. Sitting around, waiting for him to come to, would be foolish. Regardless, she couldn't leave Connie in the woods once he regained his senses. Assuming Kelli found a Good Samaritan, how could she describe Connie's location? Or answer the inevitable questions that were sure to follow?

Too much time would be wasted. They didn't have that luxury.

That meant taking the woman. Leaving her beside the road would give her the best chance of getting the help she needed.

However, Kelli agonized over deserting Jayd, even for a few hours. She racked her mind for all that she'd learned from the ALP, verifying again that no predator would attack him while he was vulnerable. Then she placed some of the agent's food packets and a water pouch within reach. After checking his pulse, she rose. Another few minutes were spent securing the rest of their food high in a tree. After stuffing a few bars into her pocket, Kelli slung the other water pouch and canteen over her shoulders. The map and compass were pocketed as well.

She untied the woman from the tree. "Time to go."

Eyes wide, Connie didn't reply.

Kelli didn't relish the idea of carrying the agent, but it was the fastest way to move her. The clock was ticking.

She took a moment to explain what she was going to do. Any movement would cause Connie pain, but it couldn't be helped. With much effort, Kelli positioned the woman on her shoulders.

They started out, the agent's shallow breathing betraying the depth of her pain. Kelli steeled her emotions to what she must be suffering. Trying not to jar the woman, she hurried through the woods, but the burden of carrying the woman sapped her energy. After a half hour, she had to set Connie down and take a break.

"Why are you doing this?" The agent's dark brown eyes bore into hers.

It was Kelli's turn to not answer.

"You should leave me."

"Don't tempt me." Kelli flexed her shoulders. Weariness hammered her body. Her ankle protested, throbbing from the extra weight.

Connie mouth tightened. "If you re-splint my leg, I could ride piggy back. It would be easier on you."

"But for you, more painful."

The woman shrugged.

Kelli considered. What she said was true. But could she trust the woman? She didn't like her throat being vulnerable. In seconds, she made up her mind.

Branches were plentiful. In no time, she'd done as Connie suggested. As she worked, she said, "You probably know none of this. And maybe don't care. But we got a lead on the man who kidnapped Ella Reese. They are both here on Xerxes IX." She paused when Connie moaned as she bound her leg. "I know you're merely doing your job, but I'm not your enemy." She met her gaze. "If I was, you'd be dead."

The woman said nothing, but Kelli could tell she was pondering her words.

She assessed the agent. Probably Intergalaxia. She was small, wiry. Extremely athletic. For some reason, she reminded Kelli of Aric. They were about the same height with long brown hair. However, this woman had brown eyes and a heart-shaped face. Kelli committed her features to memory in case she ran into her again in the future. Unlikely. Inter-G operatives were more elusive than USF.

Though the going was still rough, the arrangement was a little easier on her. She was never so happy to see the trees thinning. Finally, they broke through the brush to a road. She lowered Connie to the ground, then sat a short distance away to catch her breath.

The woman's face was pinched, lips white. She was one tough lady.

After Kelli's heart rate slowed, she tossed a couple food bars and the canteen at the woman. "Someone should come along soon. They'll get you medical help."

The agent nodded.

Kelli rose and stretched, not allowing herself the luxury of resting too long. Quickly, she cut Connie's bonds, then backed away. She still didn't trust the woman, even with a broken leg.

"Check my knapsack for an analgesic," she surprised Kelli by saying. "When Song comes to, give it to him. It'll help."

Out of habit, she bowed the traditional Xer way.

She'd taken a couple steps when she heard, "The name's Eva."

Merely grinning, Kelli plunged into the brush.

Jayd was awake when she returned. But somehow he looked worse, not better.

"I was worried." He stopped, pulling his legs up as he clutched his middle.

"Where does it hurt?" Kelli tore through Eva's knapsack, looking for the analgesic.

"Left arm. Abdomen." Jayd grunted from the effort of talking.

After she found the meds, she gave him the maximum dose. She tugged at his shirt to remove it. On his forearm was a wound, swollen and angry looking. "Does this hurt?"

Face tight, he merely nodded.

Because Jayd was more versed in medicine, she asked, "Should we treat the wound? You were injected with a modified neurotoxin."

"No. Might make it worse."

"Think you can walk? We have to move. Eva knows our location."

"Eva?"

"The one who did this to you."

A weak smile passed over his pale lips. "Remind me to never make her mad."

After Kelli gathered their things, she decided to leave the extra clothing. She also abandoned most of Eva's possessions, taking only the pain meds and food.

Finding a hollowed tree, she stuffed the items. After consulting the map again, they set off in the opposite direction from where she had left Eva. It would add time to their trip, but would be safer. Everything in Kelli said to hurry. To get out of there. Get as far from this place as possible.

When Jayd complained of abdominal cramping as well as pain where the dart had penetrated, she put her arm about him. Because of the increased activity, the toxin was probably spreading more rapidly through his system. But what choice did they have?

They reached the ravine and traveled along the bottom.

"We'll stop soon," she promised.

His body periodically convulsed. She noted with alarm that he'd begun to perspire, more than usual given the warmth of the day. When he grew disoriented, she found a place to stop. She could not keep pushing him.

Again she made him as comfortable as she could, forcing him to drink water. He refused food.

"I'll be back soon, Jayd. I promise."

From a sitting position, he looked at her with glazed eyes.

She knelt by his side. "Please, rest." On impulse, Kelli leaned forward and kissed his forehead.

"Do that again and I promise to never move." He smiled weakly.

She didn't hesitate. Leaning forward, she let her lips linger on his skin. Her fingers smoothed the nape of his neck. How she wished...

"Worth it all." Jayd spoke with his eyes closed.

When she tried to rise, his hand gripped her arm.

"Kel." His eyes fluttered opened. "Love—love you…so much." His eyelids appeared weighed down as his hold slackened.

Her heart squeezed impossibly tight. "I love you too." She traced her fingertips over his forehead and cheek.

He went limp, head lolling back. For a moment longer, she watched him before rising. She hurried away to remove any trace of their passage. Then she forged another trail to throw off any followers. Finally, she returned to Jayd's location.

He was gone.

Chapter 22

Kelli panicked. Had an agent apprehended him? She ran around the area, looking for another set of footprints. Nothing. Where was Jayd? Her heart rate pounded out of control.

Slow down. Being in a hurry wouldn't help. After backtracking a third time, she studied the spot where she'd left him. No extra tracks. Had Jayd covered his trail? Perhaps he feared he was being followed and his training had clicked in. She swept the area, moving with cautious. Yes! Faint signs showed he had traveled down the ravine, but he had hidden the evidence. Not too far away, the faded blue of his tunic caught her eye.

She ran to him.

What had happened? He was flopped over a tree stump, unconscious. And he had vomited.

"Jayd. *Jayd!*"

At first, he didn't respond. His eyes flickered open. He stared at her with unfocused eyes. Sweat drenched his skin and hair.

She grabbed his tunic and helped him stand. He rocked on his feet, then slumped against her.

"You're burning up."

Kelli helped him back to the bedroll while he leaned against her. As soon as he reclined, he started shivering violently. Though she wrapped him in a blanket, he kept drawing up his knees. He thrashed, flinging the blanket away.

"What did that toxin do to you?"

Face contorted, Jayd clutched his arm. Kelli rolled up his sleeve and looked at the wound. It was hot to the touch. A rash ringed the puncture site. She forced another dose of pain medication down his throat. Then she bathed his face and neck with water.

Dusk fell. Impotently she watched Jayd. Tremors racked his body. Under her fingertips, his pulse raced. By the time night fell, he was groaning. Relentless spasms consumed him. Kelli ground her teeth in helplessness.

In the darkness, loneliness shrouded her. Nothing she did appeared to help. Jayd's agony was her agony. And his symptoms were growing worse. Was he going to die? He had all the signs. In those solitary hours, she hugged herself.

I can't lose him.

One by one, the moons rose. Light filtered through the trees and painted the landscape in gold and purple. Time stood still while an endless night stretched before her.

He wouldn't make it until morning. Her mind raged against the unfairness of it all. Why did he have to die? It wasn't right.

As he moaned and writhed, she moved from his side. Sitting a few yards away, she merely watched, unable to tear her eyes away from the inevitable. Finally she could take it no more. After pacing away a few feet, she turned and trod back.

She looked up. "How can you allow this, God?" Now that she'd spoken, a rush of words followed. "If You're so good and loving, how can You let Jayd die? We're so close to rescuing Ella, yet You're going to take his life? If you're really God, You could stop this. You could save his life."

She marched back and forth, throwing invectives against God into the night sky. Finally, Kelli wilted, spent. The physical, mental and emotional toll overwhelmed her. Crumpled on the ground, she let emptiness consume her. Despair imprisoned her in the deadness of the night. All she could hear was her own staccato breathing and Jayd's groans. She pressed her face into the moist dirt. Her soul wailed in agony.

Couldn't God see what was happening?

Even the darkness is not dark to You, and the night is as bright as day.

The words of the psalm came back to her. He *did* see. Right now. Aghast at the thought, she looked up. "If You can see what's going on, then don't You care?"

Another line came to mind. *Rescue me, O God, out of the grasp of the ruthless man.*

He had. The remembrance, unbidden, came back to her. That night, God had not allowed her attacker to kill her. For whatever reason.

Kelli began to tremble.

"Ask Him to prove Himself." Jayd's words echoed in her thoughts. *"Ask Him."*

How did one go about praying in the middle of a forest on an alien planet? Would it be acceptable even if she wasn't in a temple? Kelli drew a shaky breath. Slumped on the ground, she again looked up to the star-sprinkled sky.

"Since You're real, God, prove it and heal Jayd."

No lightning split the heavens. No thundering voice pierced the stillness. Nothing. Her prayer felt so inadequate. Kelli had no right to ask for anything. And certainly God had no obligation to answer, especially a prayer that didn't sound sincere, even to her.

Out of the depths, I cried to Thee, O Lord.

Now she wished she'd read the rest of the psalm so she could remember what it said. *Out of the depths.* She felt as though she floundered in a deep pit. Lost. Uncertain. Stiffly, she rose. Picking out the brightest star, she spoke to it, haltingly, humbly. Tears drenched her words.

"I don't know how to ask. I know You see what's going on here. You must see how desperately Jayd needs You." She spread her hands, voice shaking. "I can't help him. So I ask. Please, God. I beg You to heal Jayd. Don't let him die. I couldn't bear it." She paused to kneel. "I surrender all to You. My life. My will. No matter what happens. Only please, *please* save Jayd."

Words faded. She had nothing left to say. Nothing left to ask. Kelli wiped tears from her cheeks. But an uncanny peace settled over her.

With unsteady legs, she tottered back to Jayd. Despite the occasional delirious groan, he appeared to sleep. Because his clothes were soaked with perspiration, Kelli covered him again with a blanket. After retrieving another, she curled against his side. She rested her arm on his chest, hoping the shared warmth would ward off the chill of the night.

Her body ached from the exertions of the day. Her ankle throbbed. She was beyond tired. Completely drained, not only physically, but emotionally and mentally. Still, Kelli didn't know if she would be able to sleep.

How precious are your thoughts to me, O God!

Could it be true? A resounding *yes* echoed in her as she pulled the blanket more closely around them. What a wonderful idea. God really cared for her?

How precious...

Sometime later, she started awake. Turned away, Jayd lay on his side, unmoving. He appeared to be resting. His skin felt warm. Finally! She repositioned herself to press against his back. Weary beyond measure, she again succumbed to sleep.

Jayd stirred as he grew aware of the warm body next to his. Cool morning air brushed his face as consciousness returned. Disorientation gripped him. What had happened? Some of the events from the day before returned. Did Kelli really sleep beside him? He lifted his head to look. Her face was lined with weariness. Anxious not to disturb her, he rose. Cramped muscles protested as he stretched. He felt as though someone had used a club to beat his lower back and thighs.

Consumed with how famished he suddenly was, he searched for something to eat in their bags. He gulped down a couple food bars, which eased his hunger. Afterwards, he walked about, loosening his stiffness.

At the sound of a small cry, he turned. Eyes wide, Kelli sat up, shock etching her face. Was someone behind him? Jayd wheeled around, prepared to defend himself. No one. Still, she stared.

He approached her. "You okay?"

She didn't answer.

"Kel?" He thought he understood her pinched expression. "Another bad dream?"

Her mouth moved as though she was unable to form words.

"Let me help you up." Jayd held out his hand to her. Slowly, she put her fingers in his and he lifted. He couldn't help it. He patted her hand and spoke to her like she was a child. "Worried we're not safe?"

"No, I..." She seemed unable to tear her gaze away. The muscles of her throat twitched.

"Want me to get you some breakfast?"

She blinked. "I guess. Sure."

While she ate, he collected their things and repacked everything. Still she remained silent, her expression strained.

He left her to her thoughts, whatever they might be. "When you're ready, I'm ready."

"I will be soon." Whatever was bothering her appeared to loosen its hold.

"How far do we have to go today?"

Moving in slow motion, she retrieved their map. "We should reach the Great Lift by afternoon, and an hour after that, the town we need."

"That's great. I hope the run-in with the agent didn't put us too far behind schedule." He smiled.

Again she got that taut look. "I hope not."

They headed out, Jayd asking her details about the agent she had called Eva. When Kelli mentioned the woman had admitted to using a modified neurotoxin, he whistled. "I'm allergic to most of them. Good thing she picked the wrong one. Would've killed me for sure."

Again her lips pressed tightly.

He rolled up his sleeve to look at the puncture wound. "Hey, look. Almost good as new." Nothing remained but a small red dot on his arm. His muscles were sore, but not bad.

That furrow again appeared in Kelli's brow.

What was wrong with her? He chalked it up to their falling behind schedule. His being down had made them late. Was she a little resentful he'd held them up?

By the afternoon they reached the Great Lift and retrieved the items they'd left at the checkpoint. An hour later, they reached the town and found the guide who had been expecting them. However, the woman had bad news.

"The girl is gone."

"What?" Kelli glanced at Jayd in alarm. "Where? When?"

"This morning." The guide's mouth tightened in disapproval. "A man, human, came with two Xerxian women. They took the girl away."

Face pale, Kelli shook her head. "Do you know where they went?"

"I'm sorry, I could not follow them."

"All our efforts. Wasted." Her shoulders slumped. Her glance at Jayd shouted an accusation. *It's all your fault.*

He stepped forward. "What about the Xerxian male who originally arrived with the girl? Did he go with them?"

The guide slowly shook her head. "I don't believe so. He may still be here in the town."

"Can you take us to where he lives?"

"I would be glad to."

Kelli's eyes gleamed again with hope. Perhaps all wasn't lost.

The guide showed them the man's house and after many thanks from them both, she departed. The building was situated on a corner lot, against the sheer wall of the plateau. It was the last dwelling in a row of attached houses, five in all.

Jayd pulled Kelli down an alley not far from the front door. "What do you think?"

"I think we should go in there and find out what happened to Ella."

He grinned. "Obviously."

"Part of me says to wait till night, but the other part

of me says we're running out of time."

"I vote we approach this guy sooner rather than later."

She nodded.

"But first, let's ascertain if he's home or not." He waited for her assent. "We don't want to scare him off. And we definitely don't want to end up on the wrong side of the Xerxian authorities."

"I'll do a perimeter search while you stay here. It might be too conspicuous if we both go."

Jayd pressed his back to the alley's wall. "If you're not back in fifteen, I'm coming to find you."

Hood pulled, he waited while Kelli sauntered away. A few passersby gave him odd looks but no one spoke to him. Lowering his head, Jayd pretended he was contemplating the stone streets. All the while, he kept glancing at the house. No movement. No one appeared to be home. He estimated nearly fifteen minutes had passed when a man walked boldly to the front door and entered the house.

Was that Kelli's attacker? The night of the kidnapping, he hadn't gotten a good look at the man who'd fled down the hallway.

Time crawling, he waited a few more minutes. Scattered clouds darkened the sky, putting him on edge. Where was Kelli?

He had to take a chance. After leaving his post, he took care approaching the dwelling. Inside, a light appeared behind drawn curtains. Pacing slowly, Jayd headed towards the rear of the house. He noted the small walk space between the building and rock wall. At the back was a half-opened window. Had Kelli gone inside?

Jayd retraced his steps, trying to see inside the windows. All were covered by shutters or curtains. As he again moved toward the back, a muffled cry met his ears. Kelli! Without another thought, he rushed toward the open window. He vaulted himself into a small pantry.

On the floor above, he heard a scuffle. Another muted cry, a woman's, and several thuds. Heart hammering, he barreled through several doors. He flew up the stairs, ears attuned to the hard panting and grunts of pain. He rounded a corner and found Kelli and a man wrestling. Before Jayd could intervene, she flipped him on his face and knelt on his back. She gripped the man's arm, his thumb bent at a painful angle while his cheek ground into the floor.

"Where is she?" Her panting voice grated with enough menace to make Jayd back up.

"Kel? You okay?"

She looked up, face relentless in the dim light. "Yeah, I am. But he *won't* be if he doesn't answer in five seconds." She jerked. The guy yelped.

"Hang on." Jayd spoke in a soothing voice. "You sure you got the right guy?"

"Oh, I'm sure."

After finding a light switch, he flicked it on. He chuckled at the now visible details.

The large man, pinned to the floor, sported a split lip and blooded mouth.

And Jayd had worried about Kelli?

He squelched his humor. First things first. "Anyone else here?"

"No."

"Anyone else expected?" He asked their prisoner.

"Answer him." With her free hand, Kelli seized his hair and thumped his face into the floor.

"No. No!"

"No, what?" She thumped him again.

"Nobody else. I'm by myself. I was just getting my stuff."

"He secured?" Jayd asked Kelli. "I'll find something to tie him up so we can have a nice chat."

Face gleaming in understanding, Kelli nodded.

He found some bedding and shredded it, fashioning enough rope to hold their man. In minutes, they secured him to a chair, hands bound to the armrests and feet tied to the legs. He glared at them with one eye, the other nearly swollen shut.

Jayd stepped back. "It's him?"

"I found a girl's tunic and pants," Kelli said. "And this is the guy who nearly killed me." She pointed to his ring, a gold band with a deep red stone. "I recognize that."

The guy's eyes widened.

"Oh, yeah." A muscle in Kelli's cheek tightened. "You're gonna wish you'd done the job right when you had the chance."

"You planning to kill him?" Jayd asked.

"Of course." Her voice dripped with sweetness. "Just not right away."

"We really should trade his life for info. You know, like who hired him. Where the girl was taken. What their plans are."

"No way." Kelli placed her hands on her hips. "I

am gonna kill him. Nice and slow. But first, I want to make him cry like a baby." She smiled grimly. "We still have that med kit, right? After I wound him a little, I'll patch him up, then go at it again."

The man's eye bulged with fear. Already, the psychological torture bored into his mind.

"You really shouldn't, Kel. After all, you are an official government agent."

"Not anymore. And I have no qualms using my training to hurt this guy." She flexed her wrists. Then she stretched, grunting in satisfaction. "I've been looking forward to this for a long time." She licked her lower lip in anticipation.

Jayd sighed. "All right. I guess you won't be dissuaded. So what's your plan?"

She smiled beatifically. "First, I'll break his fingers. One at a time. Every single bone. Won't take much effort. But it's gonna really hurt." Her smile faded. "He won't be choking women again. As a matter of fact, if I let him live, his hands would be pretty useless."

"Hmm. Effective." Jayd glanced at their prisoner. Sweat burst out on the man's forehead and ran down his nose. "Sure we can't trade his life for info?"

"Life? I don't know. You really want to let this scumbag live?"

"He might be the way we could get you reinstated with USF."

"Nah. I don't care about my job anymore. Besides, look at him. He won't talk."

"Well, 'twas an idea." Jayd straddled a chair and rested his forearms across the back. "Mind if I watch? I might learn something new."

"Sure. Although, you might not like part two. It involves removing small, unnecessary body parts. Well, unnecessary at first. Then I'll go for the more important ones." Kelli pulled out her pocketknife and began running it along the stone wall.

"What are you doing?"

"Dulling it up so it'll hurt a lot more. I'll probably have to saw a bit, but that'll be more fun. For me, anyway." She scraped the knife across the surface, the screeching sound reminding Jayd of metal dragged across tile. She tested the edge. "Ooh, almost there."

Again she ran the knife along the surface, the noise putting even his nerves on edge.

Kelli held up the blade, the metal gleaming in the light. "Ah, good. It didn't easily cut my thumb." She showed him. "I left a sharp point, though."

"Remember—breaking first, cutting second."

"Oh, yes. Mind holding this?" Kelli handed him her knife. "Thanks."

"How do you break fingers again? Haven't done it in a while."

"Grab and twist up with a quick motion." She demonstrated in the air and clicked with her tongue. "Doesn't take much effort."

"Shouldn't we gag him first? He's not talking anyway. Don't want his screams to upset the neighbors."

"Good point." She tore off a wad of bedding. "Open wide."

"I'll talk, I'll talk!" Words exploded from their prisoner, eyes fixed on Jayd. "Just don't—don't let her near me."

"So who you working for?" Jayd asked. "Make it

count. Otherwise, I won't be responsible for what she does."

His eyes darted between Kelli and him. "Mitt. Mitt Harker. He and I are friends from way back."

"That's it? Hardly worth the trade." Kelli flexed her fingers around the gag. "Open up."

The man flinched. "There's more. A guy named Barkley contacted him. He had a grudge against the kid's parents. And her." He looked at Kelli. "So he and Mitt made a deal."

Jayd planted his foot on their prisoner's chair, right between his bound legs. "Details. I'll know if you're lying."

"I was to snag the girl after I took her out." His gaze flickered to Kelli. "But Barkley double-crossed us. His guys were waiting but I escaped. My partner got hurt, so she returned to Earth. I brought the girl here myself. Kept her alive."

"That was real nice of you." Jayd spoke with cutting scorn. "What else?"

"There was a doctor on the space station. Did the operations to make us look Xerxian."

"A need a name."

"Deet-something."

"Deitman?"

"Yeah. That was him." The prisoner gave a description that left no doubt that he was the surgeon Jayd had met that night. Ironic.

In a matter of minutes, they got everything else they needed, including the security code and pass key to Harker's rented home in Xer Prime. Their prisoner, though, told them that Harker intended to leave that night with Ella on the last shuttle. He'd only stayed behind to wrap up some things before joining them.

After Jayd and Kelli reviewed the information, they had only one option.

"Let me." She smiled as she shoved the wad of bedding into the man's mouth. With more exertion than necessary, she yanked the binding around their prisoner's head.

Jayd might have done the same.

When she was done, she leaned down, face inches from the man's. "If you're lying, any part of your story, I'm coming back to pay you another visit. And this time, I *will* use this." While holding her pocketknife under his nose, she shut it with a metallic snap.

He choked and garbled some retort. Stepping up behind him, Jayd grabbed him around the neck in a chokehold. In moments, their prisoner slumped, unconscious. With some effort, they dragged the huge man, still bound, into a closet and shut the door.

As an extra measure of security, Jayd wedged a chair against the door handle. "Should give us a little insurance."

Kelli nodded. "Let's go."

Chapter 23

The night seemed excessively dark as they hurried up the narrow streets to Xer Prime. Kelli's heart raced as though she ran flat out. Was Ella still there? What if they'd left early? She racked her brain trying to remember the shuttle's schedule.

After what felt like an eternity, they reached the private, two-story residence. This was no humble dwelling like in the town below. Did it have all the security measures of a Terran home? She grew anxious as she imagined the number of guards they'd have to plow through. Would Harker hurt Ella if he thought his safety was in jeopardy?

They checked the perimeter, noting the simplicity of the adobe-like building. A small garden surrounded the place, a low stone fence separating the property from the street. Two gates, one at the front, one at the rear. No external lights. But the home was obviously occupied. Bright lights gleamed from nearly every window, even on the second floor.

Jayd touched her arm. "Let's wait a little."

She nodded. Several people still walked the streets. The evening was yet young.

Pointing upward, he acted as though admiring the night sky. Body tensing, she too looked up. If they didn't make their move soon, she would burst.

"Relax, Kel." His calm voice eased some of her tension. "Nobody's leaving this place without us seeing."

Realizing Jayd had stopped where they could view both the front and back gate, she admired his wisdom. She hoped they looked like two people who paused during an evening stroll. Casually, he hopped on the low stone wall and helped her up. She swiveled her body so she could see the rear gate while he watched the front.

"Beautiful night." His voice carried a soothing tone.

"Perfect for a rescue."

"By the way, nice job interrogating."

"You weren't bad yourself."

Jayd's eyes never stopped moving. "I'm really glad we're on the same team. Hate to think of getting on your bad side."

"No worries. Don't do anything to make me mad."

"Heaven forbid."

She smiled, some of her anxiety lessening. Time

crawled by. How much longer did they have to wait? The number of people in the streets began to thin. So far she'd seen and heard nothing coming from Harker's house. Were they too late?

To avoid suspicion, they walked around to the other side of the building and pretended once again to be stargazing.

He grabbed her arm. "Look."

Two women exited from the rear of the house. Speaking in low voices, they didn't appear to notice Jayd and Kelli. They walked out the gate and down the street.

Were these the two women who'd accompanied Harker from the town below?

A couple lights flickered off on the lower floor.

Taking a deep breath, Kelli studied Jayd. He turned his head, eyes darting downward and behind him. She got the message. Rather that using the gate, they dropped over the stone fence and crouched in the garden. Both stripped off outer robes and left their bags. She took only her pocketknife and some homemade rope, which she wound about her waist. Jayd did the same.

Before she inched forward, he spoke low in her ear. "Let's stick together."

They crept closer to the house.

A sound coming from the house pricked Kelli's ears. A child's distressed wail. *Ella!* Chest heaving, she grabbed Jayd's arm.

She could barely see his face in the night. When he tapped his forehead, she ascertained he was warning her to stay focused. She slowed her breathing. The best way to help Ella was to not let anything distract her. Even the child herself.

First they needed to remove all obstacles. While Ella's muffled crying continued to pierce her heart, Kelli set her jaw. She funneled her mounting fury into being swift and efficient. Harker would pay for every one of his daughter's tears.

After reaching the back door, they paused. From a crouched position, Jayd inserted the kidnapper's key and entered the passcode on the keypad. The lock clicked. They slipped into a salon and quietly closed the door. Squatting in the dark room, Kelli heard several sets of footsteps. Jayd held up fingers, counting the number of people. At least three, with one upstairs. Possibly more. She agreed. As she moved forward, she noted an open doorway that led to a kitchen.

With hand signals, he indicated he wanted to go through a set of double doors into what was most likely a hallway. Kelli nodded, but before they could move, the light in the next room snapped on. Both of them flattened themselves against the wall near the doorway. Out of the corner of her eye, she saw a single man pass. She waited while Jayd signaled he wanted to look as well. They listened a second, then he ducked his head forward. He gestured that only one man occupied the kitchen. At his nod, Kelli lunged forward, grabbing the guard around the neck and squeezing. He fell unconscious without sounding an alarm. Jayd deftly caught the man and pulled him into the darkened salon. With practiced speed, they gagged and hogtied him, hands behind his back. The rope around his neck to his bound feet would be enough to keep him from struggling to free himself. Or making a lot of noise.

"Not Harker," she mouthed.

He nodded.

After Jayd reached around the kitchen doorway, he flicked off the light. Since the door to the rest of the house remained open, they moved into the kitchen and again paused to listen. A quick glance into the foyer area told Kelli no one else was in sight. Approaching footsteps caused them to again flatten against the wall. A man walked by. Jayd was on him in a second while Kelli kept his body from thumping the floor and announcing their presence. The guard was quickly dispatched like the first. He too ended up in the salon.

Again they waited and listened.

"...child's aunt will arrive in the morning," a man's voice floated down from the second story. "Thank you for your services. You are no longer needed."

"Harker," she mouthed to Jayd.

He nodded, then gestured that he thought the listener would come downstairs. He was right. A Xerxian woman descended, but she was too far away from the kitchen for them to apprehend her. Kelli glanced out to see her walk down the hallway toward the front door. It opened and closed.

She signaled to Jayd. "What now?"

He motioned *wait,* then pointed down the hallway.

They made their way cautiously through the foyer, checking the other rooms on the first floor. No one else was about. That left only those upstairs.

Cautiously, they headed up the steps. Kelli no longer heard Ella, but she detected at least two sets of footsteps. When she held up two fingers, Jayd inclined his head. From her experience, Kelli knew Harker liked to surround himself with staff. The two goons they'd already knocked out looked like bodyguards, but were there more? What about domestic help?

Upstairs, they slipped into a dark room to reassess. This time, Kelli heard a third person. Jayd nodded when she mouthed her suspicion. A guard reclined in an adjoining room. Jayd took him out and hid his body in a closet.

As Jayd emerged, another guard walked in.

"Hey!" The man reached for a weapon on his belt.

Before Kelli could react, Jayd vaulted himself at the guy. As they flew backwards, the door crashed against the wall. The resounding boom echoed through the house.

The scuffle had to have alerted Harker. Leaving them, Kelli sped from the room. Footsteps retreated. She had to find him. *Fast.*

From another room down the hall, something thumped. A desk drawer? As Kelli rounded the corner, Harker's hand came up. His weapon aimed at her.

Without thinking, she leaped. The weapon fired, missing her. Adrenaline flooded her, spurred on by the realization that he was using a blaster. One shot would kill. She rolled, then sprang to her feet as he reset the gun to fire again. Too late. Her knuckles connected with his nose. Harker shrieked as blood splattered everywhere.

A satisfying crunch told her he would no longer have a pretty holo for his virtual classes.

His grip went slack. She wrenched the weapon from him.

"Where is Ella?" Kelli grabbed him by the collar. She punched him again. "Where is she?" She rained him with blows while he howled with pain. "Answer me!"

From behind, arms imprisoned and lifted her.

"Stop, Kel. Stop!" Jayd's voice grated in her ear as she fought against his hold. "He answered you. Didn't you hear him?"

Panting, she stared down at Harker. He curled into a ball, whimpering as he protected his face. Finally, she realized her knuckles throbbed. Jayd stood nearby, chest heaving from the effort of pulling her away.

"Where?" She paused to catch her breath. "Where's Ella?" For the life of her, she didn't remember Harker saying.

"Next room." Jayd pointed. "You get her. She knows you."

"We secure?"

"Yes."

Kelli didn't hesitate. After opening the adjoining door, she peered in. No one seemed to be in the dimly lit room. A small form lay motionless on a bed.

"Ella?" She spoke softly in order not to frighten the girl.

No response.

"It's Kelli. Remember me?" She went in and gently touched the girl's shoulder. Again, nothing. With care, Kelli rolled her onto her back. Ella's eyes remained shut, her body limp.

She called to Jayd. "She's drugged."

From the next room, she heard him grab Harker. She peered around the corner in time to see Jayd pulling him to his feet.

"What did you give her?" He gripped the man's shirtfront and shook him.

Harker was blubbering while his nose seeped blood. Face and clothing were drenched while his cheekbone appeared fractured.

"What was it?" Jayd shook him again.

"Mild sedative." He spoke nasally. "That's all."

When Jayd shoved him away, he whined. "Don't hit me. Please. She'll wake up in a few hours, I swear."

In minutes, they tied Harker to a chair.

"When's the next shuttle?" Kelli pulled the knot around his legs with a savage jerk.

"About…about an hour." He stared at her, eyes bulging with recognition.

"Good." She switched to a southern drawl. "We got time to look at your artifacts. Got any of them ritual beads?"

Harker sucked in a sharp breath while Jayd threw her a puzzled look.

"I'll explain later." She rose.

He interrogated Harker, but he only confirmed what his "Xerxian" henchman had already told them. Then Jayd gagged the prisoner.

"Would you mind?" Kelli flexed her sore hand. "I'd like to, but…"

"Gladly." With practiced expertise, Jayd seized their prisoner's neck until his body went slack. "I'll carry Ella. Let's hurry."

Not until they were out of the house did Kelli breathe a sigh of relief. They were free!

Jayd made his way toward the private ship's sleeping area but stopped abruptly when he heard Kelli's soft voice. Cautiously, he peered around the open doorway.

Awake now, Ella lay on one bunk. A small lamp glimmered above her head.

Kelli perched beside the girl. "I want you to hang onto this, okay? Your mom said it was yours when you were a baby." She held up a delicate golden locket that glimmered in the light. "Go ahead. I know you'll keep it safe."

Eyes wide, Ella reached for the jewelry.

Kelli smoothed the blanket over the child's thin body.

Because Kelli's back was to the door, Jayd couldn't see her expression. The girl gazed up, a small smile banishing the fright from her face. He couldn't tear himself away from the scene. Never before had Kelli displayed such tenderness. His love for her expanded until it filled the universe.

Kelli spoke softly. "We'll be home before you know it."

"Will Mama be there?"

"Oh, yeah." She smoothed the girl's hair. "I only borrowed the locket. Won't she be surprised when you give it to her instead of me."

Holding it up, Ella studied the small, gold disc. It spun and glittered in the light.

What a pair they made, both with black hair and green-tinged skin. Almost like mother and child.

Jayd gulped.

Would Kelli ever want children of her own? His kids? He pushed the thought away. Stupid question. Musings of that kind needed to be banned. Permanently.

Kelli kissed the girl's cheek. "Why don't you try to sleep now?"

"You won't leave, will you?"

"No." She rested her hand on the child's wrist. "I'll be right here."

"Promise?" Ella's voice quavered.

Caressing her arm, she nodded. "I promise."

Mouth still quivering, Ella clutched the locket. As Kelli stroked her forehead, the girl's eyelids fluttered closed.

The soft thrum of the ship's engines reverberated through Jayd while the dim lights in the room flickered. It was late. Exhaustion hammered him. Like Ella, he should be asleep in his bunk. Rest was the furthest thing from his mind. Instead, keen disappointment gripped him.

The mission is over.

He imagined what would come next. The minute they reached Earth they'd be arrested. Big deal.

What pierced his soul was he and Kelli would part ways. Eventually, she would fade out of his life. Or maybe gallop out. In light of his so-called rejection of her, she would probably put as much distance as she could between them.

It was his fault. When he had told her "no" that one critical night, she must have concluded that he wanted nothing to do with her. Not in his arms or in his life.

Somehow he'd never gotten around to explaining everything to her.

Too late now.

The stark future stared him in the face. While they worked toward the common goal of rescuing Ella, he could forget the future *someday*. Well, someday was finally here. In a few days or weeks, Kelli would wave goodbye. He'd go back to pretending she meant little to him.

How could he function at USF with her so close yet so distant? They might as well be on separate planets. That might be easier to bear.

Knowing that she believed in God eased some of his torment.

If only Sean didn't stand in the way.

She must have sensed Jayd's presence because she glanced at him over her shoulder. And smiled, sort of misty-eyed.

He gulped. *Oh, what she can still do to my heart.*

"Everything okay?" She stopped stroking Ella's head. The girl didn't move, eyes tightly shut.

"Yep." It was all he could manage to say. He moved into the room, nodded at Ella and found his voice. "How's she doing?"

"Great. She recognized me, despite the green skin. The locket from Aric helped too."

He stepped closer.

"Any word from Sean?" Kelli asked.

Of course that would be her next question. Jayd cleared his throat. The sooner he adjusted to reality, the better. "He's expecting us."

"With the police?"

"Probably. But I hope not right away. I kept the transmission short, untraceable. I asked him for five minutes of his time. Alone with Aric at the house."

"Good thinking."

"After that…" Jayd shrugged. If his friend knew what was best for them all, he'd contact USF to arrest both him and Kelli.

But at this point, he no longer cared.

"I guess I'd better start liking orange jumpsuits and halo neckbands." Kelli smiled.

How could she joke about going to prison? If she hadn't glanced at Ella at that moment, she would have caught his expression.

"If we make it through the port," Jayd said slowly, "we'll get an air taxi and zip over to the house before anyone knows we're back on Earth."

"I'd like that."

Of course she would. One more chance to see Sean. *Quit torturing yourself.*

"One last thing." He waited till her gaze rose to meet his. "Before we left the space station, I had that idiot doctor arrested. I also contacted the Xerxian High Council. They'll hold Harker and gang until they hear from Inter-G."

"Good. Although I would've loved leaving them tied up for a couple days. To make them suffer for the trauma they caused Ella." Kelli smoothed the blanket over the small form. Her brow wrinkled. "I hope she'll be all right."

"Kids are resilient. She'll probably recover faster than we will."

"Hmm." She flexed one hand as though it was sore.

"You a child expert now?"

"No, but I have a half dozen nephews and nieces. My sisters planned on big families."

Kelli's teeth caught her lower lip as though she contemplated her next words. "What about you? Do you want children of your own someday?"

Strange question. Even stranger since he'd wondered that very thing about her mere minutes ago.

Refusing to answer, he merely shrugged. It was best to pull away. Sever all emotion when it came to Kelli. If he didn't, it would hurt all the more later.

Who're you kidding? It hurts now.

Kelli dimmed the bedside lamp but remained by Ella. "You worried about prison?"

"I don't relish the idea. You?"

She appeared to study the sleeping girl. "I could face anything as long as..." She didn't finish the sentence.

Curiosity tugged at him. "As long as...?"

She slowly raised her face to his. "As long as I knew you were waiting for me."

If an asteroid hit the ship, he couldn't have been more surprised. Were his ears playing tricks? He wanted to ask her to repeat herself, but he was gripped with a sudden fear that she would mock him.

But her body language didn't lie. Her eyes were wide, lips parted. Chest rising and falling in an irregular pattern. A slow blush crept up her cheeks.

"Waiting?" He gulped.

The next moment, she rose. Wrapping her arms about his neck, she nestled her forehead against him.

The gravitational pull of a black hole could not

have stopped him from embracing her. Still he was cautious. He kept his hold loose, detached.

"If I could be sure you were waiting for me," she whispered, "then I wouldn't be afraid of anything."

He dared not hope. Not yet.

The question had to be asked. The words came slowly. "What about Sean?"

She hesitated before answering. In those seconds, his heart thudded to a stop.

Kelli took a deep breath. "I'm over him. Completely."

He wanted to believe, but couldn't.

Perhaps sensing his skepticism, she leaned back to look into his eyes. "I am. I realize now that I was just infatuated with him. I never really knew him." She pressed her cheek against his as she molded herself to him. "But I know you, Jayd. And love you. Only you."

A tremor ripped through his body. He gripped her tightly as if she were the only foundation in his universe.

Gently she ran her fingers along the nape of his neck, the gesture unspeakably endearing.

Emotion lodged in his throat. Impossible to speak!

"I need to tell you something." She again looked into his eyes. "The night you almost died…" She paused, a muscle by her mouth spasming. Her voice shook. "I prayed. I asked God to save your life. I told Him no matter what, I surrendered my life—my whole being—to Him." Her eyes glittered with welling tears. "In those hours, when you were so sick, I realized I couldn't bear to lose you."

As she spoke, truth reverberated in his soul.

Kelli's fingertips smoothed his forehead. "I know I've messed up. Lots. And I probably will again. But when I do, please remember I love you. For as long as I live."

With a soft groan, he kissed her. Nothing could stop him. It was a sweet, slow kiss. He buried his face against her neck, holding her tightly. Finally he dared to breathe. Dared to allow his heart to resume beating.

Dared to believe.

It was a long time before he spoke. "You're right. I can bear anything as long as I know you'll be waiting for me."

Fingers tracing his cheeks and chin, she smiled. "And I know—without a doubt—that God is always here. With us. I don't need to try to understand everything about Him. I can trust Him with both our lives."

Inexpressible joy bubbled up inside him. He joined Kelli in a long, drawn-out sigh.

Everything was going to be all right. He knew it.

Chapter 24

"Mama!" Ella shrieked in excitement as she ran toward her mother on the aeropad.

A stunned Aric and equally astonished Sean stood transfixed by the front door. The next second, she was running toward her daughter, arms wide. "Ella. *Ella!*"

They hugged, Aric crying and laughing at once. Moving like an automaton, Sean stiffly knelt beside his wife and daughter. He embraced them both and hid his face between their shoulders.

Kelli's heart was so full that she thought it would burst. When she felt Jayd's arm slip about her, she leaned into him. This moment was worth it all. Whatever happened next would be insignificant to the joy of seeing Ella's happy family united once again.

Jayd squeezed her waist. "Let's go inside and wait."

"For?"

"The USF agents who are likely on their way now to arrest us."

"You sure they're already on the way?"

"Knowing Sean, he probably made a deal to have them come apprehend us."

"Good. They'll be nicer than Inter-G."

Jayd smiled. Hand in hand they went into the house. He led her to a study upstairs where he rummaged through a desk drawer.

Puzzled, Kelli watched. "You adding burglary to our offenses?"

"Oh, why not." His eyes twinkled.

What was he up to?

"Don't tell me you're going to revert back to teasing and tormenting me."

He merely chuckled, the sound devilish.

"Ah, here they are." Before she could react, he slapped an ancient metal handcuff on her wrist, then his, yoking them together.

"This is interesting." She held up their wrists. "I didn't know they still made these."

"I'm merely saving USF the trouble." He grinned, dark eyes gleaming. "Don't let your imagination get out of control."

She glared with mock indignation. If she wasn't handcuffed, she might have decked him.

"Whatever." She lifted her chin. *Very well.* If he

wanted to be that way...

She clucked her tongue. "You're just worried I'll get away from you. *Again."*

"There's never going to be a repeat performance." He pulled her down on the sofa next to him. "Once was enough."

"Ha." Kelli retorted. "And you're mistaken, mister. I escaped twice. Once at the gym, once at the airport."

"Technically, the gym wasn't my fault. So it doesn't count."

"Yes, but you were in charge of surveillance. So you *are* responsible."

"It only counts if I was there. So...once."

"Uh-uh." She shook her head. "Twice."

"Once."

"Twice."

When Jayd pinned her to the sofa, she squealed. "Two times. *Two.*" She shrieked when he nibbled her neck. "Okay, okay! Only once. Stop! I give up."

A loud clearing of a throat made them both bolt upright. Sean was standing in the doorway, eyebrows raised. The silence wore on until Kelli began to squirm.

Finally he spoke. "I need to mark this event on a calendar." He moved his hand as though displaying a bannered headline. "Kelli Layne surrenders. At long last."

"Did not." Her face grew hot.

"I heard it, Jayd. Didn't you?"

"Yep. With my own ears."

She didn't mind giving in to Jayd in private, but she hadn't counted on a witness. Especially Sean. Still handcuffed, she tried to rise.

Jayd resisted.

"That's not fair!" she sputtered.

Jayd tugged her back down. This time she landed on his lap.

"Fair, schmair." He grinned. His other hand gripped her waist. "Good thing I don't always play fair."

She smiled into his eyes, all irritation vanishing.

"I can't believe she said she surrendered," Sean said. "You're the man, Jayd."

"Actually," he answered slowly, "I can't take credit. That belongs only to God."

Kelli felt her smile fade. Though Jayd had spoken with sincerity, she wasn't comfortable yet proclaiming her newfound faith.

His near death—and her plea to God—were still too precious. Too sacred.

Throat tight, she stared into Jayd's eyes, so very grateful that God had restored his life. Of that she was positive. Someday she would tell him all the details. Someday when her soul didn't well up with a reverence that could not be contained by words.

"I see," Sean finally said, his tone full of awe. "I'm beginning to believe in miracles."

"Good. Because I definitely do." Jayd moved his free hand to run his thumb softly over Kelli's jaw.

"Make that four of us–no, five–who believe in miracles." Holding her daughter, Aric stood next to her husband.

Sean put his arm around them both. "Well, we better ask God for another."

"Why?" Aric asked.

"USF agents should be arriving at any moment."

Jayd looked at Kelli. His crooked grin said, *I told you so.*

"I'm not worried." She smiled at them all. Jayd's fingers lingered on her cheek as she explained. "If God can convince me He's real and that He loves me, He can do anything."

Of that, she had no doubts. She might not know what the future held, but God did. And she was finally and fully content to surrender everything to Him.

In Book 1 in Anna Zogg's Intergalaxia series, Aric Lindquist has been abandoned by SARC on a primitive planet light-years from Earth. When an assistant finally arrives, Aric's suspicions go on high alert. Sean Reese is hiding something. Can she trust him? Or has he been sent there to eliminate the one person in Intergalaxia who wants to safeguard the indigenous humanoids - Aric?

Don't miss the next exciting book
in Anna Zogg's
Intergalaxia series!

The Terran Summit

Excerpt

Eva Hilliard sat beside the road where her enemy had dumped her. Why had Kelli Layne abandoned her here? Because Layne couldn't outright kill her? That seemed the most likely explanation. She didn't want to watch Eva die.

No travelers had come along the road as promised. As the morning waned, the possibility of a rescue faded. When a spasm of pain gripped Eva, she dug her fingers into the gravel and groaned.

Dust from an unplanted field pelted her face, agitated by the ever-present wind. Its lonely whine mocked her. The large daytime star beat down, stealing moisture from her mouth as she panted.

Time and again, her mind wandered. Why did she have to die here, on Xerxes IX? The irony bit into her soul. It seemed fitting—the planet that had birthed her sorrow would be her final resting place.

A sob tore her throat.

"Stop it." Eva spoke out loud. "Stop."

Defaulting to the rigorous Inter-G training, she forced herself to assess her situation.

Status—*stranded.*

Condition—*fractured femur, concussion.*

Medical equipment—*on the orbiting space station, in-accessible.*

Sustenance—*two food packets and a half canteen of wa-ter.*

Most likely, she would succumb to dehydration. With her injury, she wouldn't be able to crawl to the nearest town—if she even knew which direction to go. The many days previous to her accident, with little food and less sleep, weakened her further as they exacted their toll.

Her death promised to be long and excruciating.

A makeshift splint, constructed of branches and a torn robe, dug into her flesh. Beneath her thigh, a sharp stone embedded. Ramrod straight for far too long, her back protested. She swallowed the sandpaper in her throat. Agony grew.

How long before the end?

She had faced death many times in her years as an operative for Intergalaxia, but never like this.

Time crawled. Eva peered into the distance, but the road remained dismal. Empty. If a passerby would come, she could implore them for help. The humanoids of Xerxes IX wouldn't hesitate to render aid.

As her mind again wandered, agonizing memories crept back and lodged in the forefront of her thinking. Yearning slowly ate into her soul. Its twin, regret, devoured her peace.

To die without seeing her mother one more time...

Eva steeled herself. Too late to seek out the one who had deserted her so long ago. Much, much too late.

If only she could lie down. Close her eyes. Give in to blissful nothingness.

The giant sun cast the land in a hazy orange as it climbed into the afternoon. The scent of grassy fields intensified in the warmth, causing her eyes to prickle with longing. This place smelled like the Rocky Mountains. Usually they visited in the late summer to escape the heat of the city. The memory of her parents' small cabin clutched at her. If only she could go back...

The instinct to survive wrestled with her reconciliation to death.

I will not pray. I will not ask God for help.

Brutally, she crushed that childhood reminiscence. Eva vowed to welcome her passing. Dying would finally release her from the torment that had held her captive for twenty-six years.

Ripples of heat danced across her vision. In the distance, a formless mass shimmered as it rose from the ground. A specter of death?

Fear gripped her. Was she losing herself in madness? She shifted her weight. Burning flared up her leg and through her core. A primeval cry tore from her throat. Back arching, she willed her mind to subdue her body. What was that ancient, alien text?

"Pain can be controlled." She ground out the words once. Twice. The intonation eased her agony. Again, she panted, "Pain *can* be controlled. I will...will master it."

"And the one who conquers pain will overcome." A man's voice, speaking English, cut through the silence to finish the recitative.

Her head snapped his direction.

A Xerxian male stood not more than fifteen feet away. How had he appeared without making a sound? A sense of unreality pressed on her.

Eva squeezed her eyes shut. A Xerxian, deep in the heart of his homeworld, would likely not understand *Common* as they called English. Even more improbable that he spoke it. Breathing deeply, she opened her eyes.

He had vanished.

A mental picture of herself raving tore through her mind. Her body began to shake. "Pain can—can be..." She fought to utter the words. No good. The interruption had disrupted the soothing self-sedation.

A whisper of a sound met her ears as a shadow fell across the ground. Eva cried out as the phantom materialized beside her. When something brushed her cheek, she batted it away.

This wasn't real. It couldn't be.

"Forgive me my touch." The man's speech was

stilted as he again spoke in English. He knelt beside her and placed a gentle palm on her forehead.

Combating sluggishness, Eva stared at him. Where had he come from? Training again clicked in, rescuing her from the brink of hysteria.

Xerxian male. Younger than forty. Skin of the palest green, tinted with teal. Dark cropped hair. Military? No—Xerxes IX did not have armed forces. *One earring with two charms.* What did the symbols signify? Not important. *Subtle refinement in manner and expression.* Not a farmer. Laborer? *Clothing crude. Minor cuts on his hands.* Familiarity with knives. Craftsman?

Her suffering suddenly eased, cutting short her evaluation. A sigh escaped her.

This was no hallucination.

For a moment, she reveled in the absence of pain. But only a moment. While his palm rested on her forehead, she fixed her gaze on him. "Are you a healer?"

She clamped her lips together. Why had she betrayed herself by speaking Xer?

His eyes widened. In the stark sunlight, his black pupils contrasted with the deep ebony of his irises. "You speak my language." He reverted to his native tongue. "And very well."

Wave upon wave of relief washed over her. She relinquished her tight self-control to his touch.

"To answer your question, no." He spoke in Xer. "However I am versed in the practice." Though he removed his hand, her pain remained at bay. The respite would be temporary. She had perhaps minutes to beg his help.

Without preamble, she invoked the formal Xerxian plea. "I adjure you by the God you worship to grant your assistance."

"I gladly pledge it. Fully. Without reserve."

Astonished by his quick response, she gaped. He hadn't asked why she was there—a Terran on his planet. Hadn't inquired about her injury or how she ended up on an abandoned road. Nothing. But by his words, he vowed to do everything, including forfeiting his own life, to protect hers.

The Xerxian scrutinized her body as though to ascertain the full extent of her injuries. When he came to her fracture, he placed his hands inches above the splint. "May I?"

She merely nodded.

With infinite care, he rested one palm on her injured leg. Eva stiffened as a tsunami of torment battered her, even with his whispered touch. Throwing her head back, she groaned.

"Your bonds are too tight. This must be corrected. Immediately." With care he unknotted the strips of cloth.

Though he worked quickly, she couldn't stifle her cries. Spasms racked her. The more she tried to repress the tremors, the worse they grew.

The Xer grasped her hands and forced the palms together. "This practice is for Xerxians, but perhaps it will ease your suffering while I rebind your leg."

Through the haze of agony, she recognized the ancient healing ritual. How would she react? While he murmured the invocation, he pressed his palms against the back of her hands in ever-increasing pressure.

Unwilling to listen, Eva blocked out the words. God had not heeded her prayers as a child. Though she had begged and cried, He had not brought back her mother.

Cupping her jaw, the Xerxian continued the ritual. Static electricity seemed to snap between them. She resisted the uncomfortable sensation. It built and built until she could scarcely breathe.

Energy, like a lightning bolt, shot through her core.

Eva screamed and blacked out.

Books by Anna Zogg

Letters Across Time

Moon Dancing

"Gypsy Gulch" A *Moon Dancing* Mystery
(an e-only short story)

Books in the Intergalaxia Series

The Paradise Protocol

The Xerxes Factor

The Terran Summit (releasing late fall, 2016)